Still Falling
Sheena Wilkinson

Little Island

STILL FALLING

First published in 2015 by
Little Island Books
7 Kenilworth Park
Dublin 6W
Ireland

ISBN: 9781908195920
A British Library Cataloguing in Publication record
for this book is available from the British Library

Cover design by Niall McCormack
Typeset in Adobe Garamond
Printed in Poland by Drukarnia Skleniarz

Little Island is grateful for financial assistance from the Arts Council/An
Chomhairle Ealaíon and the Arts Council of Northern Ireland

10 9 8 7 6 5 4 3 2 1

For my wonderful god-daughter,
Caoimhe Browne,
with love.

ACKNOWLEDGEMENTS

This novel was a long time gestating, and I'd like to thank everyone who helped in any way to keep me reasonably sane since I started. Thanks to my family and friends, and colleagues at Methodist College and the Church of Ireland College of Education. The Arvon Foundation, the Tyrone Guthrie Centre at Annaghmakerrig and the Arts Council of Northern Ireland all played their parts.

Celia Rees, whose insight at a very early stage was crucial to the story's development, deserves a special thanks, as do all whose feedback on the manuscript at various stages helped me bash it into shape: Lee Weatherly, Bella Pearson, Linda Newbery, Susanne Brownlie, Julie McDonald, and of course my wise, eagle-eyed and long-suffering editors at Little Island, Gráinne Clear and Siobhán Parkinson. Sometimes we even laughed about it.

I've done a lot of travelling since I started writing full-time, and I'm always grateful for the invitations from schools and libraries and festivals all over Ireland and the UK. I love meeting readers and potential readers almost as much as I like sitting in a room and making things up. Thanks to Anne who looks after things when I'm away, and, as always, to Mummy and John for putting up with my funny wee ways.

All my writer and kidlit friends in Ireland, England and beyond – in CBI, SCBWI and especially SAS – continue to reassure me that if I'm crazy to do this, then at least I'm in wonderful company. And thank heavens for everyone who reads, reviews and champions YA fiction, without whom there'd be nobody to tell stories to.

Sheena Wilkinson
Co Down

I stand in the corridor, frozen with horror at the words coming out of Dad's mouth.

'Nobody saw him fall – Sandra found him at the bottom of the stairs, unconscious, blood everywhere. She thought he was dead.'

'Can I go to the hospital?'

Dad hesitates. I don't know why I'm asking, because whatever he says, whatever's happened between me and Luke, I can't walk away now.

Even though I know he might not wake up.

Esther

It's not unheard of to wet yourself on your first day at school. But not normally in sixth form.

I'm late. Should have accepted Dad's offer of a lift. It's just that arriving in school with Dad is so *sad*, especially for someone who's started being friends with Jasmine Wright. OK, maybe not friends exactly, but after results night, when I practically saved her *life* – well, she's at least going to acknowledge me. Isn't she?

The corridors are empty. Teachers' voices sing-song from behind closed doors. I hitch my new satchel higher on my shoulder and make for the sixth-form block.

Rushing down the scruffy cream corridors, I wish I had taken that lift with Dad. At least I could have drifted into the room along with everybody else and not have to make An Entrance all sweaty and flustered.

I wonder who our tutor is. Every year I pray it won't be Dad and so far my prayers have been answered. Only I remind myself I don't do praying any more. Not since I ditched God.

Despite my rejection, God – or whoever organised the classes, probably a computer program – is on my side, because the person sitting at the teacher's desk, scratching his beard, blinking at the chatting rows, counting time-tables, and looking like he's counting the minutes until breaktime, or possibly retirement, is only Boring Baxter.

All he says is, 'Ah. Esther Wilson. You can take that seat there,' and he points me to a desk where a boy I don't recognise is bent over, rummaging in his schoolbag. It's the only empty seat, behind Toby, who is shy and nice and the closest thing I've had to a friend at school until now. I slide into the seat, pull off my cardigan because sweat is suddenly pricking my armpits, and glance round. Jasmine hasn't noticed me yet. She's sitting with Cassie. Of course.

I give Jasmine a quick smile. This is sixth form and it's all going to be different. I'm going to be different. Though the tutor group is pretty much the same as the last five years. A few thick rugby players haven't got enough GCSEs to get back. Leaving space for the two new girls with ironed blond hair and lip-glossed pouts who sit in front of Jasmine and Cassie looking like they've been specially manufactured to be Mansfield Sixth Form Girls. They're so much a type that it takes me a second to realise they actually are identical. As in twins. One of them turns round and whispers something to Jasmine, who laughs. Cassie's lips tighten and she gives the twin her bug-eyed stare. Baxter and Toby are the only people who have even noticed me.

I sigh and reach for the timetable Baxter is handing me, only I miss and it flutters to the ground and I have to bend down to grab it and it feels like people are sniggering even though they aren't. It's strange to see only a few subjects. English lit, French, history and art. My crap science GCSE grades finally convinced me that I'm never going to be a doctor even though it used to be my dream.

The boy beside me sets his pens on the desk. He has four – black, blue, green and red. He lays them in a row. The red one wobbles and he frowns and edges it back into place. I glance at him from under my fringe. Blondish hair. Tall, I think, though it's hard to tell when someone's sitting down. Lean. Hot. Something inside me trembles. *Very* hot. I try to see what subjects he's doing but all I can make out is that he has highlighted them all in different colours, and his name at the top: Luke Bressan.

Not that it matters to me what he's called. If you drew a line across the class, with the cool people on one side and the rejects on the other, Luke Bressan and I would not be on the same side.

I look away, my skin burning. It's hopeless. You can't just *decide* to be cool. My legs stick to my skirt with sweat. My scalp itches even though I washed my hair this morning. Now that he's tamed his pens, Luke appears as confident as the new girls. Slightly bored if anything. I'm not used to sitting with a boy. Not this kind of boy anyway. Toby doesn't count.

I fold my arms and concentrate on Baxter. He drones on about uniform regulations and careers guidance and how we will all be treated like Responsible Adults now as long as we don't Abuse the Privilege. Then he takes off his glasses and puts on his caring face.

'And of course,' he says, his voice cosy as a cupcake, 'we hope you'll all have a great year with no problems.' He pulls at his nasal hair. 'But if you *should* encounter any little difficulties, well, *we're* here to help.'

Luke slides his hands up the sides of his face and lets them rest there. His fingers are long, but his nails are short and bitten, worse than mine. A thin silver bracelet snakes his wrist. If Baxter notices that he'll tell him to take it off.

'You all know Mr Wilson,' Baxter goes on. 'Head of pastoral care. *He's* the man to go to if you if have any – er problems.' I stare at the scratches on my desk. Around me rises a burble of mumblings. *Yeah right – Big Willy – imagine telling him –*

Imagine being his daughter.

Beside me Luke stiffens, as if my discomfort is catching. Then he gives a strange strangled cry and I turn to see him collapse sideways. His face strikes the desk as he falls and then he lies on the floor, limbs juddering and jerking.

Instant panic. Cassie screams. People gasp and flock round. I slip down from my chair and kneel beside Luke.

'Don't touch him!' Toby cries. His normally pink face is white. I remember him throwing up in third year when we dissected a rat.

'Are you meant to put something in their mouth?' somebody asks.

'Oh my God, he's going to die!' Cassie shrieks. Which is exactly what she said when Jasmine passed out on results night. Helpful.

'Shut up. Give him space,' I order. My voice comes out clear and strong like I expect everyone to obey and they do, even Baxter. Even Jasmine and Cassie, huddled together, their eyes nearly popping out of their mascaraed sockets. I pull the chair well away from Luke and shove my cardigan under his head to cushion it. Blood blurs his cheek, from the desk I suppose. I yank at the tight knot of his tie, open his collar. His head flails, froth blooming from his mouth, his arms and legs spasming in a mad jerking dance.

I lean back on my heels. I've made it as safe as I can. This isn't his first time. I've seen that bracelet properly now, and it's an epilepsy medical alert one.

'Phone an ambulance,' Cassie cries.

'You shouldn't need to,' I say.

Already the shuddering limbs are slowing.

A high clear voice, one of the new twins, says, 'Oh my God, he's *wet* himself.'

A dark stain spreads across Luke's trousers and over the floor. It lies on the newly polished start-of-term tiles and doesn't soak in.

The jerking stops. I manoeuvre Luke's body, limp now, into the recovery position. Almost at once his eyes flicker open. They are dark greyish-blue and very confused. I swallow. I'm not so confident; now the crisis is over. I'm fabulous at emergencies. It's just the normal bits of life in between I'm crap at.

'It's OK,' I say. 'You just had a seizure.'

I stroke his arm to reassure him. We both look down at my hand on the white cotton of his shirt for a second before I pull it away.

'You're in the classroom,' I go on, partly for something to say and partly because Luke's eyes are still bewildered. 'You've cut your cheek, but it doesn't look too bad.'

He lifts his hand and rubs at his face, then looks at the blood on his fingers.

The others crowd round; curious, excited even, now that nobody is actually dying or anything. Luke struggles to sit up. 'I'm fine,' he says calmly. He glances up at the crowd of faces, then down at the ground. I catch the exact moment when he realises he's wet himself – his lips tighten. He lifts up the cardigan I had put under his head, dusts it down and stares at it.

'It's mine,' I say, and he hands it to me.

Baxter seems to remember he's in charge. 'Esther, you've been wonderful,' he says.

He glances at Luke, who is standing up now but still looks as if he isn't too sure what to do. Except that he wants out of here. I can feel the desperation oozing out of him into the stuffy classroom air.

'Sir,' I say, 'shall I take Luke to the nurse?'

'Yes.' Baxter is clearly as desperate to get rid of Luke as Luke is to escape. 'All right to walk there, Luke? It's not far, just the next corridor.'

Luke nods. He packs his schoolbag slowly. Blood trickles down his cheek. Jasmine springs forward and hands him a tissue.

'I'll take your bag,' I offer. It's light, brand new, a plain black rucksack. I think of the pens inside, all new.

I can't think of anything to say on the way to the sick bay. I trial loads of stuff in my head – *Don't worry, it isn't that bad, nobody will have noticed that you wet yourself; it happens all the time* – but in the end I don't say any of it. Partly because I never can think of what to say to boys and partly because it isn't true.

Luke

By the time my brain is working half-normally we've reached a door labelled SICK BAY and the girl knocks. A middle-aged nurse opens the door and sighs as if she hadn't planned on having the first day of the school year messed up with an actual medical situation. But as soon as the girl tells her what happened the nurse sends her back to class and switches straight into professional mode.

She dabs the cut on my face with something stinging. Every time her arm moves I catch a whiff of her deodorant. Or maybe perfume. Sickly and sweet. Hard to imagine anybody *choosing* that smell. But Christ knows what *I* smell like. A seizure can be quite a workout. I look past her, itemise the room to stop myself flinching. Sickly green walls. Cheerful posters about STDs and self harm and eating five a day. Two beds against the far wall. Cupboards neatly labelled but it makes me dizzy to try to read them. Already the familiar headache is nibbling at my temples.

'I can sponge those trousers for you,' she says.

I chew my lip.

'They'll dry on the radiator in the time it takes someone to come and pick you up.'

'It's OK,' I mutter. 'You don't have to.'

'It's no bother. I've got some spares here, from Lost Property. You'd be amazed what people leave lying around.'

'*No.*' What is she fussing for? I'm sitting on a hard plastic chair. She can wipe it when I leave.

'Of course,' she says, riffling through a box of plasters, 'you won't be on the computer system yet. You'll have to give me a phone number. Is someone at home? Mum? Dad? Or can they come from work?'

The backs of my legs are cold and wet, but I don't *think* there's a smell. 'I don't have parents.'

She pulls the backing paper off a plaster. 'There must be someone?'

'Sandra.' The headache bites harder, its teeth sharpening by the second.

'Right. Sandra. She's your …?'

I suppose this will all be *on the system* soon enough, along with God knows what else.

'Foster carer. Can I get some painkillers?' At least she seems to have forgotten about wanting me to take my trousers off.

She frowns, sticks the unnecessary plaster over my cheek. I suppose they have to make it look like they've ministered to you properly.

'You sure you don't have concussion? Your eyes look OK but if you hit –'

'It's just a headache. I always get one afterwards.' Along with: feeling knackered enough to sleep for a week; bumps and bruises from bashing myself around like a mad thing; occasionally throwing up; and, worst of all, mortal humiliation. The thought of going back into that classroom tomorrow is enough to make me walk out of this school now, for ever. I grit my teeth, then stop because it hurts.

She's talking again and I realise she's asking for Sandra's number. I don't know it, but I hand her my phone. I zone out and then she's handing the phone back and saying something about Sandra being in a queue at Lidl but she'll be here as soon as she can.

'And she says it's fine to give you Paracetamol,' she finishes, even though she's the one that's meant to be a nurse, not Sandra, and Sandra's never even see me have a seizure because I've only lived with her for three days.

Anyway, she gives me the pills, thank God, because the pain is gnashing lumps out of my brain now, and she makes me a cup of tea and says I can lie down on one of the beds and rest while we wait for Sandra. But I say I'd rather stay where I am. I sip tea and watch the nurse fill in a form and hope that Sandra won't be annoyed at having her morning interrupted.

The nurse looks up from her desk as if she's had a bright idea and her biro jumps out of her hand. 'You can keep a spare pair of trousers here,' she says. 'Just in case.' She beams at her brilliance.

'I don't plan to make a habit of it.'

She picks up her biro again and says, 'Hmmm.'

Sandra reverses her Skoda carefully out of the space marked VISITORS. She keeps her eyes fixed on the driveway and slows down to avoid two tiny suicidal brats whose huge bags make them look like hunch-backed turtles. She beeps and they cower. In my last school they'd have given us the finger. I know she wants me to say something but I can't summon up any words. Sandra indicates left out of the school drive and heads down the South Road.

'God love you,' she says. 'That's bad luck on your first day. What do you think triggered it?'

I shrug. 'Dunno.'

'Were there any bright lights or –?'

'*No*. It's nothing to do with anything like that. It just *happens*.'

She should know this; she must have read my file. Plus there must have been lots of cosy chats with Brendan before he persuaded her to take me.

'You took your medication OK?'

I sigh. 'I always do.'

'Stress maybe?'

'We hadn't *done* anything. Just got our timetables. Sat in a classroom. It wasn't exactly stressful.'

'Och, aye, but it's a big day for you, Luke.'

I hadn't even spoken to anyone. Only answered 'Here' when the teacher called my name. And then that girl came and sat down beside me. She was quiet, not all tossy hair and makeup and giggles like other girls. And then I got that feeling – I can never describe it: it's not a smell, or a noise, nothing so romantic as an *aura*; I just *know*. But it's always too late.

I close my eyes and lean back against the seat.

'Are you sure we don't need to take you to Casualty?' Sandra asks. It's the first time I've seen anything faze her.

I open my eyes again. 'No. I just need to sleep it off. I'll be fine in a few hours.'

As always my heart sinks when we turn into Sandra's street. My street now. It's a bit miserable, a lot of concrete and the gardens are titchy. At least Sandra's has flowers in it – not bins and old bottles like the one next door. A few tattered flags, left over from summer, droop from the lampposts.

A bedraggled skinny black kitten is sitting in the middle of Sandra's path.

'There's that wee cat again,' Sandra says. 'It's been hanging round for a few days.' She bends down but the kitten scarpers.

By the time I get to my room – refusing another cup of tea; Sandra is a great believer in the healing powers of tea – the headache and the tiredness have blotted out everything else.

Sandra calls up the stairs, 'Leave me out your uniform so I can give it a wash through.' She doesn't mention the words *trousers* or *wet* and I think vaguely as I pull everything off and leave it in a heap outside the bedroom door that that's a brownie point for her. I don't know if this is just the honeymoon period or if she and Bill are going to keep on being this nice.

The plain blue duvet still smells of washing powder. I haven't been here long enough for it to smell of me. When I close my eyes I see the ring of shocked, scared faces; chair legs; human legs; dust skittering in the sun on the polished wooden floor tiles. And then the girl's face, calm and still with brown eyes. Her wide slow smile. Her hand on my sleeve. The new warm smell of her cardigan.

Esther

I dodge through crowds of boys playing football and girls standing in groups to find a space on the wall outside the library for a quiet read. But no sooner have I taken out *The Great Gatsby*, which we've just been given in English, than someone looms over me. Blond hair swings over the page.

'Budge up, Esther,' Jasmine says. She smiles her beautiful cool smile, and my own lips stretch into what I know is a goofy grin.

'Hey.' I make room for her. I set the book down before she can see it's a school one.

Cassie and the new twins come up behind her. I know they're called Zara and Zoë because they're in my art class.

'So what's he like?' Jasmine asks. She takes out a plastic lunchbox and offers me a carrot stick like we have lunch together every day.

I take one. I love the idea of being someone who eats carrot sticks with Jasmine, even though it's probably obvious to look at me that I've just had a gravy chip with F Scott Fitzgerald. I hope I don't smell of gravy.

'What's who like?' For a stupid moment I think she means Gatsby.

'The *new* boy, of course,' Jasmine says. She hugs her knees.

'Um.' I crunch my carrot stick. It's not like I've *talked* to Luke.

Zoë or Zara leans back and sighs. 'I *came* here for the boys,' she says, 'and so far they've been a bit of a let-down.' She glares at me as if this is somehow my fault.

'The upper sixth are a better-looking year group,' Cassie says with an expert air. She licks the lid of her yogurt, and moves closer to Jasmine.

'Well, *I've* been banking on some fit new boys,' Jasmine says. 'Because I've gone through all the acceptable boys in our year *and* the upper sixth.'

As I don't know how many boys she's *gone through* I have no idea if this means her standards are very high or very low.

'There's a real hottie in our art class,' a twin says. 'I bagsy him.' She starts describing him in rapid, hushed tones. It's obvious she's describing Mihai, who's Romanian, and gorgeous, but hardly ever speaks. She'll be lucky. But I don't say anything.

'Anyway, Esther, as you can see, it's slim pickings this year,' Jasmine says, 'so we want to know more about – what's his name?'

'Luke.'

She nods. 'Nice.' She waits. 'Well?'

'But I ... I don't know anything about him. I walked with him to the nurse. That's it. '

'But you – the way you *were* with him. We thought you already *knew* him.'

Zoë or Zara says, 'You took all the handouts and all to keep for him.'

'I was just being nice.'

'*Told* you, Jas.' Cassie's voice is triumphant. 'Just Esther being a good Christian girl.'

I open my mouth to say, *No, I've given up on all that*, but how stupid would that sound?

I have all his handouts safely in a folder. There was an envelope with his address. 11 Lilac Walk. I have no idea where that is, but I like knowing it. I might Google it later. No, I won't. That would be weird.

'But you were all – when he had that fit thing, you knew what to do. You talked to him like – like you knew him really well,' Cassie says.

'You were like – *touching* him, adds Jasmine.'

She makes it sound dirty. I knew I'd sounded weird. I bet *he* thought I'd been really forward. I have a sudden memory of my hand reaching out and rubbing his arm. I hadn't planned to do that; it was just instinct. I only did what I've always done.

I shake my head. 'I helped out at the special school's summer scheme. Where my mum teaches? Some of the kids there have seizures. It's no big deal. You know me, Jasmine – I'm good at looking after people. First aid and stuff.' I give her a private kind of smile.

She looks at me blankly, and I realise she actually doesn't remember results night, she was too drunk. Then I see the warning in Cassie's froggy eyes and I know *she* remembers; she remembers every detail, but her eyes are telling me It Never Happened. Cassie was pathetic that night, and she clearly doesn't like the fact that I wasn't.

'So you *don't* know anything about him?' Cassie asks.

'And you're *not* going out with him? – I told you she couldn't be,' says Jasmine.

'Nope,' I say. 'He's all yours.'

The four of them exchange glances.

'*I'd* give him one,' Jasmine says. 'Definitely.'

'Me too,' says Cassie, who always agrees with Jasmine.

The twins look at each other. 'I don't know,' says one. 'What if he had a fit on the job?' She shudders and wriggles her fingers like she's touched something gross.

'Zoë! That's minging,' Zara says.

'He can't help it,' Jasmine says. 'And he is *very* cute.'

They've lost interest in me now I've nothing to offer them, but they aren't rude enough to get up and leave – or maybe they just can't be bothered. Lunch is nearly over.

'Would you, Esther?' Cassie asks.

'Would I what?'

'Give him one?'

Give him one *what*? I nearly ask. I shrug. 'Probably,' I say nonchalantly.

'Well, bagsy *me* first go,' Jasmine says. She gives me a narrow look that makes her eyes look all mascara and no eyeball.

The bell clangs and I stuff *The Great Gatsby* back in my schoolbag. I know, as I watch them all dash off to class without asking me where I'm going, that it's the last time they'll bother to be friendly.

As for *giving him one*. My chances with Luke have never been great, but now those four have decided he is *very cute* they're non-existent. And I'm certainly not going to make the mistake I made with Jasmine and think we're *friends* or something just because I helped him out. I have got some pride.

This is all too hard. It was never like this with Ruth or the other girls at our Christian youth group. But I can't think about Ruth now, and I'm not thinking about Luke Bressan either.

Much.

Luke

'Take the day off,' Sandra says next morning when she catches me looking for painkillers in the kitchen drawer. I don't know where things are in this house yet.

'I'm fine. It's just a headache.'

'You can't be fine if you need painkillers.' She reaches up into a high cupboard and hands me down an old biscuit tin. I check out the array of tablets, go for the strongest ones. She hands me a glass of water. I swallow two pills and sneak a couple into my pocket for later. The headache's fading, but it's as well to be ready.

I sit at the table and pour some cornflakes into a bowl. I ache everywhere. Why don't I ever have a seizure in a nice soft padded cell? Or even on carpet?

Sandra puts the tin back up in the cupboard. 'Bill, you tell him.'

Bill looks up from *The Belfast Telegraph*. 'Tell him what, love?'

'That he's not up to going to school.'

Bill takes off his glasses. 'Looks all right to me. Sure isn't it great the lad wants to go?' He sets the paper down. 'She can't get used to somebody wanting to go to school. Half the kids we've had, you'd to beat them out the door.'

'Not literally *beat*,' Sandra cuts in, as if I'm going to get straight on the phone to the Social. She leans over Bill and pours herself a cup of tea, but she doesn't sit down. 'Is there any point in going in on a Friday? Sure it's nearly the weekend.'

I spoon cornflakes determinedly into my mouth. No wonder she ended up only being a foster carer with that attitude to education. 'I've already missed most of a day. All the AS courses will be starting. I don't want to get behind.'

And if I wait until Monday, if I have all weekend to remember waking up in a puddle of piss on that classroom floor with everybody staring at me, I might not have the courage to do it. I have to get it over with now. But I can't tell her that. I can't let her see I'm bothered, that in my stomach, pecking uneasily at the undigested cornflakes, is a fluttery bird that won't keep still.

'Well.' She shakes her grey frizzy head and folds her arms across her big chest. I know she's used to getting her own way. I know that's one reason I've been put here. *Sandra and Bill won't stand any nonsense.* But I'm insisting on going to *school*, not staying out all night drinking. 'At least let me drive you.'

When we're driving out of the estate, she says, 'You're a stubborn one. Brendan warned me about that.'

I wonder what else he's warned her about, but I'm not going to ask.

———

I hesitate at the door of the sixth-form centre but I can't make myself open it.

'Hey, can we get past?' Two girls push by me in a whirl of perfume and long blond hair. They may or may not be in my tutor group. Most of the girls here look the same. The door slams behind them.

There must be a library but I don't know where. I decide to try to find my tutor-group room. I take a couple of wrong turns – all the corridors are identical tunnels of scuffed cream walls punctuated by black bins and blue doors. But at last I find it, Room 33. It's empty. I head for the same seat I had yesterday. There's nothing to show what happened – no stain on the floor; no marks on the desk. It's only in my head that the seizure lingers. I take out my timetable and study it. History. English lit. Maths. Economics. Good solid subjects. Brendan encouraged me to keep on art but that would be a waste of time. It's not like I'm good enough to make a living at it. 'It's good for you to express your feelings,' Brendan says — which is the kind of puke-making thing social workers always say. I take out a pencil and doodle in the corner of my timetable, without thinking, just a little Celtic knot, and then I'm annoyed because it was all neat and perfect and now it's messed up. I check in my new pencil case but I don't have an eraser.

The door creaks open and the bird fluffs out its feathers and beats its wings against the bottom of my stomach.

It's The Girl. She's carrying an art folder, and her dark-brown hair is pulled back in a short pony tail. I look down at my timetable and then force myself to look up. She's right beside me. She hugs her folder. I read her name upside down. Esther Wilson.

'Hey,' she says.

'Hey.' I swallow.

Esther stares at her feet. 'Are you OK now?' Her cheeks are very pink.

'Fine. Thanks for ...' I wave my hand.

'You didn't miss much. We got some handouts. I took copies for you. I thought Baxter might forget. He's a bit senile.'

I wish everybody would forget. I wish they were all a bit senile. This girl, setting her folder down on the seat, rummaging in her bag, is embarrassed just *talking* to me, her face burning and her words tumbling. And she was the one who'd been so cool. What's everyone else going to be like? The bird inside me starts having a seizure of its own.

'Here.' She hands me over three sheets of A4, slightly crumpled, and an envelope with Sandra's address on it. 'Sorry. The folder got a bit squished in my bag.' Her voice is gruff and low and quick, not the reassuring calm voice I thought I remembered.

'No, that's great. Thanks.' I glance at them. Term dates. PTA. Coursework Deadlines. 'Are you going to sit down?' I ask.

'Oh.' She looks uncomfortable. 'I don't think Baxter will make us stay in the same seats.'

The bird sticks its head under its wing and stalks off.

'Suit yourself. Thanks for the handouts.'

I start reading them to show her I don't need company, I'm only being polite.

But she hesitates. 'Do you *want* me to sit here?' She pulls at her growing-out fringe.

I shrug. I read about how parents can help raise money for the new changing rooms, and how late coursework will not be tolerated. The chair beside me clatters as she pulls it out. She sits down. Glances across at me. Nervously. I can't believe this is the same girl. But the warm clean smell of her cardigan is the same.

'You're quite safe,' I say. 'I'm not going to have another fit on you.' I cross my fingers under the desk because that's a promise I can never make.

Her cheeks blaze. 'Look, you could have ten seizures a day and it wouldn't bother me. That's not what I meant.'

'Oh.' I fold the handouts; slip them into my blazer pocket.

The clock over the door says five to nine. Already the corridor outside is filling up with chatter and buzz. Before I can ask her what she *did* mean the bell clangs. Baxter comes in and dumps a bulging briefcase on his desk. Other people mooch in past him, yawning, chatting, slipping phones into pockets, pulling earphones out of ears. I look down at my timetable so I don't have to make eye contact with anybody. Double English first. Maths. Break. I read the meaningless room numbers and teacher initials and wonder when it will all make sense.

'Hey.'

I think someone must be saying hello to Esther, but when I look up, there is one of those girls they mass-produce here. Tall, blonde, tanned, beautiful, short black skirt skimming perfect thighs. Beside her a skinny girl with big eyes and mousey hair. Definitely looking at me. They don't seem to notice Esther, who's leafing through *The Great Gatsby*.

'Oh my God, are you OK?'

'We thought you were dying.'

'We were so worried about you.'

Their fussing tentacles around me. The headache throbs at my skull again.

'Jasmine, Cassie, sit down,' drones the teacher before I have to say anything, and the darker girl sighs but obeys him.

'You're in my English class,' the blonde girl says. She smiles. 'I'll show you where to go if you like. After assembly.'

'Jasmine!'

'Sorry, sir.' She flounces past my desk, her silky hair floating after her. She looks back and smiles before sitting down.

Esther chews the side of her thumbnail.

'Do you have English first?' I ask her, guessing from *The Great Gatsby* that she's doing English. 'With – um – Mr Donovan?'

'Yes. He's new. But I suppose they'll all be new to you.'

'Will you show me where to go?'

She smiles a slow wide smile. 'What about Jasmine?' she asks.

I shrug. 'What about her?'

The boy in front turns round. He has a face like a pink cushion. 'Wow,' he says. 'Two girls fighting over you on your second day.'

Esther

'And we pray, Lord ...'

Everybody in senior assembly gives up the will to live. Dad's on form. Every time you think he's prayed for the whole world he takes another breath, and says, 'And we also remember, Lord ...'

I wriggle my buttocks, which are already sore from listening to Ma McCandless's uniform lecture and the headmistress's usual new-year-new-start talk, hunch further over and study my hands.

I try to blank out Dad's holy voice but he's moved on to natural disasters and unfortunately there's been a hurricane somewhere this week and a flood somewhere else. Beside me Luke whispers, 'Are they having a competition to see who can be the most boring?'

'They're always hyper at first. It wears off by half term.'

'How many clichés can you get into one prayer? Is this wanker on speed or something?'

I don't say, *Try living with him*; I just smile and then thankfully Dad runs out of people to pray for, and five hundred people scramble up in numb-bottomed relief.

In English, Luke pulls out the seat beside mine without asking. I try to hide how pleased I am by switching into helpful-swot mode, showing him the notes we made yesterday.

'Can I borrow your book to copy this up?' he asks.

'Of course.'

People drift in around us but I don't see Jasmine. Mr Donovan, pink and baby-faced, comes in, nearly hidden under a huge pile of handouts. Luke goes up to ask for a copy of *The Great Gatsby*. Donovan can't find one and gets flustered, his cheeks blooming redder by the moment. As Luke stands by the teacher's desk, waiting, I try not to stare at him, but I can't help it. A shaft of sunlight slants through the window and finds gold lights in his hair. It's too warm in the classroom, and Luke pushes his shirtsleeves up to his elbows. I remember stroking his arm yesterday and my neck burns.

Get a grip, Esther, I tell myself. I doodle on my notes, then remember I'm meant to be lending them to Luke and stop before I draw something embarrassing.

Jasmine dashes in, clutching her books to her chest because her designer schoolbag is too tiny to actually hold anything. She pauses beside Luke at the teacher's desk.

'Oh.' she says, 'You're *here*. I thought something must have *happened* to you. I couldn't find you.'

'No,' he says. 'As you can see I managed to get here in one piece.'

Jasmine looks disappointed. She glances at Donovan, who has just located the spare copy of *The Great Gatsby* under the pile of handouts, and is trying to pull it out without making them all topple, which involves a lot of huffing and frowning, and seems to decide he isn't worth apologising to. She scans the room, her eyes sliding over me like I'm invisible, and goes to sit with Cassie.

Luke's eyes follow her down the classroom. He might be a bit brusque with her but he clearly hasn't failed to notice her attributes.

What about my *attributes, Luke? I might be plump and quiet but I'm brighter than she is. And quite a lot nicer.*

As if that ever counted for anything.

Would you give him one, Esther?

If only.

I have to catch myself on. I've had crushes before – crushes are all I've had – but never on someone I've actually spoken to. Never on someone real.

I dodge McCandless outside the locker room door, and have to step over outstretched ten-denier legs. Because our names are close together – Wilson and Wright – my locker is near Jasmine's. I try to manhandle my art folder so it fits in.

Jasmine leans back against her locker and opens her make-up bag. 'Don't move, Cassie,' she says. 'I'm going to prop my bag up on your leg.'

'Go ahead, babes.' Cassie looks as if life can hold nothing better than being a human make-up table for Jasmine Wright. Her nose has been out of joint since Jasmine's been letting the twins hang round her.

'Watch out for McCandless,' I say. 'She's on the warpath.'

Cassie makes a who-asked-you? face.

'Huh!' Jasmine says, squeezing foundation on to her hand. 'I'd like to do a makeover on *her*. Can you imagine trying to cover up those whiskers? So, *Esther*,' she goes on, in something more like the friendly voice she used yesterday lunchtime, 'are you *sure* there's nothing going on between you and Luke?'

I shake my head, willing my cheeks not to burn.

'You were *very* quick to take him under your wing.' She smooths foundation over her already perfect cheeks.

I shrug. 'We were just going the same way.'

'Right.'

I remember what Toby said to Luke this morning, *Two girls fighting over you on your second day*. He was joking. But if this *is* a fight – and it does feel a tiny bit like one at this moment – what weapons have *I* got against Jasmine Wright?

———————————

As always, my spirit relaxes the moment I enter the library. It's old and pretty, with stained glass windows and scratched wooden tables, and tightly packed shelves running up to high ceilings.

The only free seat is in the far corner under the picture of the school's founder, Elias Mansfield. I take out *The Great Gatsby* and one of Donovan's handouts about the Jazz Age. I chew my pen and look up at Elias. I've never really noticed him before. He's one of those Victorian guys with weird swoops of facial hair. Hands clasped across a huge stomach. Big teeth resting on a too-red under-lip; droopy eyelids. If you look closely his eyes are kind and suggest he'd enjoy a joke – a nice clean Victorian one – but I reckon most people, if they notice him at all, just see the ugliness. If Luke looked like *that*, or like that pizza-faced boy in the upper sixth, who I always feel sorry for though I don't know his name, those girls wouldn't be so keen.

I frown at my notes. Why am I so annoyed? Do I *want* Luke to get a hard time because of what happened yesterday? No, of course not. I was relieved this morning when nobody stared or whispered. I'm delighted for him that the cool girls want to make friends.

OK, not *delighted*.

A shadow looms beside me. It's Luke, as if I've conjured him up. My stomach flutters.

He sets his bag on the table. 'D'you mind?' he asks. 'All the other tables are full.'

'Course not.' I pull the handouts towards me to make room at the desk. I try not to over-analyse his remark about the other tables. Did he mean he *wouldn't* have sat here if he'd had a choice?

He takes out a file block and the notebook I lent him. It's funny seeing it in his hands, my loopy scrawl and doodled margins. He leans back in his seat and looks up at the high vaulted ceiling and stained glass.

'Wow,' he says.

'Shh,' hisses Miss McGurk, the librarian, who's probably been here since Elias Mansfield's time. '*Silent* study.'

We exchange grins, and Luke gets down to copying out my notes. He works with a fierce concentration, even though it's only a few basic biographical notes about F Scott Fitzgerald. His handwriting is so clear I can nearly read it upside down. I wonder what school he went to before and why he moved. A boy at the next table goes up to ask McGurk something and she starts tapping at the computer on her desk, chatting to him.

I take advantage of her distraction to ask Luke, 'What school were you at before?'

He hesitates. 'Belvedere High.'

'Oh.' Unexpected. The Bearpit, as everybody calls it, is one of the roughest schools in Belfast. It's always being threatened with closure, and its pupils are more likely to graduate to prison than to the sixth form of Mansfield. That's *statistically* true, not me being snobby. And he doesn't *sound* like he went to the Bearpit. 'Why did you move?'

Luke raises his eyebrows. 'Why d'you think?' He underlines a subheading in red. 'Can I ask you something?'

'Yes.'

'Yesterday – how come you knew what to do? I mean, do you do first aid or something? People don't usually have a clue.'

'I helped out at a summer scheme for kids with special needs. Some of them had epilepsy as well as other stuff. One kid fitted nearly every day. I just got used to it.'

On McGurk's desk the printer hums and then stops. She frowns at it. 'I'll have to go for paper,' she says.

As soon as she leaves, the noise level in the library creeps up, which makes it easier to talk.

'Have you always had it?' I ask.

'Only since January.'

'Is it controlled? I mean, normally?'

He frowns. 'I keep hoping it is and then …' His mouth twists.

'Bad luck on your first day.'

'Yeah.' He seems to think about this, then shrugs it off. 'Good luck to be sitting beside *you*, though.'

'Any time.' Stupid thing to say.

Luke doesn't reply but just continues writing. I highlight key points in yellow on my handout. I wish I wasn't so *aware* of him across from me. I try not to look at him, but I can't stop my eyes from glancing up every so often. My brain makes notes without me asking it to.

Grey-blue eyes, dark lashes – darker than his hair. Pale, freshly shaved skin. His lips are dry, a few tiny flecks flaking away from the skin. He should put some Vaseline on them. My tongue imagines licking his lips, and I have to swallow hard and concentrate on *The Great Gatsby*, but my eyes and brain keep up their inventory. A tiny cut on his cheekbone – from the seizure. I can't help comparing the self-contained boy sitting here taking neat notes with the other Luke, unconscious and convulsing on the floor.

And how weird am I, to have been so much more confident with *that* Luke?

Luke puts his pen down and leans his elbows on the table, cupping his chin in his hands. 'What?' he asks.

My face burns. 'Sorry – I'm just …'

Just wondering what your lips feel like. Just remembering how close I felt to you yesterday when I was the only one who knew how to help you. Just remembering the feel of your skin under my hand. Just wondering how to deal with all these feelings zinging through me.

'… wondering if my notes are OK?'

'They're fine,' he says. 'Thanks.'

Luke

Another good thing about Sandra: she always knocks.

'Come in,' I say, looking up from *The Great Gatsby*.

Sandra puts her head round the door and smiles. 'Up and dressed already?'

'I'm always up early.' I slide my finger between the pages to keep my place.

'Bill always does a fry on Saturday mornings. And then he does the hoovering for me. We just wondered – would you take a wee fry? What do you like?'

It's weird, living with someone who doesn't know what you eat or when you get up.

'I don't mind. Anything.'

Sandra looks round the room. It looks exactly as it did when I moved in on Monday, except for my new MacBook Air sitting on the small IKEA desk, and the pile of books beside the bed.

'You can put up any posters you like,' she says. 'We want you to feel at home.'

The walls are OK, freshly painted magnolia. Hardly worth messing them up.

'I could do with some bookshelves.'

'Och, aye,' she says. 'We should have thought of that. Brendan said you were a great one for your books.' Not for the first time I wonder what else Brendan has said. 'Bill can sort you out something,' she goes on. 'He's hands for anything. Sure, come on down and we'll ask him.'

Bill, cracking eggs into a pan, face shiny with heat, smiles when he sees me. 'Och, that's great,' he says. 'Nothing like your fry.'

We never had fried stuff. Stir fry maybe, but not an Ulster fry – the full heart attack on a plate – all bread and shiny egg and processed pig, glistening with grease on Sandra's old-fashioned flowery plates. Not that you can see the pattern for the food piled on top. You'd think Bill and Sandra would be obese, eating this stuff, but she's just grannyishly plump and he has only a bit of a belly.

I stick my fork into the egg, and yolk spurts out.

Sandra pours tea from a huge brown pot, then squeezes into her seat. 'That wee cat's on the windowsill again,' she says. 'I'm going to have to start feeding it.'

I look up at the window but the black kitten jumps down when it sees me.

'So, what do you normally do at weekends?' Sandra asks, attacking her own fry.

'Och, Sandra, leave the lad alone. He probably just likes to – what do they call it – hang out. Isn't that right, son?' He gives me an all-boys-together smile. A bean is lodged in his moustache.

I shake my head. I'm certainly not going to *hang out* on this estate.

'Homework,' I say, cutting up a sausage. 'Reading.'

Sandra looks alarmed. 'Aye, but you don't sit in all the time, do you? Young fellow like you?'

'No.' I try to think what I *did*, back when I had a normal life. Drawing is the first thing that comes to mind. But there's no point now. 'I go running. Or cycling.' Suddenly the idea of the day – the weekend – two years – stretching ahead in this tiny house is unbearable. 'I think I'll cycle to the library.'

'Sure the library's only round the corner,' Bill says. 'Take you two minutes to walk round.'

I've checked it out already. It's small and full of celebrity biographies.

'I meant my own library – the one I used to go to.'

'*Cycle?*' Sandra says. 'Is that a good idea?' She means should someone who's liable to smash to the ground without warning be allowed out on the roads in charge of a bike.

I shrug. 'I have a helmet.'

'I know, but ... if something ...'

'Sandra. Love.' Bill sets down his knife and fork, burps and covers his mouth. 'Pardon me. You can't wrap the lad in cotton wool.'

'But if he fell off – in the traffic? He'd be killed! That main road!'

'He could cycle on the footpath.'

I'm seventeen, I want to scream. *I am not riding my bike on the bloody footpath.*

'Did the doctor say you could ride a bike?' Bill asks, pouring out another cup of tea.

I frown at my plate. Despite this very annoying conversation, I seem to have eaten most of the fry.

'She said, be sensible. She said' – I take a deep breath; I've heard this a million times – 'there's no reason not to lead a perfectly normal life as long as I don't take unnecessary risks.'

'Well.' Sandra's mouth tightens in triumph, 'I think that counts as an unnecessary risk all right.'

'She *meant* drink and drugs and stuff, I think,' I argue. 'Which I don't do.'

Sandra and Bill exchange glances as if they know better. Which means Brendan must have let rip with the gory details.

I mop up the last of my tomato sauce with a piece of soda bread I've been saving. I make a huge effort to sound calm.

'Look,' I say, 'I hardly ever have seizures on this new medication. Maybe one a month. Not even.'

Bill seizes on this. 'See, Sandra, the lad knows his limits.'

'Bill, he's a seventeen-year-old boy. Of course he doesn't know his limits.'

'I am in the room, you know. And I don't think anybody can actually *stop* me. I'm not a child.'

Sandra bangs down the teapot. 'For crying out loud! Look, you're right. We can't stop you. But we're responsible for you. We don't want anything to happen to you.'

'It *won't*.'

And really, what does it matter to them? They'd still get paid even if I was in hospital. They met me for the first time a few weeks ago, a polite meeting with Brendan doing most of the talking; I've lived in their house for five days. They can't pretend to *care*. And at the end of the day they can just send me back.

Except.

Except this is Last Chance Saloon. I'm not stupid, and Brendan has been pretty up-front. 'It's not easy getting foster carers for older teenagers, Luke,' he'd told me. 'We're very lucky that Sandra and Bill are willing.' *We*. Like it mattered to him. 'Put me in a flat,' I told Brendan. 'I can look after myself; I don't need *carers*.' But Brendan told me not to be stupid; they don't set seventeen-year-olds up in flats. 'Especially not ones with epilepsy. Can you imagine if you had a seizure in the shower? With no one around? Or hit your head?'

'A hostel then,' I suggested. I didn't need to be in a *family*. I don't *do* family. 'All I need's a room. Some meals. Just somewhere to stay till I go to university.'

Brendan laughed – not at the idea of me going to uni; he'd realised by then that I'm not as thick as most of the losers he works with. 'Luke, you wouldn't last two days in a hostel. They'd eat you alive. No. Our recommendation is another foster placement. And Sandra and Bill are great; you'll like them.'

The stupid thing is I *do* like them. They're a bit old and a bit (let's face it) common, and their house is too fussy for me, with all those photos of their daughter and even their old foster kids – but they are *nice*.

It's the bloody epilepsy that is the trouble. Nobody knows how to deal with it.

Including me.

'Everybody else my age is learning to *drive*,' I point out. 'I need to have *some* independence.'

'And he probably wants to see his old friends. That's only natural,' Bill says. I don't know yet if I should welcome Bill being on my side, but he's got it wrong about the old friends anyway. People at Belvedere didn't live in South Road. People who lived in South Road went to Mansfield. And now *I* go to Mansfield and live in the same kind of estate as people from Belvedere. But on the far side of town. I can't keep up with my own social mobility.

Esther's face swims into my head. Talking to her yesterday was the first conversation about epilepsy that hasn't done my head in. For the first time I kind of understand why Brendan is always trying to pack me off to support groups and things. Not that I'd be seen dead at one.

With a supreme effort at self-control and maturity I say, 'Well, I suppose I don't *have* to go today.'

Bill looks relieved; Sandra triumphant.

I look at the flowery wipe-clean tablecloth and wonder how I'm going to survive weekends in this house, on this estate, for two whole years.

I sit on my bed and take Esther's notes out of my schoolbag even though I know the two pages by heart. Her writing is loopy and girly, slightly backhand, and there are doodles in the margins – a flower; the letter E made fancy and swirly like something out of the Book of Kells; a cat. Nothing revealing. Blue ink. Red underlining.

I smooth the two sheets of paper and put them in a plastic folder.

'Luke?'

Bill's knock comes a fraction *after* his voice and the head round the door. I frown but say, 'Uh-huh?'

He looks round. 'Phooo!' He lets out a long breath. 'I've never seen this room so tidy.'

'I'm a tidy person.' I wonder how many kids have slept in this room before me.

'Sandra said you need shelves for your books.' He takes a tape measure out of his back pocket and puts his glasses on. 'Now,' he says, 'we can put some up above the desk – three maybe? Would that be enough? About – what – three foot long each?'

'Thanks.'

I don't know why he wants to mess up his walls. It'd be easier to buy a bookcase in IKEA, and probably cheaper. Maybe he has loads of wood lying round in his shed. Maybe he likes a project. Or maybe he's trying to get in with me.

He leans across the desk. 'Just grab the other end of this, would you, son?' He indicates the tape measure.

I stand up and hold it. He mutters measurements, lifts a pen from the desk and scribbles them down on his hand.

He clicks the tape to make it slide back into the plastic casing and puts it back in his pocket. I wait for him to go. I can probably finish *The Great Gatsby*, or read my history textbook. One full day at Mansfield has been enough to show me that people are far cleverer than I've been used to. At Belvedere it was easy being top of everything – most of the others were barely literate; now I know I'll have to work my ass off just to keep up.

Bill doesn't leave; he grabs the chair at the desk and nods at me as if asking for permission to sit down. I can't say no, so I nod back. He sits. I stay standing.

'Look, lad, I'm sorry if Sandra came across a bit– overprotective.'

'It's OK.'

'It's just – some of the kids we've had – well, they've been handfuls. Drinking, stealing, mitching school. Drugs. Fighting. You name it.'

'I wanted to go to the *library*.'

'I think she feels – you're educated and all. She feels a wee bit … you know …'

'I have nine GCSEs,' I point out, 'not a flipping PhD.'

'Och, aye, but Sandra and I – we're more used to …'

'I'll get drunk and trash my room,' I offer, 'if it'll make her feel more comfortable.'

Bill laughs and for a long horrible second I think he is going to reach up and ruffle my hair or something. But he stands up. 'We'll all get used to each other, son. It's early days.' He looks round the walls. 'I did them magnolia just to clean them up,' he says, 'but if you wanted a different colour …'

'It's fine. Thanks.'

'There's a good match on. Man U and Arsenal. We've got BT Sports.'

'I don't really follow football.'

'Rugby, is it?' I can see him trying to cover up the thought, *snobby wee get*. 'Oh, well, kick-off 's at three if you change your mind.'

I don't change my mind.

Esther

I spend too much of my weekend thinking about Luke Bressan. Some of the thoughts embarrass me. I lie on my bed, hugging Mac, my ancient cuddly dog, and listening to Taylor Swift. All the boys in her songs make me think about Luke.

I try to distract myself with baking. I make gingerbread men, and their lovely spicy smell draws Mum into the kitchen, smiling in approval, which she hasn't done much of lately. But when the time comes to decorate them I hesitate. That was always Ruth's job: I baked, she iced. We had quite a production line going for Youth Fellowship socials and church cake sales. Back in my sad old life.

Only, looking back, it doesn't seem that sad. At least I always had somewhere to go and someone to be with. If only Mum and Dad weren't at the same church.

I know if I texted Ruth she'd be glad to hear from me – we never fell out or anything. It's just – well, I didn't know how to tell her I was dumping Jesus: I knew she'd want to *analyse* it all and probably *pray* – and I get enough of that at home. So I just kind of walked away, and I don't really think I can just walk back again. Even though I miss her.

The gingerbread men sit on the cooling tray all evening looking faceless and forlorn. I could bring them into school – Toby would love them – but it'd look pathetic and mumsy.

On Sunday morning Mum and Dad go to church. They've stopped asking me to come. They've said they respect my misgivings, and doubt is part of faith, and they know teenagers often rebel against their parents' beliefs. They've said

I may think I've given up on God but God hasn't given up on me. I think Pastor Greg must have given them a leaflet or something: *What to do when your child won't go to church.*

I might as well have been there because they relive every moment of the service just so I know what I'm missing.

It's quite a relief to get back to school on Monday.

Luke

I take my timetable out of my blazer pocket. RE. It's the class before lunch and I'm hungry, and tired in that dozy, cotton-wool-headed way that is my medication's way of reminding me it's inside me, doing a not-wholly-successful job of stopping my brain going haywire. I'm half-tempted to skive, except that'd be playing into the hands of everybody who thinks someone like me won't be able to cut it at a school like this, so I hack my way through a clump of shrill brats and find the right room.

The crowd milling round outside the door looks familiar, and my chest flutters. We must do RE in tutor groups. In subject classes I can just be an anonymous new boy, but with this lot there's no hiding from being the loser who lost total control of himself on the first day. It's Wednesday now but they still eye me nervously, like I'm going to start frothing at the mouth and rolling round on the floor. Maybe even now they're checking me out, wondering what the likelihood is of me getting them out of a boring RE class.

But tutor group also means Esther. She isn't here yet but when the teacher – that old baldy bloke who was praying for about sixteen hours in assembly on Friday – herds us into the room, I keep a seat for her. There's the usual turning round and chatting, so it looks like people don't take RE any more seriously here than they did at Belvedere.

Esther dashes in, and her face floods with colour when she sees Baldy.

'Sorry – um, sir. I had to wash paint off my hands.' She holds up her hands as if for proof, but the teacher, sorting through bits of paper, hardly glances up, just tells her to sit down quickly.

I catch her eye and she slides into the seat beside me. She has her hair in stubby pigtails and her cheeks are still red.

'Now, lower six B,' Baldy says in a voice totally different from his praying one, 'Miss Carr is off today so it falls on me to be taking you.' He beams round as if we should all be praising God about this. 'Now, this term you're doing Ethics.'

On and on he drones. Something about the sanctity of life. He manages to squeeze in even more clichés than in his prayers. The classroom is boiling. A fly flings itself at the dusty window. My eyes prickle and the effort to stretch them open seems hardly worth it for this.

Beside me, Esther looks equally bored. In fact she looks sort of distant. Not like herself at all. There are streaks of purple paint on her hands. I wonder what she's painting and if it's more revealing than her doodles. I have a sudden anger that she gets to draw and paint and I don't – but giving up art was my own decision.

Baldy waffles on about every person being unique and valuable and special to God. The boy across the aisle is texting. Jasmine and Cassie look at an iPad under their textbook. Esther is staring down at her notebook, her dark lashes semi-circles on her cheeks. They look soft, not sticky and mascaraed like most of the other girls'.

'You! Yes, you – what's your name?'

'Me? Luke.' Baldy doesn't seem satisfied. 'Bressan.' Still looking at me expectantly. 'Sir.'

'And is it too much to expect a modicum of attention?'

Well, yes, frankly, when what you're talking about – last time I tuned in – is such a load of clichéd wank.

'Sorry.'

'And you have joined us from …?'

'Belvedere High,' I mutter.

Someone giggles.

'Ah yes. Quite. Well, the standards of Belvedere High are not the standards of Mansfield Grammar. Permit me to point this out to you, since nobody else seems to have done so.'

Bastard.

Just to annoy him I focus raptly on what he is saying – euthanasia, or abortion or something. My head turns to concrete with the effort. There isn't enough air to go round, and someone in front has farted. At Belvedere people used to fart out loud and laugh and wave it around but of course that doesn't happen at Mansfield, where the standard of farting is so much higher.

I prop my head on my hands. A yawn stretches out.

'Mr Bressan!' Baldy swoops down. 'Am I boring you so much?' He doesn't wait for an answer. 'So what is your opinion on this? I'm sure it's worth sharing.'

'My opinion? On …?'

'Abortion,' he snaps. Beady brown eyes bore into me.

'I'm in favour.' My voice comes out louder than I expected. Esther gives me a surprised look. A giggle punctuates the air.

'In every circumstance?'

I bet he is wishing someone had aborted me seventeen years ago. I haven't exactly been keeping up with the discussion, but I'm not too dozy not to know he's trying to catch me out.

'Obviously not.' I try to mimic his tone. 'But if the mother doesn't want it, yes. If she isn't going to be able to give it a life.' I do feel qualified to have an opinion on this.

'She should have it adopted, not kill it,' says someone behind me.

Girls get involved, all smarmy voices.

'Oh, but how could you give up your baby?'

'Better than murdering it. At least it can go to someone who wants a baby.'

'They don't just get adopted, though.' I recognise Jasmine's confident voice. 'I saw this programme about it. They get shunted around in foster care for years. By the time you get them they're not even babies and they're, like, traumatised.'

I frown at my desk. This isn't the way the conversation should be going.

'Well.' Baldy's voice is very confident. 'I know Social Services do their best.'

He's looking at me. I swear the bastard is looking right at me. And he's the pastoral care bloke, isn't he? That means he must know all about me. I can't let him go there. In front of everyone. An anger I've sat on for months surges through me. Sweat pricks my palms. My chest tightens.

'You know fuck all.'

At first I don't realise the words have actually come out of my mouth. Or that I'm standing up, hand curled into a fist. Breath huffs down my nose. Baldy's face is a few inches from mine. I can smell his breath.

Someone gasps. Baldy's face patches red and purple. The air in the room kind of solidifies. It's almost like the split-second before a seizure when everything feels different but you don't get time to wonder why.

But no seizure delivers me from this. I wish I could walk out, but there's nowhere to go.

Baldy recovers first. 'Sit down, Mr Bressan.' His voice is high-pitched but controlled. 'As I said, the standards of this school are clearly not what you're used to.'

I sit down. I wait to hear what they're going to do to me. Swearing at teachers happened every day at Belvedere – but I was always the good boy there. I don't want to be the bad boy here. I just want to be invisible. Baldy tells us to make notes from Chapter 3, and everyone settles down. Esther hunches over her work and pulls her chair round so she has her back to me.

Baldy escapes the moment the bell goes. He doesn't speak to us again except to tell us to finish the notes. I bend down to lift up my bag and when I straighten up, Esther has disappeared too. People drift out, not looking at me.

I lean back in my chair.

Toby stops in front of me, his pinkish face very earnest. 'I think Esther's upset because you were so rude to her dad.' His reedy voice is uncertain.

I don't get it. 'Her dad?'

'Yeah. Mr Wilson. Didn't you know?'

I shake my head. 'Of course not.' We know nothing about each other, really. But now – she must think I'm some kind of psycho.

Toby gives me a sympathetic grimace. 'I'll go and find her and explain,' he offers.

'I should –'

He hesitates, then seems to make up his mind. 'We sometimes go to that new juice bar on the main road – turn right at the school gates.'

'Thanks.'

I grab my bag and run.

Esther

Toilets – sixth-form centre – canteen – even library – zoom through my mind as places I can't bear to be.

And I *mustn't* bump into Dad.

My legs carry me out of the main building, round by the mobiles, down the back drive and right out of the gates. Straight onto the main road and into Jus, the juice bar where I've started hanging out a bit at lunchtimes with Toby when he's not at chess club.

I slip into a corner seat. A waitress with pink hair and a pierced lip takes my order. I'm too wired to choose, and she gets impatient, so I go for boring orange, even though Toby and I have been having a competition to see how many weird fruit combinations we can come up with. All the while my brain flashes messages: *Don't think about it! Don't think about it!*

Yeah, like that's possible. I keep replaying the scene: one minute a boring RE class, with that undercurrent of discomfort I always feel when I have to be in the same room as Dad in school, and the next something ugly and violent. Luke had looked like – someone I didn't recognise. Someone who was about to thump my dad.

'Esther?'

I glance up. 'Oh.'

Luke's hands stroke the top of the chair opposite. I try to forget the fantasies I've had about those long fingers. And the fact that I've just seen them curled into fists.

'Can I sit down?'

I hump a shoulder. 'If you want.'

He pulls out the chair and sits. His hair is rumpled, like he's been raking his hands through it. I want to reach across the table and smooth it back, kiss his eyelids, run my finger over his lips.

No. I don't.

The waitress comes up and Luke orders a carrot, ginger and apple juice. A detached part of my mind thinks, *Toby'd like that, I must tell him.* I have a sudden worry that Luke might be gay, like Toby. Maybe being able to choose cool fruit combinations under pressure is a gay thing. Not that Toby's ever actually said it, even to me.

'I'm sorry,' Luke says.

The cold inside me starts to melt. A tiny bit.

'I ... I didn't know he was your dad.'

'I thought you were going to *hit* him. Just – out of nowhere. It was horrible.'

'I know.' His juice arrives, sludge-coloured. He lifts the glass, then sets it down again. His lips are taut. 'He – I suppose he touched a nerve.'

I try to process this. What had it even been about? 'So – are you, like, adopted or something?'

He sighs. 'I'm in foster care. I didn't want people to know.'

'Why not?' I've never met anyone in care before. Well, Mihai's adopted – he came here from Romania when he was three, but I suppose that's different.

'I just want to be the same as other people,' he mutters. 'Blend in.'

I wrap my hands round the cold glass. 'That's going well, isn't it?'

He gives a short unamused laugh.

'So how come you're in care?'

'Oh.' He bites his lip. 'My mum died.'

'I'm sorry.' But I'm glad too. It's such a *respectable* reason. I've seen the same TV programmes as Jasmine. I've seen the hopeless alcoholic parents and their flotsam and jetsam kids. I'm so glad that's not Luke's background.

'How long – I mean when did she . . . ?'

'January.'

The waitress bustles up again. 'Do yous want anything else?'

'When do we need to be back at school?' Luke asks.

'Oh – kind of in five minutes,' I say regretfully.

His hand uncurls itself from round his glass and lies on the table between us. One finger twitches. More than anything I want to stretch out my own hand towards it. January. That's only nine months ago.

'So what are your foster parents like?'

Parents? Is that the right word? Or is it carers? This is a bit of a minefield and I definitely don't want to *touch a nerve* like Dad.

Dad's head of pastoral care. He must have *known*. Then I think back to the scene in the classroom. Of course he knows. That's why he let Luke off with it.

I wonder what else he knows.

I realise Luke's talking. 'Sandra and Bill.' His face relaxes. 'It's fine. They don't bother me; I don't bother them. It's a bit like being a lodger, I suppose.' He somehow manages to make me feel childish and pathetic for still living with my parents at the age of sixteen. 'Come on,' he says, standing up. 'We should get back.' I think he might hold out his hand, and if he does I will take it.

But he doesn't.

Luke

Brendan leans back in the faux-leather sofa, making his small paunch more obvious. Let himself go a bit. Better not get hooked on Bill's Saturday fry-ups if I don't want to go the same way. We're in a café for our monthly meeting. Brendan's idea. I think it's meant to make me feel blokey and matey and adult. It doesn't make me feel any different but it makes him look like a sad bastard, having coffee with a seventeen-year-old boy. He's too young to be my dad. Maybe he looks like he's *grooming* me.

Or maybe it looks like exactly what it is: try-too-hard social worker and monosyllabic teenager-in-care. Client. Service user. All those stupid words they use to make you feel like you've *chosen* to have Social Services creeping all over you.

Still, I'll say this for him: it's a lovely café. All exposed brick and old photos. It's called Coffee Spoons. I know that comes from a poem. I don't suppose Brendan does.

'So?' he asks. His goatee beard trembles with anticipation.

'So what?'

'Come on, Luke. The new school. Sandra and Bill. Everything.'

'Fine.'

Brendan raises disappointed eyebrows. There's a bit of scurf in one. I scratch my own eyebrow.

'It's good. They're nice.'

'Luke – you got an A star for English GCSE. You didn't get that saying *good* and *nice*.'

I sigh and blow foam across the top of my cappuccino. What else is there to say? Sandra and Bill are doing a very satisfactory job. Why can't he just tick a box saying so and leave me alone? He must have other kids to see.

'I'm sure the new school must be – challenging?'

'It's OK.'

'Luke. Please? Give me just a *wee* bit more?'

I sigh. Then try. 'It's like a different planet. From Belvedere I mean.'

He nods. Waits. Like he's probably been trained to do.

'They have *music* lessons. And prefects. And houses in Donegal. And they carry their *oboes* round the way people in Belvedere carried knives.'

Actually there had been just that one incident with the knife in Belvedere. But I like to remind Brendan of it whenever he implies I'm a soft sap who can't *cope*.

'*You* can have music lessons. There's a special project called Fosteri–'

'I don't want bloody music lessons.' It's enough coping with the normal lessons. But that is what I don't want Brendan to know. Mansfield is the best school in town; I proved I could get in and now I *have* to prove I'm up to it. Even without Helena pushing and helping. I never think about Helena, so I rush on. 'I just mean – they play *rugby*. It's like Eton or somewhere.'

Brendan bites off a grin. 'Luke. It's a Belfast grammar school. It's nothing like Eton.'

Like *he'd* know. He comes from Ballymena. 'But the work, the standard – you're coping with that OK?'

'Yep.'

I look down into my cappuccino. I know he isn't fooled. Brendan's not a genius but he has known me for three years.

'It's bound to be a big jump – from GCSE. I'm sure everybody –'

'It's fine.' But he's fixing me with that terrier look, and I won't get him off my case until I give him a bit of what he wants. 'It's just – at Belvedere it was easy to be top. Everybody else was thick. Nobody even wanted to work. So I thought I was smart. And now – everybody's smart.' I shrug, to show I accept this, to show that I was never so naïve as to think I was anything *special.*

'But you got great GCSEs.'

I can't explain. That all I had to do for GCSE was learn everything. And Hel– the teachers helped: they couldn't get over the fact that someone actually *wanted* to work, and they used to give me extra help at lunchtime. It was something to do, and somewhere to go away from all the psychos. Even after the epilepsy, apart from that first load of meds that turned me into a zombie, I could still learn enough to do well. I got the best GCSEs anyone in Belvedere had ever got in the entire history of the school. Four A stars and five As. The teachers were practically *crying* on results day. The headmaster shook my hand.

But now. I do everything they tell you. Read over my notes every night. Spend all my free periods in the library. But I don't understand everything. Not all the economics and maths anyway. History and English are OK. Walsh, the history bloke, gave me A- for my first essay. I've read all the set books in English even though we're still on *The Great Gatsby.*

'Only Sandra mentioned you seem to be working very hard. In your room for hours every night. She's worried you're not getting enough sleep.'

Aha. I should have known he'd be having cosy chats with Sandra.

'Sandra's just not used to people doing homework.'

'She says your light's on when she's going to bed.'

'Brendan – I can't believe I'm getting hassle for doing *homework*!' And the idea of people spying on me makes my skin shrivel.

'I just don't think you should be working so hard. Maybe if I had a word with the school you could drop a subject –'

'Don't you dare!'

He changes tack then, slickly. 'And the epilepsy?' He always keeps this for last.

'OK.'

'Seizures?'

'One. First day of term. In school.'

Sandra will have told him this; he just wants to make me talk about it.

'Ah.' He nods sympathetically. 'Unfortunate.'

'Yep. You only get one chance to make a first impression.' I say it as lightly as I can and for once he takes the hint and drops the subject.

'Friends?'

'Yeah. Some.'

Toby, I suppose. I first started talking to him because he was Esther's friend, but now I like him for himself. He always keeps me a seat in economics and he has a way of seeming uncomfortable in his body that I sort of under-stand. And Esther, though I don't know how I feel about her now she knows so much about me.

'You know –' Brendan leans across the table as if he's about to share some amazing insight – 'you should give yourself a break about the academic side of things. Why not *join* something?'

I shrug and say maybe, just to get him off my back, and then it's time for him to go, thank goodness. Brendan offers me a lift but I say I'll get the bus.

I don't get the bus; the thought of having a seizure on a bus is too horrible, so I'm getting used to doing a lot of walking, which is probably why, despite Sandra's meals, I'm thinner and fitter than I've been for ages. Unlike Brendan.

Maybe that's what makes me think, next morning, about Brendan's suggestion. Social workers always want you to *join* stuff; it probably gives them an extra box to tick. But there's one thing here at Mansfield that I wouldn't mind joining. One thing that seems to give you instant acceptance.

I put my name down for rugby.

Last week we didn't have games because of some careers talk, so this is the first proper games class. There are five other new boys. We stand at the edge of the pitch, sizing each other up with sidelong looks. One of the boys is built like a gorilla, with black stubble that seems to grow as you watch it.

Holden, the coach, surveys us like an identity parade. When he gets to me he looks me up and down. I concentrate on standing tall in my new Mansfield sports kit.

'Played before?'

'Soccer.'

He curls his long upper lip. 'We don't play *soccer* here.'

That's why I've put my name down for rugby, you dick.

'I'm fast,' I say.

'Name?'

I tell him. He scans the list in his hand, then looks up. His red jowls wobble in discomfort. 'Ah, you're the epileptic boy?'

'No.'

'No?'

'No. I *have* epilepsy; I'm not *defined* by it.' OK, I know I sound like a wanker. I suppose I'm quoting Helena.

A couple of the other boys titter.

'Och, aye, son, you know what I mean.' He taps his pen on his list. 'Look, lad, rugby's a contact sport. Very physical. I don't think it would be a good idea. If you had a – problem – in the middle of a scrum – no. Too risky.'

'I *wouldn't*.'

'Sorry, son. What about hockey?'

'It's a girls' game.'

Holden looks like he secretly agrees with me. The other boys have fallen out of line into chattering groups.

'You don't have to do games,' Holden says. 'Not in your condition.' He makes it sound like I'm nine months pregnant. 'You can sit it out in the library. Probably safer.'

'Sir, I have a right to join in.'

'And I have a right to say who plays what. No, son. Different, maybe, if you'd a bit of experience.'

'You have to let me exercise. It's a statutory right.' Shut up, Helena's voice. You're not in my life now.

But Holden is already wetting himself in glee at whatever the gorilla is telling him. He barely glances back at me. 'You say you can run? Well, join the cross-country group. Over there.' He points down the steps to the far corner of the grounds, where a clump of people are hanging round chatting, doing the occasional warm-up stretch when they catch him looking over.

Another battle lost. I might as well wrap myself in a blanket and wait to die. In the meantime – well, cross-country running doesn't sound *too* bad.

I set off at a steady pace.

Esther

I squidge myself into a more comfy position on the wooden bench. Over on the pitches, people are doing real exercise. Ugh. Beside me, Toby and Cassie half-heartedly swing their arms to warm up. Two spotty asthmatic boys push their glasses up their noses and carry on talking about *Minecraft*.

'My counsellor says exercise is good for me,' Cassie says after two swings. She waits, clearly wanting me to ask why she has a counsellor. If it's to help her not to be a jealous psycho bitch it's not working. She looks mournfully into the distance where Jasmine, captain of the second eleven, is doing her hockey thing. I think I see the twins buzzing round her with their matching long blond plaits. 'But I have to be careful not to *overdo* things.' After another swing, she flops down beside me with a groan and stretches out so there's hardly room for me. 'Time of the month,' she mouths.

Toby looks mortified and shuffle-wobbles away towards the fence, exercise clearly being the lesser of two evils. The other boys sniff and study their phones. Suddenly Cassie narrows her eyes. 'Someone's coming,' she says. She's still lying on the bench, but she's turned her head in the direction of the rugby pitch up above us.

'So?' Sometimes Miss Dickie comes and checks up on us, but as long as you aren't actually horizontal she never minds much. We're too hopeless to bother with.

And it isn't bad out here in the air. It gets nasty by November, but right now, on a golden September afternoon, with the sun warm on my bare arms, it's OK.

I look in the same direction as Cassie. The figure walking towards us isn't Miss Dickie. It's a tall, determined-looking blond boy.

Luke.

Immediately my skin prickles. I haven't seen him since the day in the juice bar last week. I mean, I've *seen* him, but we haven't spoken apart from, *Did you read Chapter 3?* and *Isn't that essay title impossible?* He has definitely backed off.

I pretend not to notice him and even consider following Toby round the fence. But no matter how much my brain might order my feet to run in the other direction, they are rooted to the ground, and my heart has swelled to about three times its normal size.

'It's the new boy,' Cassie says. Without Jasmine she's a lot friendlier, because she always needs an audience.

'So it is.' I sound like nothing could interest me less. I open *Tender is the Night*.

'Hi,' Luke says, to me more than Cassie, since Cassie has her eyes closed and is groaning faintly. He looks down at her with an expression of distaste and moves away. 'Is this the cross-country running group?'

'Well,' I say. To my amazement my voice sounds bright and confident, even though my heart is banging against my chest. 'I wouldn't *exactly* call it that.'

The asthmatics slope off. Cassie waits for attention, eyes closed.

'So what is it, then?' Luke demands.

Obviously I'm not going to *say* it's a rejects club. Instead I say, 'Running *is* an available option. Cross-country – not so much.' I spread my hands as if to show him an amazing view. 'You have the perimeter of the netball pitch, round behind the bike sheds, the main driveway, down by the war memorial – that's quite nice actually – up past the mobiles and then the glorious sweep round the rugby pitch so everyone can actually *see* you and laugh at you, because by then you're half dead and hyperventilating.' I don't know where the words are coming from. I seem to have been colonised by a helpful alien power – some sassy, confident girl. 'Or,' I carry on, turning a page of *Tender is the Night* even though I haven't read the one I'm on, 'you can read.'

'So,' he says, 'you're not in training for the Belfast marathon?'

'Marathon *skive*,' I say. Or rather, Sassy Girl says it for me. 'And some people don't need much training.'

Cassie lets out a little groan and Luke moves further away. 'What's up with her?' he asks in an undertone.

'You're *meant* to ask her how she *feels*. Only I wouldn't advise it, because she'll tell you. In detail.'

'I don't give a damn how she feels.' He gives a sudden grin. 'So – are we going for this run, then?'

'Um.' Sassy Girl scarpers. I want to spend time with Luke but I'm not so keen on getting red and puffy and sweaty in front of him. 'I'm not much of a runner.' He looks at me quizzically and I'm suddenly very aware of how unattractive I must look in my black track bottoms and white polo shirt. The track bottoms are huge – bought by Mum to last – and the shirt strains across my chest. When I look down I can see the Mansfield crest stretched out of shape by my left boob. 'As you can see.'

Toby huffs pinkly towards us, looking hopeful and sweaty and exactly the way I don't want to.

'So shall we go for a *very* gentle jog?' I ask. I feel a bit bad, wanting to get going before Toby comes back – how often have I been grateful for Toby? – but if he starts talking to Luke, this lovely chance will evaporate.

'It can be a very gentle stroll, if you like.'

We set off at a fairly brisk walk. I don't want him thinking I'm a complete couch potato.

'War memorial?' Luke suggests. 'That sounds better than the netball pitch and the bike sheds.'

The war memorial, a tiny hedged garden with a marble Celtic cross, is at the other end of the grounds, beside a side gate that is always kept locked. I haven't been here for ages. I had a phase of hiding out here in fourth year, when I was obsessed with the war poets, and when Cassie was being so mean. I loved the clean white marble and I used to know the order of the eighty-three names almost by heart.

'Look.' I sit on the wrought-iron bench and point to the bottom of the cross. 'My name – nearly. My middle name's Grace.'

Luke kneels down and reads aloud, 'Wilson, Edward G.' He traces the carved initials with a fingertip. The letters are green and mossy. 'Any relation?'

'Not as far as I know.'

Luke's lips move as his eyes scan down the list. 'Eighty-three. That's like – nearly all the boys in our year.' He leans back on his haunches, and then sits on the bench, his long legs stretched out beside mine. I suck my tummy in as hard as I can.

'I know. If that was today – you'd all have to go.' I think of all the boys I've been in school with for years – marching off to die or be maimed or maddened. I can't imagine it. Even the rugby boys, though they think they're tough, have their kits washed by their mummies every week. Toby, marsh-mallow-soft, bowed under the weight of a rifle and pack, sickened and terrified by everything.

Luke's face gives one of those strange twists. 'Not *me*.'

'Why? Oh. I suppose not.' An epileptic seizure in a trench would have been pretty catastrophic. 'Well ... that'd be one advantage, I suppose.'

Luke raises one eyebrow. 'Being left out of a war that happened a hundred years ago?' He kneels down again, and runs a finger over the name under Wilson – 'Wright. Like Jasmine.'

'Ugh,' I say without thinking. *No!* scolds Sassy Girl, appearing from nowhere. *Don't let him think you're the kind of girl who bitches about prettier girls*, so I turn it into, 'Oh, yeah, so it is.'

'Esther?' he says suddenly, without turning round. He is hunkered in front of the cross, one hand still stretched out to the white marble. 'Can I ask you something?' His voice is serious.

My breath curdles in my throat. He *can't* be going to ask me – He isn't.

'Is there always this much homework and that?'

I try not to let my disappointment show. I shrug, stupidly, since he still has his back to me. 'I don't do the same subjects as you.'

'English and history.'

'We don't get *that* much.'

He sighs. 'It takes hours, though. Every night.' He scrapes at a piece of moss under the words PRO PATRIA.

'Well, that's what you get for doing maths and economics. They sound really hard.' Actually Toby says economics isn't too bad except that you're meant to read the boring financial bits of the newspapers.

'Yeah. But even history ...' He leans back from the cross but he still keeps his back to me. 'How long did that essay take you?'

I try to remember. Walsh gave the essay on a Friday to be handed in on the Monday, and all the ones with social lives grumbled that it wasn't fair. I put it off on Friday night, and made excuses not to do it on Saturday because it was a lovely day and I went to the Botanic Gardens to take photos for my art project, and then ended up doing it on Sunday afternoon, partly to annoy Mum and Dad, who don't approve of schoolwork on a Sunday.

'Two hours? Something like that.'

'OK.' He goes on scraping at the moss.

The sun is shining on my back, but the war memorial is in shade, and my arms are goose-pimpling in the cool air. I rub them.

'That essay took me all weekend,' Luke says. 'Well – about six hours.'

'That sounds a bit much.'

'I can get the grades,' he says in a sudden burst of words. 'So far. But I didn't think it would be this hard. And I wondered if … if it's the same for everybody or if I'm just –'

'What?'

'Stupid.' He flicks some moss from his fingers and it lands on the gravelly path. 'Like your dad said – the standards of Belvedere High are *not* the standards of Mansfield Grammar.'

He imitates Dad's voice and I wince.

'Luke – of *course* you're not stupid. You wouldn't have got in here if you were stupid.'

'I learn it all, but then I forget it. We had this economics test and I spent all night revising and then I got a C.'

'A C's OK.'

'Do *you* get Cs?'

I guess I'm not really meant to answer this. Instead I say cautiously, 'Luke, could it be your meds?' I've been kind of reading up on epilepsy, but I don't want him to know that.

'I can't use that as an excuse.'

'But it might be a *reason*. Maybe they can change the one you're on?'

'I don't want to change again. This is the best one so far. The first one turned me into a zombie. The next one made me – ugh! – fat and spotty.' He shudders. 'This one is the best.'

I can't imagine Luke fat and spotty. Even his back view is so desirable that I have to sit on my hands to stop them reaching out to stroke the nape of his neck where it rises from his white PE shirt.

'Well, maybe you could drop a subject. Some people only do three. Half the rugby team. You could ask my dad. He's in charge of –'

'No.' His ferocity startles me. 'I don't want *special treatment*.' He says it like it's something disgusting. 'I'll just work harder.'

I lean forward so I'm kneeling beside him. 'Don't work *all* the time,' I say, and some instinct – or desire – makes me put my arm on his shoulder. It's rigid. He turns his head. His face is so close I can see the smattering of tiny freckles on the bridge of his nose.

'Why not?'

'Because …' I'm just reassuring him; I'm just being good old Esther, and then suddenly I'm not. Sassy Girl, just when I need her, takes over. 'You won't have time for other stuff.'

'Like what?' His shoulders have relaxed and his hand comes up and rests on my arm. My hand slides from his shoulder to the back of his neck.

'Well – like this.' I lean in and nudge his lips with mine.

His body stiffens and for a split second I think, *Oh no! I have read this wrongly, Sassy Girl has plunged me in way, way out of my depth*, and then his hand tightens on my arm and he's kissing me back.

Luke Bressan is kissing me.

Something sings inside me. I can't believe I'm kneeling here, at the school war memorial, holding this beautiful boy, who is kissing me back as if he really wants to, as if what he feels for me is the same as I feel for him. I feel so brave – I, who've never been kissed by a boy, have made the first move. Luke pushes my hair back from my face and looks straight into my eyes.

From inside the building, the bell blares out.

Luke

Sandra dries her hands on the towel hanging off the front of the cooker and goes to fill the kettle. The cat, now named Jay by me because, like Gatsby, he seemed to come from nowhere, meows up at her. 'How was the rugby?'

'Rugby?' I've forgotten. 'Oh! Hopeless.' I hang my schoolbag over the back of a chair.

Sandra gives me a quizzical look. 'You don't seem too bothered. Tea?'

'Yes, please. No, I don't mind. You should have seen the rugby players. Morons. And the coach is a fascist.'

This is possibly the most I have ever said to Sandra in one go, and she looks delighted and sets out two mugs on the table. I want to go straight upstairs and lie on my bed and think about Esther – relive that incredible moment when she curled her hand round my neck and kissed me.

We hadn't said anything – the bell went, and we sat up, and she pulled at her hair, and we walked back to school, and I wondered if I should take her hand, but the drive was suddenly invaded by home-going juniors, jostling and texting and grabbing each other's schoolbags, so I didn't.

'Luke?' Sandra waves a hand up and down in front of my face. 'I said do you want a Hobnob? Tea won't be for a bit.'

We'd separated at the girls' changing rooms, and she'd stood for a moment at the door and said *Well*, and I'd said *Well*. And she'd said, *See you tomorrow then*, and I'd said, *Yeah,* and that had been that.

I don't even have her number.

'I'll take the tea up with me,' I say. 'I have loads of maths to do.'

I sit in the bedroom which is starting to feel a bit more like mine. Bill's put up the shelves he'd promised, and they are full of my books. I've spent ages arranging them properly.

It doesn't matter that we haven't said anything; I'll see her tomorrow in tutor group. Only – the room will be full of people; the whole *day* will be full of people.

I lay my maths book on the desk, well away from my mug, and turn to a clean page in my notebook. I read the first problem, but the words and figures dance around on the page and in my head. I stare at it until the tea scums over and my neck cramps with tension. I knead it with my fingers and remember the pressure of Esther's hands there. My hands can't produce the same feeling hers did.

Maybe the maths will make sense after tea – a meal that used to be called *dinner* at Helena's. Meanwhile I can read over the economics. It's very boring and very complicated, but at least I understand the *words*. There's an English essay – I'll leave that until the weekend, but I can go over my notes. As soon as I start reading the biographical notes on Fitzgerald I remember copying them down from Esther. Even though I'm looking at my own neat writing, I'm seeing her loopy, girly script.

It's no good.

I can't wait until tutor group. I could look up her landline number in the phone book – but there must be hundreds of Wilsons, and her dad might answer. But I have Toby's number and Toby, surely, must have hers. I text him before I can change my mind.

My phone pings back immediately. I look at the screen for ages and think about my message. I don't want to sound *desperate*. Maybe I shouldn't bother.

You definitely shouldn't bother.

It's a voice in my head I haven't heard for years. For a moment my brain doesn't even recognise it. My guts, turning to ice, are quicker.

Shut up, I tell it, and tap out a text:

Hope you don't mind me
getting your number off Toby.
Just wondered if you
are free on Friday night?
Luke

As soon as I press Send I toss the phone down on the bed behind me and force myself to read *The Great Gatsby*. It isn't a great distraction: Gatsby yearns for Daisy. Nick kisses Jordan, though he's not in love with her. The phone stays silent. So does the voice.

Sandra calls me down for tea. I leave the phone on the bed.

Sorry: phone on silent.
Yes, free Friday.
See you tomorrow.
E x

I lie on my bed and read the message over and over again, and forget all about the maths.

I frown at my cornflakes. Where can I take her? Where do people *go*? She lives on the other side of town, near school. The pubs that aren't fussy about ID will be crawling with

Mansfield sixth-formers. I can't really afford to take her for a meal, but going for a coffee doesn't feel *dateish* enough.

'Luke? I said do you want a lift?' Bill sounds impatient. 'I'm off today and I've to go into town. Save you getting the bus.'

Sandra and Bill don't know I always walk. It would sound so stupid to say I'm nervous of going on a bus in case I have a seizure. If I make it for a whole month without one I'm going to rethink.

But for now – well, it's hardly worth it, just for one day. The walk will give me a chance to come up with a brainwave about Friday night. Actually, that Coffee Spoons place – that was cool; that might do.

'It's OK,' I say. 'Thanks – but I always see my mates on the bus.'

Sandra and Bill exchange pleased looks. I finish off the last of the cornflakes and wonder how the lies can fly out of me so easily.

Esther

I stand in the shower and screw up my eyes as the hot water pounds me. I'm far too early but I've factored in lying-on-the-bed-in-my-dressing-gown-becoming-less-pink time. I run through the list of topics that are too grim/uncool for a first date.

War.

Homework.

Pretty much everything we've ever actually talked about.

Suddenly panicky, I reach for the conditioner. Then, as I smooth it through my hair I relax. It will be fine, I tell myself. He likes you. It's a *date*. He *invited* you. He *fancies* you.

I try to summon Sassy Girl but all I get is a bitchy voice that sounds like Cassie. *Of course he doesn't fancy you. Look down at yourself. Look at that wobbly body; those big thighs, glowing red in the heat.*

He kissed me. He asked me out.

You kissed *him. Of course he asked you out. You've made it very clear you're available. He's a seventeen-year-old boy. They're after one thing and you've made it clear he can have it for the taking.*

No! Did I let him think that? How far will he want to go? How far do *I* want to go? I really fancy him, but ... I wish I could talk to Ruth about this. How far is too far? If he only wanted – *that* – he wouldn't bother taking me out.

He's taking you out to a café.

So?

So he *knows he doesn't have to try too hard. Because you're desperate.*

Shut up shut up shut up.

I turn the shower on harder and let the pounding water silence the voice.

––––––––––

The café, Coffee Spoons, is in a side street in the centre of town. As soon as I push open the door I relax: this is such a me place. It isn't like Starbucks or Costa; it's all white paint and exposed brick and mismatched tables and crockery and quotations from poems on the walls. The music is low and sounds like someone singing in French.

Of the million fears I've had since we made the date, the worst is that Luke won't show and I'll have to sit on my own for ages with everybody looking at me. But I see him almost at once, sitting on a leather sofa in front of a coffee table, looking at his phone, but checking the door too. He looks up and smiles.

'You found it,' he says.

'It was easy.'

I sit beside him on the sofa and wonder if that's why he chose this particular table. There are other tables free, but they are just normal ones, with chairs facing each other.

'Is this table OK?' Luke asks and I feel myself blush.

'Perfect.'

He puts his phone in the pocket of his hoody, which is folded on the sofa beside him. He's wearing dark green jeans and black Converse, with a check shirt over a black tee-shirt. His hair looks blonder under the dim wall-lights. I have agonised about what to wear. My wardrobe isn't exactly extensive and it's never included date-clothes. I have one beautiful dress that's too fancy for a café; smart clothes for church – lately unworn – which make me look like a secretary; slobbing around clothes; and not much in between.

So I've mixed and matched jeans with a vintagey-looking blouse and cardigan. I hope the effect is cute and quirky and not slightly weird. My period is due which makes me feel fatter than ever. I don't have much make-up but I've done my best, and my hair is on its best behaviour for once.

I look round the walls and say something inane about the photos and something even inaner about the bus being late, and then the waitress comes and I order tea because I think fiddling with the pot and everything will give me something to do.

'For two,' Luke says.

'Tea for two,' I say stupidly. 'We know how to have a good time.'

He frowns. 'Is this OK? I didn't think you were a pub kind of person.'

'I love it.' For the first time it occurs to me that he might be nervous too. I smile. 'And you're right. I'm not very – um, pubby.'

Ruth and I and all our church friends were great ones for cafés. It was one of the comforting things about being in a Christian crowd – no pressure to go into pubs or drink. I feel a sudden pang. I never imagined I'd be getting ready for my very first date without Ruth to reassure me and get excited with me. But it's my own fault.

'Do you want something to eat?'

'Maybe later.' I don't think I'll ever relax enough to eat in front of Luke. I have no idea where the confidence has gone which let me kiss him by the war memorial. I remind myself of my good resolutions – no depressing talk. No making the first move. *That's* not going to be a problem. Sassy Girl has cleared off.

I try not to look at Luke too much, but I totally can't stop myself. We talk about *The Great Gatsby*; the weather; the sixth form ski trip which has just been announced – which neither of us has the slightest interest in. Nothing personal. There's also a fair amount of not-talking. Looking round the café and pretending to be interested in the other people. I'm so distracted by how much I long to *touch* Luke. We're slightly turned towards each other on the sofa. His shirt traces the contours of his chest and flat stomach. His arm lies across the back of the sofa; it would take a very slight adjustment for him to slide it round me – but he doesn't.

I drink three cups of tea until my stomach protests and I have to go to the loo.

I check myself in the mirror and replenish my lipstick. My cheeks are as red as strawberries and I try to calm them down with a dusting of powder. I give myself a good talking to – not out loud. *Look at you*, I say. *You're not pretty, you're not thin, you're not cool. You can't afford to be dull as well. No wonder he isn't making any moves on you. Just kiss him! You did it before.*

Which is *exactly* why I can't do it again.

When I get back, having resolved nothing except my bladder and my lipstick, there's a fresh pot of tea at my place. And a tiny gingerbread man with cherry buttons down his front. To my horror, my throat thickens and my eyes fill with tears. Please let him not notice.

He notices. 'Esther? What's wrong?'

'It's stupid.'

'Tell me.'

'It – um – reminds me of someone. My friend Ruth.'

'Is she dead?'

'No!' I start laughing and crying at the same time. Snot bubbles in my nose. 'We just fell out – we didn't even *really* fall out.'

He gives me a *girls are weird* look that I can't blame him for. I mean, he has a *dead mum* and I'm crying over someone I've only been avoiding because I'm embarrassed about the way I left the church.

'You don't have to eat it.' He leans towards me and now he does put his arm round me, which feels delicious but it isn't the way I've thought of it at all. I don't want to be comforted; I want to be *desired*.

'Esther.' Luke frames my face in his hands and pushes the tears away gently with his fingers. 'I'm so sorry. I've upset you. Again.'

'You *haven't*. I promise.' The week before my period it takes a lot less than that to make me burst into tears – but I don't say that out loud.

He pulls my face towards him and kisses me very gently. It isn't like at the war memorial – for a start we're in a public place – and he pulls away pretty much as soon as I've registered the fact that he *is* kissing me, but all of a sudden things are OK. More than OK. The tea goes cold, and the waitress keeps giving us meaningful dirty looks, but we talk and talk, like I've never talked to a boy before.

I tell him about Ruth, how not being in a crowd at school never mattered because she was such a good friend.

'So what happened?'

I hesitate. 'I'm kind of – not in that group any more.' I don't want to admit it was a church youth group, in case he thinks I'm some kind of religious nutter. Had enough of that when Cassie started on me in fourth year. But then I think, no, there's no point pretending, and I admit that my whole life until this summer revolved around my parents' church.

'I don't go any more,' I say. 'I just – grew out of the whole scene I suppose. It all seemed a bit – smug. Sure of itself.'

He doesn't look *totally* horrified. I suppose if he can survive me crying all over him, he can take a wee bit of Jesus in his stride.

'So are you a Christian?'

I shrug. 'I don't know what I am. Or what I believe. I mean, I still believe in God. I *think*.'

'I don't.' Luke sounds very definite. 'I mean – sometimes I think it might be nice. But the evidence against is pretty overwhelming.'

'You mean suffering? The Holocaust and all that?'

'Yeah. And the Middle East. Kids being bombed –'

'I *know*.' This chimes so exactly with my feelings that my words tumble out. 'And at the summer scheme – some of those kids had terrible disabilities. Some of them were in pain all the time. And I've always been brought up to accept that God knows what he's doing, but – for the first time I just couldn't.'

I forget all about being shy and self-conscious. It's a relief to try to explain this to someone who isn't – unlike my parents and Ruth – going to take it as a personal rejection. We argue and talk and it's as easy as being with Toby or Ruth, only much more exciting. He takes my hand and he doesn't let go. His skin is drier than mine, his fingers long.

Eventually we can no longer ignore the waitress's looks because she has started to brush the floor, and there are no other customers left.

'Have you got a curfew?' Luke asks.

I look at my phone in alarm. 'Oh gosh, yes – eleven. And it's half ten now.'

'That's OK. I'll walk you home. We'll make it.'

'But if you walk me home you'll miss the last bus back to your house.' I never like to say 'home' because I'm not sure if he thinks of it that way. And I'm still not sure *where* Lilac Walk is except that it's on the far side of town from my house and school.

'I'll walk. I like walking.'

'But – it's late.' I *want* Luke to walk me home; I want the night to last longer and I love the idea of being alone with him, holding hands and stopping to kiss in the privacy of dark streets. Though not my *own* street, just in case …

But I don't want him walking home on his own afterwards. When you hear stories about people being attacked at night, it's nearly always young men. 'I know – we can get a taxi – it can drop me off and then you?'

'There's no need,' he insists quickly, and I'm aware of two things.

One, he might not have enough money for a taxi.

Two, if I was with Toby or Ruth, they could have walked back with me and then Dad would have given them a lift home. He'd have grumbled a bit but he'd have been happy to do it, really.

But Dad thinks I'm with some girls from my art class.

'I can pay for the taxi,' I suggest.

'No. *I'm* meant to be taking *you* out.'

'It's the twenty-first century, Luke.'

He frowns and drums his fingers on the tabletop. 'I wish I had a car.'

'I'm getting driving lessons for my birthday. Next month. I can't wait.'

'Lucky you.'

His mood seems to have darkened and I can't think why.

'Are you seventeen yet?' I ask, just to change the subject. The waitress hovers and I stand up and shrug on my hoody.

'Yeah. In August,' he says, 'but I'm not *allowed* to drive.'

'Why –? Oh. What – *never?*'

He sighs and picks up his own hoody. 'You have to be seizure-free for – I don't know – two years or something. So far the most I've managed is three weeks.'

'But things will change! Sometimes people just grow out of it.' I hope it's not too obvious that I've been googling epilepsy websites.

'Yeah.' He gives his head a little shake, as if he can shake off the epilepsy, or maybe just the mood. 'Come on.' He holds out his hand. 'Let's get you home before Big Willy does his nut.'

Luke

It's pouring. The sky outside is so black that the stained glass in the library windows looks dull and grey. The war memorial is our usual school hang-out, but not today.

Esther frowns as she looks through the economics notes she's meant to be testing me on. 'Quantitative easing?' She giggles. 'I always think that sounds like some kind of laxative.' She grins her lovely wide slow smile, which makes her teeth rest on her lower lip. 'I'm not surprised you find this hard to learn. It's so *boring*.'

I hesitate and chew the end of my pen. 'I just need to work harder.'

McGurk sashays past with an armful of sociology books, her tightly trousered bum pushing against Esther's seat. 'The library's for working, not talking,' she says. 'You mustn't disturb other users.'

I look round pointedly: there are precisely *no* other users, apart from a rugby player who is dozing with his head resting on *Where's Wally?*

Esther takes advantage of McGurk being at the other end of the library to stretch across the desk and give me a quick kiss.

McGurk's voice drones from behind the sociology shelves. '*That's* not what the library's for, either.'

'Pervert,' I whisper. 'She must have been peeking through the books.'

Esther bites her lip and starts to giggle. 'Right, fiscal policy,' she whispers.

When the bell goes we have to go in different directions, me to economics, Esther to art. I try not to imagine what it would be like to be going to art now. I haven't drawn for weeks. Maybe I should just buy a sketchbook – the bus money is mounting up. My fingers itch to draw, to get involved in that synthesis of eyes and hand and brain, where everything else disappears. At the library door Esther reaches up and gives me another quick kiss, just as the office door beside the library opens and Wilson comes out. He's frowning over a sheaf of papers, so I don't know if he sees, but when he does look up, his eyes narrow. 'You are late for class,' he says. 'Both of you.'

And yes, part of me enjoys looking him in the eye and seeing the sudden fear written there when he said *Both of you*, and thinking, yes, you prejudiced bastard. I *am* with her. I'm going out with your daughter and there's damn all you can do.

And what wouldn't he do, Lukey, if he knew what you really were?

Maybe *that's* one of the things that would disappear if I started to draw again.

'Does he *know*?' I ask. 'About us?'

Esther hesitates. 'I haven't told him.'

'Are you ashamed of me?'

'Don't be daft! I just don't see the point of giving him ammunition. If he knows, he'll be far more strict – he might even try to stop me seeing you.'

'You make it sound like *Romeo and Juliet*. And look what happened to them. Anyway, he can't stop you. You're nearly seventeen.'

She sighs. 'It'd just be easier. For now.' She leans against the door of the girls' lockers. 'I have to go.' She reaches up and kisses me. 'I like things how they are,' she says, with one hand on the door. She sounds suddenly very young. 'I don't want anything to change.'

Esther

'So. Esther.' Jasmine and Cassie lean against the lockers beside mine. Cassie is playing with her phone but Jasmine's eyes, wide and blue, framed with impossibly long lashes, are fixed on me. And I hate myself for warming up inside at her attention, but I do. I always have.

'Oh. Hello.'

'You and Luke?'

'Um – yeah.' I give a stupid little laugh, and try to pull my art folder out from where it's got wedged behind my history textbook.

'It's *so* nice,' she goes on. 'Isn't it, Cass? Cass? Weren't we saying that it's so nice? Luke and Esther?'

'Yeah.' Cassie doesn't look up from her phone.

'Anyway– we're really happy for you.' Jasmine's eyes shine with sincerity. 'And you must come out with *us* some time.'

'Maybe.'

'You mustn't keep him *all* to yourself!' She giggles. 'But seriously, Esther – it's *so* lovely that you've found each other. I mean' – she lowers her voice, though there's nobody else round the lockers apart from two Chinese girls talking so animatedly in Chinese that they couldn't possibly be tuning into anything else '– the way you can deal with – you know. It must be so *reassuring* for him.'

I walk to art, seething with indignation. Patronising cow. I play the words over and over and by the time I'm at the art corridor the words she hasn't said but clearly meant are rolling round my head too. *He's too attractive for you. Everybody knows that. He only likes you because he knows you won't freak out if he has a seizure. Because you're so sensible. Good old Esther.*

But Luke hasn't had a seizure since the start of term. He told me yesterday that he was starting to relax and think they were under control. And I squeezed his arm and said that was brilliant.

Which it is.

Because any suggestion that a seizure-free Luke would have the confidence to look well beyond a girl like *me* – a sort of comfort-blanket girl – well, that's just ridiculous. That's just a spiteful, shallow, *jealous* girl trying to undermine my new-found confidence, and I am not going to listen.

Dad puts his head round the kitchen door. 'That's me away,' he says. It's his men's bible study night, and I wish he'd hurry up and go. He's been in a weird mood all through dinner. In the intervals of telling us all about the controversial passage from one of Paul's letters he is looking forward to discussing with the other men – Dad has very decided views on the passage, surprise surprise – he's been giving Mum strange meaningful looks.

He gives her one now. 'Pamela, remember we agreed you'd …?'

'Oh. Yes.' Mum pauses in emptying the dishwasher.

'What?' I ask, but Dad's gone. I hear the car start in the drive.

'Your dad told me he saw you in school with a boy.'

'It's a co-ed school, Mum.'

'So – is he your – well, *boyfriend*?' She says the word like it burns her mouth.

'I guess.' *Why* am I sounding like someone in an American teen film? I take a deep breath. 'I mean, yes.'

'And – what's he like?'

I busy myself with the cutlery rack, pulling out knives and settling them in the drawer.

'Essie?'

'He's lovely.'

'And where does he …?'

She means, *Does he go to church?*

I sigh. 'Mum. Not everybody goes to church. *I* don't go to church.'

'Well, you should. There are some lovely young people in the Youth Fellowship. There's a new leader – Adam. He's at bible college. You'd like him. And you never bother with Ruth these days.'

I swallow down indignation, and sadness at the mention of Ruth, and wish Mum could understand that Luke being completely unlike any of her beloved Lovely Young People is one of the reasons I like him.

'And Pastor Greg asks about you every Sunday. It's getting hard to keep thinking up excuses.'

'You don't need to *make* excuses. And actually Luke and I talk about religion and everything. He's very intelligent.'

She puts the last of the plates into the cupboard and closes the dishwasher. When she straightens up again, I see how tightly her skirt strains across her bum. I wonder if Dad still fancies her – *ew*.

I realise Mum is still speaking.

'… the deceit. That's what I don't like, Essie. You've always been truthful.'

'I didn't *lie*!'

'You've been *seeing* this boy behind our backs.'

'Because I wasn't sure how you'd –'

'Your father said he's not the sort of boy –'

'Mum – ignore Dad! They just got off on the wrong foot.'

I put the kettle on for tea. Anything for distraction. 'I'm nearly seventeen. It's *normal* to have a boyfriend.'

She looks at me and her face collapses into a frown. 'You've got so – I don't know. So grown-up and far away.'

I put mugs on the counter. Grown-up and far away. I wish.

'Does he respect you, Esther? You don't know anything about boys. He could take advantage of you. *You* know what I mean.'

'Mum, he treats me like a princess. Honestly. He's not at all – well' – this is mortifying, and true – 'pushy. You know. In *that* way.' I feel my face burning.

'I should hope not! And I hope you respect *yourself*, Esther.'

'Mum! Of course I do.'

We've never *been* anywhere private. He's never invited me to his house, even though Sandra and Bill are bound to be less Victorian about these things than my parents. Probably when we are somewhere – appropriate – Luke will relax – we both will – and things can get more physical. Aren't boys supposed to be gagging for it all the time?

Not if they're with plain plump girls they've chosen because they're *reassuring*.

I lift the steaming kettle and pour boiling water into the teapot.

Luke

'So,' Ms Andrews says on Monday morning. '*Not* the most impressive test you've ever done. Anyone who got less than forty per cent will come back and repeat it at lunchtime today.'

There's an indignant muttering, and people look round at each other. I look at my paper. Thirty-seven per cent. Shit.

'*How* are we meant to get magically better by lunchtime?' I ask.

She raises one eyebrow at me. Andrews is not one of the teachers people argue with, and so far I have been invisible and silent in economics, but the look she's giving me suggests that Wilson's blabbed about my meltdown in RE.

'That,' she says, 'is *your* problem.'

The period before lunch I go to the library to look over the economics notes. They don't make any more sense than on Friday. The bell clangs and I stuff my books and notes into my bag with a sense of impending doom.

Coming out of the library, I meet Wilson going into his office next door. He must lie in wait.

'Your top button's undone,' he says, nodding at my school shirt.

This is my cue to give a wry smile, say *Sorry sir* and button it.

But I don't. I raise my eyebrows as if to say *How fascinating!* and push past him, walking fast. I half-listen for him following me but the corridor has erupted into a frenzy of pupils pushing their way to lunch.

The economics room is at the other end of the school, and I'm less than halfway there before I know I'm not going. What's the point? I'm going to fail again.

I don't go looking for Esther, but I suppose I hope she might be at the war memorial. She isn't. I sit there looking at the names, semi-aware of the lunchtime school life going on all round, heard but not seen – the thuds and yells of a football match; younger kids shrieking; girls laughing. An old teacher I don't know walks past and gives me a funny look, but the war memorial isn't out of bounds so when she sees I'm not smoking or anything she just sniffs and says, 'Make sure you don't leave any litter,' and goes on her way, her head bobbing up and down as if she's having a conversation.

Senile old bat. What does she think I'm going to leave litter *with*? I turn to the back of my economics file and take a pencil from my bag. I try to capture the hardness of the stone, the lines of the cross, the way the carved names look darker than the rest of the marble. I'd like to be able to write all the names accurately – it seems wrong, somehow, not to – but the scale is far too small.

I forget all about economics. The voice that's been bugging me is silenced by the sweep of the pencil. Everything fades except making my eyes and brain and hand and pencil work together to show the truth of the object. But it's not as good as it should be. Partly not having the right materials; partly being out of practice.

The school bell is an intruder from another world. I drag myself up off the cold stone seat, stuff the file and pencils into my bag and join the back-to-school flow of people.

Esther isn't in the handful of people chatting outside the history classroom. I lean against the wall and look at my phone: the classic way to pretend you don't care that people aren't talking to you.

When I realise that someone is.

Jasmine and Cassie stand in front of me, their illegally high heels making them almost my height. 'Luke!' they say like they haven't seen me for months. 'How *are* you?'

'Fine.'

'Still seeing *Esther*?' Jasmine gives a strange half-smile as if she finds the idea faintly ridiculous.

'Yes.'

'Hmm.' She touches her front tooth with a pink fingernail. 'Oh, well.' She shrugs and turns away.

I bend lower over my phone. I can't believe she's so blatant and I can't understand why she bothers me so much.

Oh really? Like me to tell you?

Shut up.

When Esther arrives, out of breath and pink – 'I was finishing something off in art. I didn't hear the bell' – I put my hand on her shoulder and kiss her. Her eyes widen in surprise, but she kisses me back warmly and then pulls away when Dr Walsh, moulting books and paper, bumbles round the corner, saying 'Sorry, people. Recalcitrant photocopier – won't bore you with the details.'

'Oh, sir, do,' Jasmine says, and even though Walsh is about a hundred and ninety she flashes him a smile that makes him cough and drop his keys.

'How was the test?' Esther whispers as we get our books out. I shake my head, writing my name neatly across the top of my homework. Now that lunchtime is over – and all I have is a futile picture nobody will ever see – it seems stupid that I've avoided the test.

We have a film about Parnell. Walsh always has the volume up pretty high, so he doesn't notice when someone knocks at the door.

'Sir,' Jasmine says. 'The door.'

Before Walsh can go and answer it, the door opens and Andrews stalks in.

'Dr Walsh,' she barks. 'I do apologise, but may I see Luke Bressan outside please? It won't take long.' She makes this sound like a threat.

Esther's face is a question mark. Walsh looks put out but nods. Sighing, I follow Andrews out of the room.

She starts before I've even closed the door behind me, so people are bound to hear.

'So?' she says. 'You aren't ill?'

'I forgot.'

'You forgot? Is this some sort of side-effect of your – condition? I mean' – in a softer tone – 'are there special circumstances?'

I hesitate. But I'd rather have trouble than special circumstances.

'No,' I say. 'I just forgot.'

'I gave up my lunchtime.'

'It wasn't only me,' I mutter.

'That is not the point! And the others had the courtesy to turn up. *You* will repeat the test in after-school detention on Wednesday. An ignominious punishment for an A level student, but …'

It's no more than I expect really. I go back into class.

What's up? Esther scribbles on the corner of her file block.

Nothing. Just the test. Boring, I write underneath. Then, catching Walsh's eye, I concentrate very hard on the film.

I push open the door of the detention room. The teacher bent over his marking doesn't look up at first, and I see only bald head, navy suit – could be one of a dozen of them – and then he sits up and looks at me and it's Wilson. Great.

'Mr Bressan,' he says in a pleased voice. He skims through a file on the desk and marks something off. 'Humph.' He hands me a copy of the economics test. 'Sit on your own,' he says.

Since all the others in the room are kids, I'm hardly going to want to sit with them.

The test isn't any easier this time round, though I have tried to swot up for it. Every time I glance up Wilson's eyes are on me. They're exactly the same colour as Esther's, which is all kinds of wrong. The room is uneasily silent, the quiet broken by sniffs and coughs and sighs, and like most classrooms too hot. The curtains are pulled tight. The class before us have probably been watching something on the screen and nobody has bothered to open them.

At four o'clock Wilson says, 'Right. Half hour's up. Leave.' As the juniors heave glad sighs and stuff books into bags he raises his voice and adds, 'Not *you*, Bressan. Your test is an hour long, which means that I too am punished for an hour. Thus the rain falls on the just and the unjust alike.'

'I've finished,' I mutter. 'You don't have to stay.'

Wilson doesn't even look up and his voice is cool and bored. 'You are not finished. You will stay here until four thirty. Whether you do or do not complete your test is a matter of the utmost indifference to me.'

I'm not going to give him the satisfaction of putting my head on the desk or anything, so when he goes back to his marking I slide out my lovely new sketchbook. My tin of pencils. I can't bear to draw the classroom and I never draw anything that I can't actually see in front of me – my teacher at Belvedere told me I was a superb draughtsman but I had no imagination – so I start sketching him. I forget that I hate him, that he's Esther's dad, who hates me, and just focus on him as problems to be sorted out with my pencil – how to get the shine on his bald scalp, the way the light reflects off his glasses, the slump of his shoulders as he hunches over his marking. When I've done I look at it critically. He doesn't look mean, which annoys me – just sort of hunched and fed up. I feel a ridiculous flicker of sympathy – for the picture, not the real man. I put the sketchbook away and read over the test. When – after what feels like three hours of the room getting hotter and hotter and honestly I can *smell* those junior kids even though they've gone – it's finally half four and I hand the paper in. Wilson takes it as if it's contaminated. He stands beside me. I can smell his aftershave and a faint sweatiness. Maybe he's responsible for the whiff in the room. He glances down at the neatly written but admittedly brief answers.

'Hardly worth your while or mine,' he comments. 'Still, I suppose …'

The standards of Belvedere High are not the standards of Mansfield Grammar.

I escape into the corridor. Esther is waiting outside. She's reading a book and doesn't see me at first. When she does, she looks surprised. 'Luke? What are you doing here?'

'What are *you*?'

'I'm getting a lift from my dad. I had art club; he had detention.'

'Me too.' I fiddle with the strap of my bag.

'*You?*' She looks at me like I'm some kind of loser. Which is exactly why I didn't tell her. 'What for?'

'Mitched that test the other day.'

'But you –'

'Esther. We're going to hit the traffic if we don't leave *now*.' Wilson locks the classroom door. 'Hurry up, Bressan,' he says. 'Time you were away.'

Esther

It doesn't take long for Dad to start. Steering out of the school driveway and into the traffic he says, 'Look, Esther, I know you're fond of that boy.'

'Dad, it's none of your business who I'm friends with.'

We have to stop at the lights. Dad drums his fingers on the steering wheel. 'I know girls your age have boyfriends. That's fine. But preferably not – not that particular boy.'

'You can't *stop* me seeing him.' I sound like a petulant child.

The traffic starts to move again and Dad puts the car into gear. 'Maybe not. But I can encourage you to – to set your sights higher than a boy in care from one of the roughest schools in Belfast. A boy with such an – unfortunate background.'

The unfairness of this stings me.

'*Dad*. You're talking as if being in care makes him some kind of different species. Imagine if something happened you and Mum. *I* could end up in care suddenly. I mean – it's not long since his mum died.'

'Is that what he told you?'

'What do you mean?' A tiny cold worm of doubt wriggles inside me. 'It's true. January.'

'And he told you *that's* why he's in care?'

'Well – of course. Why else?'

'Ah …'

The worm grows bigger and colder. 'Dad – what does *Ah* mean?'

He indicates right into Palgrave Crescent, and doesn't say any more until we're pulling into our own drive. Then he stops the car, puts the handbrake on, and unclicks his seatbelt. As he lets it slide into the holder he turns to me and, pulling on the end of his nose, says, not unkindly, 'Look Esther, as head of pastoral care I am privy to certain – information. Confidential information.'

The worm is growing into a huge icy snake. But I swallow hard and try to make my voice come out normally. 'So?'

'So – I don't think Luke has been – entirely – honest with you.'

'What do you mean? Dad – I *trust* Luke.'

Dad reaches into the back seat and lifts up his briefcase. 'I can't divulge confidential information. You know that. Anyway,' he adds cleverly, 'you say you trust him. So there's no need for you to worry, is there?'

There is no answer to that.

I lie on my bed hearing the thrum of conversation from the living room, but not the actual words.

Does Dad really have so-called *confidential information* about Luke? Or is he just bluffing to put me off him because he doesn't like him? And what *sort* of information?

I try to remember what he said. Very little. *My mum's dead. I live with this couple called Sandra and Bill.* OK, it's – basic – compared to everything I've told him, but I know boys don't *share* the way girls do. That's fine.

But I can't get Dad's voice out of my head. *I don't think Luke has been entirely honest with you.*

I peel myself off the bed and go to the window. The streetlights are just coming on. Palgrave Crescent looks its usual smug self. But even here, I'm sure, behind all the expensive blinds and tasteful paint, people must suffer and have secrets. The girl in the corner house, the one with the really pretty hair, came home from her first term at Oxford like a skeleton and didn't go back, and now she never leaves the house.

I wish I had someone to talk to. I even get as far as digging my phone out from the bottom of my bag to call Toby, but in the end I throw it on the bed without using it. Toby *knows* Luke. He's always saying how much he likes him. It isn't fair to voice my doubts to him. Make him speculate and wonder about Luke. Especially as Toby isn't exactly over-endowed with friends. If only *I* had the normal quota of supportive girlfriends who would come round and listen to the whole story and reassure me I'm not being daft – or even better, tell me I am.

I try to distract myself with homework but I find myself on Facebook. It makes a change from the epilepsy websites I've become obsessed with. Luke's about the only person I know who isn't on Facebook. For the first time in ages I go to the page for our Youth Fellowship. Lots of photos come up of their summer camp. The first one I ever missed.

I click on a photo of Ruth bending over her guitar, her red curls gleaming in campfire light. A dark-haired boy sits beside her, holding up a song book for her.

Good clean fun, mocks a voice – Jasmine's? Cassie's?

Who cares? It *was* fun.

I glance at the panel down the side. Ruth's online.

My fingers itch to message her. She'll probably ignore me. I've ignored her enough times.

But she messages back right away.

Gr8 to hr frm u bn ages wot
hv u bn up 2? Lotsa goss! LOL ☺

I look at her message for ages; it seems to belong to a simpler life. Good clean fun. Ruth is kind and straightforward. She will give me her honest opinion without being judgemental. And she doesn't know Luke so I'm not breaking any confidences by talking to her about him. I type:

Wd love to see you F2F.

And back comes Ruth:

Cum rnd rite now!!!!!

Mum is delighted when I tell her I'm going to Ruth's, even though it's a school night.

'I was hoping you two hadn't fallen out,' she says. 'Ruth's a lovely girl. Such a good … friend.'

She was about to say *influence*. I almost see her catch the word halfway out of her mouth. She wants to give me a lift but I say I'll walk; it's less than a mile. I wish Mum didn't want to be so *involved* with my life. I think of what Luke said about Sandra and Bill, that it was like being a lodger; that must be kind of peaceful.

Ruth's bedroom hasn't changed: it's still lavender with fairy lights strung round the bed frame and the curtain pole, the same fairy lights I have, and a few inspirational posters above the bed: *Be still and know that I am Lord.* I don't know if it's reassuring or disturbing that Ruth, at nearly eighteen, still favours kittens and rainbows and bible verses. It's exactly like my room used to be, I suppose. We had a lot of the same posters. Now I've given mine a makeover, but it's a bit bare. I don't know how I want it to be.

Ruth shrieks and hugs me. 'I missed you,' she says simply. She clasps my hands and leans back to look at me properly. 'You look the same.' She sounds surprised.

'Why wouldn't I?'

She puts her head on one side like a bird listening. 'We-ell. It's been ages.' She smiles, then frowns. 'Look, Essie, did I *do* something?'

'No! Of course not.'

'We were meant to go out and celebrate our results and you just didn't turn up.'

'I … I went with people from school.' That stupid results party. Toby had dragged me along – it was the first time there'd been anything social that was open to everyone, and I'd ended up abandoning him to play nursemaid to Jasmine.

'I know you don't want to come to church,' Ruth goes on. 'But I didn't think that meant you'd just walk away from your best friend.'

'*You've* always said it was hard being friends with non-Christians.'

Ruth wrinkles her small nose. 'I said that when I was, like, *thirteen*. Anyway, are you actually saying you're *not* a Christian now?' Her eyes widen.

'I … I don't know, Ruthie. Honestly. I told you I stopped being able to just *accept* it all –'

'So it's not just that you want to get away from your parents? Them being so involved in the church and all?'

The crisp comment reminds me how well Ruth knows me. 'I don't know.'

It's true I started wanting to assert myself more. Working at the summer scheme made me feel so much older. And – well, I suppose I was fed up being the sad Christian girl at school. It's OK for Ruth: it's not social suicide to be religious at her school the way it is at Mansfield.

Maybe coming here was a stupid idea. I look round the room for some inspiration. There, beside Ruth's (neat) desk is her photoboard – years' worth of Sunday-school trips; coffee bar nights; weekends away. There are quite a few old favourites – me and Ruth at the annual barbecue, aged about eleven, hair in matching bunches, holding out sausages on sticks in a way that now seems faintly obscene; outside Castlewellan Castle on ponies – but there are new ones too and more than one seems to be of a stocky, dark-haired boy with a wide grin. In one he has his arm round Ruth and they are beaming into the camera with matching smiles. It's the boy from the Facebook photo.

'Who's this?' I ask.

Ruth flumps onto her bed. She picks up her white cat nightdress case and hugs it.

'That's Adam,' she says. 'I *told* you I had lots of gossip! And, oh my gosh, Esther, I have had *so* much hassle about him!' Her voice is suddenly serious.

I sit down on the bed opposite her. Where have I heard the name Adam recently?

'The new youth leader?'

'How did you know? Esther, he is lovely. He just gets me, you know?' She hugs the cat again, clearly wishing it was Adam.

'So what's the big deal? I mean – who's the hassle from? Are the others jealous? There's always far more girls than boys, aren't there?'

'Not them. Mum and Dad.' She lowers her voice as if her parents are on the landing.

'But …' I look again at the clean-cut, open face in the photo. The jolly jumper. The clear affection for Ruth that shows in the way he looks at her. My parents would wet themselves in delight at the very thought of me being with a boy like Adam. 'What's not to like? He looks – perfect. And Mum said he's at bible college. Surely your parents would love that?'

Ruth sighs. 'He's *twenty*, Esther. They say that's too old.'

I consider. 'It's not *that* old.'

'But they think – oh, you know, because he's older he'll want to take things, well, more seriously.' She blushes.

'You mean sex?'

'Well – yes. I mean – we *wouldn't*. Obviously.'

'Why obviously?'

'Esther! You *know* why not.'

We'd had lots of talks about this since we started noticing boys. Respect. True love waits, etc. But it had all been completely theoretical as neither of us had even been kissed.

'But if you're so close, doesn't that make it very – well, hard?' As soon as the words are out of my mouth I wish I could take them back.

But I catch Ruth's eye and she giggles, biting it back self-consciously at first and then giving herself up to it. We clutch each other's arms. It's suddenly easy to say, 'I have a boyfriend too. And *my* parents aren't exactly his biggest fans.'

She immediately looks interested. 'Esther! Tell all! Have you got a picture?'

I take out my phone and scroll through the gallery. 'Here.'

Luke doesn't like having his picture taken, even with a phone, so it's a pretty rubbishy, rushed photo. Ruth looks at it carefully, her red curls falling over her face, then hands it back.

'Hmm,' she says. 'Cute. Not the type I would have imagined you going for.'

If Jasmine or Cassie had said something like that, the subtext would have been, *He's too good-looking for you*, but Ruth doesn't do nasty subtexts.

I don't tell her *everything*. But quite a bit. More than I would have told her if she'd been at school with us, or if I'd had any notion of her meeting him in the future. Is that a bad sign – that I don't have fantasies of Ruth and Adam, Luke and me all cosying up for double dates?

You mustn't keep him all to yourself, Jasmine had said.

'So you see, I don't want to pry,' I say when I tell her about Dad's hints. 'Because it might just be Dad being – well, overprotective. You know what he's like.'

Ruth frowns, which doesn't suit her button nose and freckles. 'I don't see why you can't just ask Luke to tell you more,' she says. 'Relationships are about *trust*.'

I fiddle with a fairy light on the bedhead behind me.

'Adam's always honest with me.' Ruth curls her legs under her. 'We've talked about sex.' She smoothes her school skirt down over her grey tights. 'But there's other ways to feel close to someone.'

'But do you not – you know, *want* to?'

I think about how I feel when I'm kissing Luke. Feelings I've never had before. Delicious, scary feelings.

'We *talk*, Esther. That's the whole point. And pray of course. Praying together is very special. And we both believe sex is only for marriage, so that helps. Do you and Luke –'

'*No.*' Hardly any kissing even. I can't possibly admit this. But does Luke *want* to? Surely it's supposed to be the boy wanting it all the time? Even this Adam – it must at least be a temptation if he has to *pray* about it. Have I come across as so inexperienced that Luke's scared of coming on too strong? Or does he just not fancy me?

'I think,' Ruth says, 'that if he respects you, he should be more honest with you. There's *nothing* Adam wouldn't share with me.' Her face shines.

I wonder what it must be like to be that confident about someone, and if I'll ever know.

Luke

'So. Luke. You should totally come to my birthday party.'
Jasmine leans back in her chair and I can see the outline of
her bra under her white school shirt. Esther's at the dentist
and Jasmine made a beeline to sit with me when Donovan
said we had to work in pairs.

'We're meant to be comparing Gatsby's parties – do you
want to do Chapter 3 and I'll do Chapter 6 – halve the
workload?' I wave my copy of the book.

'Luke – it's pair work; that means we *talk* to each other.'

'About the *book*.'

'Donovan's down the back of the room. He won't know
what we're talking about. And it's going to be an excellent
party. We've hired caterers and a band and –'

'We should probably –'

Jasmine pouts. 'I don't invite just *anyone*. Only the people
who *count*.'

'Right.'

I suppose a few weeks ago this would have meant something. I'd wanted to count. Or at least to be accepted. But it
doesn't seem to mean much now I have Esther.

'I'm sure *Esther* would love to come,' she says, speaking
very quietly and pretending to write at the same time so
that Donovan, lumbering round the room, nods at us and
says 'Good show.'

'Twat,' Jasmine murmurs and gives Donovan a dazzling
smile. 'Esther doesn't get invited to many parties,' she goes
on. 'I mean, *she* deserves a bit of fun, doesn't she?'

I underline a sentence in my book. Does Esther have *fun* with me? The gap between how I want to be with her and how I really am – does she feel it too?

'OK. You're right. We should totally talk about *Gatsby*. But I'll make sure you're on the guest list.' And she gives me a wide, innocent, I'm-being-nice-to-you-even-though-you're-so-rude smile which shows perfect teeth and makes me hope Esther gets back before history. I have this weird feeling that if Jasmine wants us at her party, we'll be there.

'You *want* to go?'

We're under a tree in the park, trying to pretend it's not freezing. Esther's cheeks bloom over a woolly red scarf. She hugs her knees and opens her eyes wide.

'Well – duh. Don't you?'

I shake my head. I can't keep up with girls, not even Esther, who's more like a normal person. 'I thought you didn't like Jasmine.'

'It's – complicated.' She looks down at the grass at her feet. 'Sometimes with girls it's not as simple as liking and not liking. But she has a birthday party every year. And I've never been even close to being invited until now.'

'So?'

She sighs, and digs her brown suede boot into the grass. 'When we were kids everybody always used to obsess about Jasmine's parties – they were always the *best* parties, never just cinema and pizza, but pony-trekking or ice-skating or –'

'I get the idea.'

'And every year I used to wish I'd be invited. Because all the girls who did – it was only girls then of course, until she was fifteen, when she had a *ball*, with the guys in DJs and –'

'Yuck.'

'– and they always flaunted their invites all over the classroom and there was, like, this divide between the ones who were invited and the ones who weren't. Jasmine was always top dog. She was much nicer before Cassie came. Cassie hates Jasmine being friendly with anyone else. That's why she's so mean to the twins, but they don't seem to care.'

'Hey. Where did Esther go? You look like her. You feel like her' – I lean over and touch her cheek – 'but you don't *sound* like her.'

She laughs and pushes my hand away playfully, but keeps hold of it. 'I'm sorry. I suppose it sounds stupid. Told you girls were complicated. And you're right, I don't exactly *like* her, but ...' She sighs and slots her fingers in with mine. 'I used to compare her birthdays with mine. Because they were only a few weeks apart. And mine ...' She wrinkles her nose.

'No ice-skating ponies?'

'I had parties with my friends. But they were a bit lame. And then one year ... I ... I used to be kind of friends with Cassie. I know – hard to believe. She was new in fourth year and she kind of latched on to me. I didn't really have a schoolfriend and I was so pleased. I invited her to my party.' She stops and shrugs. 'This is a really boring story. You don't need to hear it.'

'Yes, I do.'

She chews her lip. 'Well, people were having parties with drink and boys and – you know. *Real* parties. Only me and my friends from church, well, we were still pretty innocent.'

'Like, pass the parcel and Ribena?'

'Not quite. We had a barbecue in the church grounds. Toasted mallows. Singsong – OK, it was probably a *bit* sad.

But I thought it was great. I was so thrilled that I had a friend from school there and everybody was really nice to her and' she blushes '– well, we prayed for her and thanked God for bringing her into our midst – and she sat there and smirked, loving all the attention, and then on Monday someone found out she'd been at my party and they started taking the piss, and she said she'd only gone because she felt sorry for me. She said I was a religious maniac.' She shakes her head. 'I think, looking back, she was desperate to get in with the cool crowd, specially Jasmine, and she knew this was a way she could do it. By laughing at the sad Christian girl. And she and Jasmine have been joined at the hip ever since.'

I hate the idea of anyone laughing at Esther. I squeeze her hand.

'I'd always just kept my head down at school. It was embarrassing having Dad there. But now – it was horrible. It was actual bullying. Not Jasmine really. Mainly Cassie and a girl called Melissa. Some of the boys.' She wrinkles her nose. 'In the end I went and told the head of year. I said I was being persecuted for my beliefs. And Cassie got into *loads* of trouble.' She smiles, but kind of sadly. 'So being invited now – it's like – like I finally get accepted.'

I hug her, and she kisses me, her lips fluttering on mine, then getting more urgent. Her hand finds its way inside my hoody, fumbles with my jumper.

I wriggle away.

'What?' she says. 'There's nobody around.'

'You're very forward for a good Christian girl.' I keep my voice light, but my heart's pounding. A weight has settled in my stomach and I know if we go any further there'll be trouble.

'But I'm *not* a good Christian girl any more.' She strokes her hand down my chest.

'Esther – not here. I don't …'

She sits up as if I just slapped her. 'Sorry. I – uh – I thought …'

'So. It's *your* birthday soon too. Tell me what you want.' My voice is high and forced. 'And we'll do something – really special. Anything you like.'

'I don't mind. Please don't put yourself out.' She sounds cool.

I twist away from her and lean against the trunk of the tree, waiting for my breathing to slow. 'Come on – say what you'd like and I'll make it happen. Only *no* ice-skating ponies.'

She tosses her head and pretends to pout. But something in her eyes has died, and I know she's only pretending not to be hurt. 'If I can't have ice-skating ponies,' she says, 'then I don't want anything.'

She pulls off her scarf and hits me with it. I grab it off her and hit her back but, laughing, she snatches it and then shoves it safely under her where I can't get it. But she's trying too hard. We both are.

She grins at me, her hair all messed up. 'So, what did you do for your seventeenth?'

I hesitate. 'Nothing special.' I moved to Sandra's the day after my birthday so all I did on the actual day was pack my stuff. 'I got my MacBook,' I say. I knew when I opened it that it was more than a birthday present – it was a guilt present. And a goodbye.

'Nice! My old laptop keeps freezing, but they're already getting me driving lessons, so I'll have to put up with it till Christmas.'

'I can't afford to buy you a MacBook,' I say, trying to push down the usual cold frustration I get when someone talks about driving. 'Choose again.'

'Eejit! You know that's not what I meant. I'd like a surprise.' She smooths her hair. 'Could we maybe go out for a meal?'

'Course.'

'But not anywhere dear,' she says quickly. 'I mean – Pizza Express would be fine. I actually love Pizza Express.'

'I'll take you somewhere nicer than that.'

Suddenly I'm fired with the desire to make Esther's birthday as perfect as a birthday can be. I'll pick her up and take her out to a really nice restaurant. I'll book a table and everything. I'll take her home in a taxi, and we'll both get dressed up and I'll buy her something gorgeous. I'll make up to her for not being a proper boyfriend in other ways.

Nice one, Lukey: keep her sweet with a nice birthday and she won't notice –

Shut up.

I hate asking for advice, but I have to get this right, so later, when I'm washing the dishes and Sandra's drying, I say, 'I have to buy a birthday present.'

'For your girlfriend?'

I feel my face blaze. 'How did you –?' I've never mentioned Esther.

Sandra laughs. 'Luke. I've brought up a daughter and you're our seventh foster child. I know the signs.'

'I didn't think I was so predictable.'

'So what's she like?'

'Lovely.' I smile at the suds.

'Good.' She hands me back a saucepan. 'There's a bit of potato still stuck to that. You can ask her round here, you know, Luke. This is your home.'

'I suppose.' I scrape at the crevices of the pot.

'You don't sound very keen.'

'I am!' But I'm not sure. I saw the shock Esther tried to hide when she found out I was in care, and I can't imagine her being comfortable walking through this estate. After all, *I'm* not.

I must look doubtful because Sandra says quickly, 'Look, we won't embarrass you. You can bring her up to your room. As long as we can trust you to – you know. There's condoms in the bathroom cabinet.'

'Sandra! It's not – not like that.'

See? She knows what you're like. She can tell.

Shut up.

She takes the rewashed pot I hand her and rubs her cloth over it. 'Behind the cough medicine. Just for future reference.'

I frown into the dishwater. 'Anyway, it's her birthday. I wondered if you'd any ideas …'

'Well, you should know what she'd like.'

'She just said a surprise. I don't – I've never – all I can think of is a book.'

'A book?' She looks doubtful, but then she's not exactly literary. There's a few trashy novels in the house, the *Guinness Book of Records*, a gardening encyclopedia and that's about it. 'I don't know,' she says. 'I think most girls'd rather have a nice bit of jewellery.'

'Jewellery! Is that not a bit – I don't know – *much*? Like I'm trying too hard?'

'Och.' Sandra rubs the cloth round inside a big saucepan. 'There's no harm in letting her see you've made a bit of an effort.'

Esther doesn't wear much jewellery. A watch. I try to remember if I've ever seen her wear anything else but I can't think. Is that because she hasn't got nice jewellery or because she doesn't like it?

Sandra picks up a handful of cutlery and fans it out, burnishing each individual piece till it shines like the jewellery we're discussing. 'Honestly, Luke. Take it from me. I've had three foster daughters as well as our Joanne. There isn't one of them didn't love getting a wee bit of bling. Even Megan – and she was a tomboy, never out of a tracksuit. You should have seen her face when she was showing us her engagement ring!'

Engagement ring.

Something glitters in the corner of my right eye. Diamond ring. I saw it and I knew. That was it. No hope now. I shiver and close my eyes against the relentless sparkle.

Water splashes and slops on the floor.

'Luke?' Sandra's voice is far away. 'Are you OK?'

She thinks I'm about to have a seizure on her.

I plunge my hands back into the hot soapy water and fish around for the last couple of lurking spoons. 'I'm fine.'

I think she'd like a book. Books are safe.

Esther

'Blasted thing!' I press a few keys randomly but the screen stays frozen. If I don't get this essay finished tonight I'll be in trouble with Donovan tomorrow.

Usually when you turn it off and on again it's OK, but this time it won't even turn off. 'Damn it!' I throw my copy of *The Great Gatsby* – *not* my laptop – at the wall and the noise brings Mum fussing to my door.

'Esther? Is everything OK?'

'Yes.' I pick up the book and smooth the bent cover. I never used to throw books at the wall. 'This stupid laptop's playing up again. Can I not get a new one for my birthday?'

Her face creases. 'What about your driving lessons? You can't have both.'

I sigh. 'I know.' And I'm excited at the prospect of driving. 'It's just – this thing isn't going to last much longer and I need it to be reliable. I wondered if ...'

'I'm sure we could manage a new one for Christmas, Essie, but we're not made of money.'

'Maybe it could be a kind of *early* Christmas present? I need it for school. I don't just use it for social networking and crap.'

She frowns at the word *crap*.

'What's going on down there?' Dad appears behind Mum, his glasses pushed up on his forehead. He lowers his voice. 'We're *trying* to have a prayer meeting in the living room. Pamela – we'll want tea in about twenty minutes.'

'All right, Alec.' Why doesn't she tell him to get his own bloody tea? Then I think of the way I am with Luke – don't I pussyfoot around him a bit? No. I'm just – I respect his privacy.

'Dad – it's this bl– flipping laptop. It keeps freezing and I'm trying to type up this essay for Mr Donovan, and the deadline's *tomorrow*.'

'Oh, for goodness' sake, use mine,' Dad says, 'but quieten down. You're not helping to create a very prayerful atmosphere. And Esther – keep my laptop in the study; I don't want you lugging it round the house, and remember, no tea or coffee anywhere near it.'

Using Dad's work laptop is not exactly the treat he imagines. It's ancient and about the size of a grand piano.

The study is a tiny box room; Dad's desk takes up more than half of it and there's a huge IKEA bookcase all along the opposite wall, stuffed with the most boring books you could ever imagine, mostly about the bible, some of them about teaching RE, a few shiny new ones about pastoral care.

The study also whiffs a bit. Dad doesn't believe in opening windows. The first thing I do, when I go in with my sheaf of notes, is to fling open the window even though it's a blustery autumn evening.

The essay isn't that hard – 'Is Fitzgerald's presentation of the women characters in *The Great Gatsby* misogynistic?' I think they're all pretty horrible but then so are the men, so that's what I write. I get it done before ten and I can hear from their chatter that the praying men are still here. Their voices rise and fall, all very sure of themselves and their God.

I send the document to the printer, which decides at first it doesn't want to print it, so I have to do a bit of faffing around and, while I do, I scan Dad's boring list of documents. All to do with RE or church stuff – PAUL; ETHICS; MEN'S GROUP; GCSE, that kind of thing. I cast my eye over them idly.

And then I see it. PASTORAL CARE/CONFIDENTIAL.
My finger hovers over the keyboard.

I can't. I wouldn't.

The men's voices rise and fall. I recognise Ruth's dad's
laugh. *If he respects you he should be more honest with you,*
Ruth had said.

If *I* respected *Luke* I wouldn't be thinking of hacking into
private pastoral care folders, just because of some ridiculous
hints Dad dropped.

It's not hacking. Dad knows I'm using his computer. If
there was anything sensitive he'd have it password-protected. It's not my fault if he left this lying open for anyone
to see.

There are three subfolders – JUNIOR; MIDDLE;
SENIOR. I click on SENIOR. I don't know what I expect
– lots of documents with people's names maybe, containing
all kinds of private info – but it's not like that. There's only a
couple of documents. One is called POLICY-PAST/CARE
and I ignore it; the other one is simply labelled 2014/15
– PC NOTES FOR STAFF. If it's for *staff*, I argue, that
means all the teachers, it can't be confidential.

You're not staff, Esther Wilson.

So? I'm more entitled to know things about my own boyfriend than some random teacher who doesn't even know
him.

You're entitled to know what he chooses to tell you.

I click on the file.

It's a spreadsheet. The first column is just a list of names. I
can see at once that it's all of our year group in alphabetical
order. The second is labelled HEALTH ISSUES; the third
OTHER ISSUES. Most of the names don't have anything
beside them.

Mihai Antonescu – Adopted (from Romania)
Rosie Arnold – Allergic penicillin – father dec. 2011

Dec. must mean deceased. I remember Rosie's dad dying; we all raised money for lung cancer for our charity effort that year.

I only need go as far as the Bs, though it's tempting to imagine what he's got on Cassie. *Personality disorder (incurable). Pathological jealousy.*

Ha!

Luke Bressan – Epilepsy (occasional tonic-clonic seizures) – mother dec. 2014; local authority foster care 2008

Well. My shoulders slump in relief. Nothing I didn't know. Nothing he's lied about. And then the date thrusts itself at me, mocking my naivety.

2008.

Six years ago.

'*Esther!*' It's Dad's voice. 'Have you finished in there?'

I close the file. Close the folder. 'Just printing my essay.'

I take the three sheets of A4 as the printer spits them out and, hugging them to me, I shut down the computer, close the window and go out into the hall. The front door is open and Ruth's dad's broad back is moving down the path. Mum and Dad are waving.

Mum closes the door and smiles at Dad. 'Well,' she says, 'Jim was in good form, wasn't he, Alec?'

'He was saying you were over with Ruth the other night,' Dad says, looking at me with something closer to approval than I've seen for a while.

'Why don't you invite her over for your birthday, love?' Mum asks. 'I could make you a cake and you could have a sleepover?'

'Mum! I'm not *seven.* I've already made plans.'

'With this Luke, I presume?' Dad still says Luke's name as if it's in speech marks.

'Yes.' I turn to Mum, as the one more likely to be supportive. 'He's taking me out for dinner. He's booked a table at Boccaccio's.'

They exchange glances.

'Boccaccio's is lovely, Alec,' Mum says.

'Not cheap.'

'No, Dad. *Luke's* not cheap, whatever you think about him.' 2008. Six years in care. Why not just *say*? And of course *that's* what Dad meant by *unfortunate background*. Not just having no parents.

'We're going out anyway,' Dad says. 'Remember, Pamela? The missionaries?'

'Oh yes.' Mum turns to me. 'Some missionaries from Kenya,' she says. 'They're home on a visit and they're going to give a presentation about the orphanage they look after there. There'll be a supper and a promise auction – bit of a fundraiser for them. I wasn't going to go, love, on your birthday, unless you wanted to come too?'

'No, thanks.'

'But if you already have plans …'

'It sounds great,' I say with a big smile. 'You should go.'

Dad gives me a look as if he thinks I'm being sarcastic but actually I'm not. It *is* great that they are going to be out on my birthday, leaving me free to go out with my boyfriend.

My lying boyfriend.

———

In bed I think I've worked it out.

Maybe his mum had something wrong with her for years, something that *eventually* led to her death in January and meant she couldn't look after him since 2008. Multiple sclerosis maybe. My thoughts dash and flit like the birds waiting for Mum to put bread out on the bird table.

OK. But didn't he say *My mum died so I went to live with Sandra and Bill?* How long has he actually *been* with Sandra and Bill?

I'm back where I started when I first began to worry about all of this, except now I know for sure he's lied. Or at least not been very forthcoming with the truth.

But haven't I done that too? Edited my past? I'd told him about leaving church but I'd never admitted how much I'd loved it, and how I still kind of miss its certainties.

But editing out *six years*?

I sleep badly, waking up every hour or so, and arrive at tutor group late, gritty-eyed and edgy. I stand for a moment at the door and look through the glass panel. Luke is sitting alone at the desk we've shared ever since Baxter put me there on the first day. Jasmine leans across the aisle and says something to him, her long blond hair sweeping the desk. I wonder what they're talking about.

I push open the door and the moment I do he looks up and catches my eye and smiles, and my heart skips and I wonder how I could ever have doubted him.

'I thought you must be sick,' he says as I slide into the seat beside him.

'Slept in.' I yawn. 'Sat up too late doing that *Gatsby* essay.'

'Me too.'

At lunchtime we go to the war memorial, which we pretty much always do now, though it's starting to get cold and we always keep our blazers on.

'Luke, can I ask you something?' I turn towards him on the bench and a blast of cold air sneaks up inside my blazer.

'Yes. As long as it's not what I'm getting you for your birthday, because that's a secret.'

'How did your mum die?'

He frowns and leans back. 'Oh. A car crash.'

'A *car* crash?' My careful theory skids off the road.

'On New Year's Eve.' He says it very casually but a tiny muscle twitches in his jaw.

'I thought – well, I just wondered.'

New Year's Eve. Didn't he say his epilepsy started in January? And epilepsy can be caused by a head injury.

'Were you – were you with her?'

He shakes his head. A million questions are flitting through my mind – like who told him? How did he react? I hadn't been expecting anything so dramatic, so *sudden*.

'And so did you just go straight to live with Sandra and Bill? I mean I ... I don't know how these things get – well, organised.'

He half turns away. 'Look,' he says and his voice is – well, it sounds more *bored* than anything, or cross maybe, 'I hadn't been living with my mum since I was eleven.'

Relief floods me. 'Why not?'

'She just wasn't very – you know. Capable or whatever.' His face twists. 'She had me too young.'

'So – you've lived with Sandra since you were *eleven*?'

'No. Only since the start of term.' He sighs. 'Someone else.'

I wait for more but it's clearly not coming.

'So why did you move?'

'It didn't work out.'

'After *six years*?'

He shrugs, and I know he's reached the limit of what he wants to tell me.

I reach out my hand to touch his arm. It's totally rigid. 'So why didn't you *tell* me you'd been in care for so long?'

'It didn't come up.'

'That's ridiculous! It's not like some little detail you could just forget.'

'So you think it's a big deal?' He turns back to face me and his eyes are sparking with some expression I can't read. I remember his meltdown that day in RE.

'I – I …' I don't know how to answer.

He pushes his hands into his pockets. 'Look – I saw how you reacted when I first told you I was in care. You were shocked.'

'Not *shocked*. I just never –'

'You don't *know* anyone in care.' His voice is hard. 'Kids in care don't go to Mansfield. Kids in care get into trouble and –'

'Stop it! That's not what I think.' But I suppose until I met Luke I never really thought *anything* about kids in care. They just weren't on my radar. Maybe that's why he didn't tell me.

'It's what your dad thinks.'

'I'm not my dad.' I look at him very steadily, and slowly the anger dies out of his eyes.

He shakes his head. 'I already told you – I don't want to be different. I didn't want people to know.'

'So am I just *people*?'

'No,' he says after a pause. 'Of course not.' But when I go to kiss him he jumps up and says it's cold and we should get back to class.

Luke

I jump awake. The room's lighter than it should be. And the house is noisier: hoovering on the landing; TV blaring from downstairs. I fumble for my phone on the bedside table. 10.38.

10.38? I scramble out of bed. The roar of the hoover increases. Bill must be right outside my door. I pull my dressing gown from its hook on the door.

'All right, lad?' Bill turns the hoover off and it growls a bit before subsiding. I have to sidestep to get past. The landing is tiny, just a square. 'Not like you to be getting up at this hour. You missed your fry. Sandra wanted to wake you but I said let the lad have a lie-in for once.'

'I mustn't have heard my alarm.' Now the day's going to be over two hours shorter than usual. I have to revise for another economics test, do a history essay – I've been wasting too much time drawing lately. I have to pick Esther up at seven, and I'm never going to have everything done by then.

Panic flares in my chest, then subsides when I think of the neatly wrapped present sitting on my desk. Thank God for the Internet. I could have wandered second-hand bookshops for months before finding anything as perfect as the little old copy of Wilfred Owen's poems. It's not a first edition but it's leather-bound and special-looking.

I think about Esther as the hot shower blasts down on my shoulders, and as I get dressed, throwing on any old thing, and dragging my duvet up roughly, not smoothing it the way I normally do. It was stupid not to have told her before, about being in care so long. I think I'm glad she knows now.

Yes, but you wouldn't want her to know *everything*, Lukey boy, would you?

Shut up. Give me a day off. Please.

The card should arrive this morning. It took ages and it wasn't my usual kind of thing at all, but it looked good in the end. I wonder what time her post arrives. As I run two at a time down the stairs I see that ours has come, but I don't bother lifting it, because the only thing that ever comes for me is stupid boring stuff from Social Services.

'Och, there you are.' Sandra turns round from putting dishes away in the cupboard. She still has a drying cloth over her arm. 'Not like you to sleep in. That's all those late nights. I looked in on you about half nine but you were dead to the world. I said to Bill, no point in putting his name in the pan, I said, not today.' She smiles, pleased and motherly.

I try not to process the thought that she looked in on me. I try not to think of those lost hours.

'Luke?' Sandra waves her drying cloth in front of my face and laughs when I blink and jump back. 'I said, do you want me to do you something now? You know we're going to Megan's wedding, but I've time to do you an egg or –'

'It's OK, I'll just grab a cereal bar. I need to start work.'

She shakes her head. 'Well, I've got you a bottle of wine for tonight.' She gestures to the table where a bottle of red sits beside the fruit bowl. 'Is it OK?'

I know nothing about wine and I don't suppose Sandra does either, but I imagine her checking out the wine in Lidl, maybe asking someone for advice, telling them what it was for.

'Thanks,' I say. 'That's really nice of you.'

One of the reasons we chose Boccaccio's was because you can bring your own.

'Och, well, it's a big night, isn't it? Now what about some toast?'

I escape before she can complain about balanced meals.

———————

It's funny when they go. I've hardly ever been in this house alone and I don't know all its creaks and hums. I like being left alone to work with nobody nagging me to come and eat or have a cup of tea or go and lift leaves in the garden. But I must have slept for too long, because my eyes are gritty and the words in the economics book blur and ripple. I try the history essay instead. I know what I want to say, but the argument chases itself round the screen and I end up deleting the whole thing.

I give up. If I don't go out and get some fresh air I'm going to fall asleep. I put on my running gear. It's cool and drizzly outside, which means the streets of the estate are quieter than usual. I love running. I love the way my whole body does what I want it to. I love the way I don't think. I love how the music in my ears helps my feet to pound out a rhythm on the damp pavements and drowns out everything else. And today's rhythm is *Esther's birthday Esther's birthday Esther's birthday*.

Esther

'I can't believe my wee girl's old enough to drive,' Mum says for about the sixth time.

'It'll probably take me years to learn,' I say, looking at the voucher in my card. It's for ten lessons. The card says, TO OUR BEAUTIFUL DAUGHTER, and there's a picture of a princess on the front. A nine-year-old princess. Mum's made a big cooked breakfast even though I'm trying to diet and Dad's meant to be watching his cholesterol.

'It's not just the lessons,' Dad says. He sets down his laptop at the end of the table we aren't using, and comes and sits down beside me. He usually only works in the study, but he's decided to come over all family man today which means he still spends the morning doing schoolwork, but he does it in the kitchen instead. I wish he wouldn't. I can't look at his laptop without remembering. 'It's costing a fortune to have your mum's car insured for you.'

I slip my phone out of my jeans pocket and check it under the table. I was expecting an early-morning happy birthday text from Luke – he's always up way before me – but so far there's been nothing and it's after 9.30.

'Esther – not at the table.'

I sigh and slide the phone back into my pocket.

'Och, Alec, it's her birthday.' Mum leans over and sets down a plate of egg and bacon and toast. 'There you go, love.'

I pick up my knife and fork. I don't want to want this, but the salty smell of the bacon is irresistible. And it *is* my birthday. In my back pocket my phone bleeps. Mum and Dad exchange glances.

'Sorry.' I chew my lip and spread butter on a fresh slice of toast.

The smack of the letter box releases me. 'I'll go!' I dash into the hall, and even as I register that there are four cards on the doormat – no, one's a brown envelope for Dad, but three look very like birthday cards – I'm pulling my phone out of my pocket.

Happy birthday pal,
have a good 1.
Be good LOL ☺

Ruth. Oh, well.

I pick up the envelopes. I always get three cards through the post: Gran, Aunty Jenny and Toby. The pink one is Gran, the Cath Kidston spotty one is Aunty Jenny, and the big white one must be Toby. I've neglected Toby a bit since Luke came on the scene, and I feel guilty.

But it's not Toby's spidery writing. It's a neater, clearer style. Luke. My face spreads into a grin. Who cares about a silly text message when he's gone to the bother of posting a card?

The picture is hand-painted on thick card. Kind of cartoony but delicately detailed. Ink and watercolour. It's a silvery-white pony with flowing mane and tail. Ice-skating. There's a tiny signature in the corner: LB. I gasp out a giggle, and sit back on the bottom stair to open it. All it says inside is *Happy Birthday Esther. All my love, Luke.* The letters are outlined in ink and painted. It's the most beautiful card I have ever had. And it's much, much better than anything I could do, or anyone in my AS art class, even Mihai, who's Beauman's golden boy. I didn't even know Luke could draw. Why does he waste his time on economics and maths?

I sit on the stairs and run my fingers over the hand-painted letters.

Leabharlanna Fhine Gall

All my love, Luke.
All.
My.
Love.
I can't wait until tonight.

Luke

As I set my keys on the hall table, I hear a tap dripping from the kitchen, and the hum of the central heating. It's five to six. Just time for the quickest shower ever.

God, my bones are like lead. I ran for way too long; just didn't want to stop.

The tap drips louder; it's really annoying. I need to turn it off before I do anything else. I push open the kitchen door.

The smell from the fruit bowl on the table is overpowering. Something must be going off. I reach over to lift out a black banana, when everything shudders. The kitchen blurs. I have a split second to think, *Shit* –

Blood in my mouth. Eyes open on – what is that? I blink. Rough wood. Why am I under the table – well, half under? The underside of the table is rougher than the top, and wavy. It doesn't stay still. It makes my eyes funny to watch it. I might just close them again. Might just lie here.

What am I all tangled up in? Hands scrabble on rough cotton. Tablecloth. I've pulled it down with me. I force myself up, ducking my head clear of the table, freeing myself from the cloth that's gathered under my arms. The fruit bowl is lying upside down in the middle of the floor. Apples and oranges dot the lino. The sickly smell of banana fills my head.

What's the damage? Elbow tingly, must've banged it on the table leg. Usual foam of bloody spit, but I've only bitten my tongue, nothing major. I rinse my mouth at the sink.

The teapot-shaped clock on the kitchen wall says it's just on six. So I've only been out for a minute or so. The house feels too big and empty round me, even though I still haven't got used to how small it is. I wish Sandra was here.

No. That's stupid. I make myself pick up the stuff from the floor, though bending down makes my head swim. The wine bottle has rolled across the floor and is wedged against the fridge door. Amazingly it hasn't smashed. I take this as a good omen, and set it carefully on top of the fridge. I put all the fruit back in the bowl apart from one squashed banana which I put in the bin. The cloth is wrinkled and grubby so I stuff it in the laundry basket and find a clean one.

This is what they've all been scared of, why everyone's so bloody overprotective – that I'll have a seizure when I'm alone and not be able to *cope*. Well, look at me: coping. You fall. You land. You get up.

And if Sandra was here she'd only say I couldn't go out. She'd take the decision away. It's up to me; it's my body, and I can look after myself.

I reach up to the high cupboard and take down the tin of tablets. I take two painkillers, then another two for luck.

My limbs feel like they're clogged with liquid cement, so I have to do everything slowly, but I do it. I stand under the shower (again) longer than I probably should because it feels so lovely. There's a red mark on my elbow that will be a bruise tomorrow but that's nothing. I'll get away without anyone knowing I've even had a seizure. A secret between me and my brain.

I check myself in the mirror in the hall. No marks on my face at all. I smile. Pick up the bag with the book, check that I've got my keys, wallet and phone, remember the wine and go back to the kitchen for it.

The kitchen is clean and tidy and the tap isn't dripping any more. There isn't a single sign of what's happened. And for once, no losing it in public. A rush of something – pride, determination, or maybe just adrenalin – carries me down the street to the bus stop. Because that's another good thing – I can get the bus. It won't happen again tonight. Everything's under control.

Three wee kids, all smoking and laughing, come towards me. I have to stop because they're taking up the whole footpath.

'Oy, mister. Give us some of your wine.'

'Aye, go on.'

'Piss off.' I jostle past them. Wee shits can't be more than eleven.

'Piss off yourself, you snobby get!' they shout after me.

It's a stupid, nothing encounter, but as I walk on down to the main road my head starts that tell-tale throbbing.

Stop it, I order it. *You can't do that. I gave you the pills. Stop playing dirty.* But it ignores me, and the pain beats out my footsteps.

By the time I'm in the bus the adrenalin or whatever it was has deserted me and something queasy and ominous has taken its place. The bus is quiet so I have a seat. I close my eyes as the juddering hum of its vibrations find their way into me. I breathe deeply and keep telling myself it's my imagination, it's just the movement of the bus, it's because my head's sore, it doesn't mean anything. Because the only thing nearly as embarrassing as having an epileptic seizure on a bus would be puking on a bus. But it's *not* going to happen.

It doesn't. I get to the stop near Esther's house safely. The fresh air, the walk down her street, will revive me. Her street is pretty much how I thought it would be. I count off the identical cream bungalows, distract myself by doing a survey of the cars in the drives – matching Mercs in one; then an Audi and one of those cute little Alfa Romeos; a boring Renault people-carrier thing festooned with Baby-on-Board stickers. As I pass it I glance in and see the detritus of juice cartons and baby wipes all over the seats. My insides lurch. I shouldn't have taken those pills on an empty stomach. I close my mind to the reality of sitting in a restaurant for hours, with the smell of food all round, and drinking this wine – oh God. If someone could magic me back to my own bed, I would let them, birthday or no birthday.

Then I square my shoulders. It'll be *fine*. The pills will kick in soon. Esther doesn't even need to know.

The car in Esther's pristine driveway isn't Big Willy's Golf, it's a Clio; must be the mother's. I hope they really are both out. I don't want to meet even the mother, and I especially don't want to meet her now when I feel so weird.

Esther opens the door, and the small part of my brain that isn't focussed on trying not to throw up registers that she looks nervous but gorgeous in a proper girly dress I've never seen before and her eyes all sparkly.

'Happy birthday,' I say with startling originality. 'Sorry I'm late.' I smile widely, ignoring the way the movement of my lips sets the headache off on a sharper spiral of pain. 'You look beautiful.'

But the talking undoes me. Huge surge of nausea. Cheeks tingle. Just time to turn away before I'm puking all over the doorstep. I clutch the wall with one hand and stay bent over, because it doesn't feel like I'm done.

If anyone throws up near me my only thought is to get as far away as possible. But Esther does the opposite. I feel her hands on my shoulders. She doesn't flinch when it happens again, just rubs my back and says it'll be OK in a minute.

When I'm pretty sure it's over I straighten up. 'Oh God. I'm so sorry. Shit.'

I punch the wall of the house but the pain doesn't help. I glance down at myself. There's puke on my trousers and I want to die.

Esther sees where I'm looking. 'It doesn't matter. We'll sort it out. Come inside.'

Esther's hallway is all pastels and beige. She steers me past closed white doorways to a bathroom. 'Take your trousers off,' she says. 'It's only a wee bit. I'll wash it off and put them on the radiator.'

I obey. I can't say I've never thought about taking my trousers off in front of Esther – **No I bet you haven't**. *Shut up, not now* – but never like this, in a pale green bathroom smelling of Toilet Duck, and me mortified and shivering, my legs looking ridiculous. Why don't girls' legs look stupid?

Something catches at my nostrils. Orange. Bubble bath. I have to breathe in hard to stop myself throwing up again.

Esther throws my trousers into the bath. 'I'll sort them out in a bit,' she says. 'Are you ill, or was it a seizure?'

'Seizure.'

'Have you taken anything? Painkillers?'

I try to remember. My head is fuzzy. 'Yeah,' I say. 'But they're probably – you know, on your doorstep.' I can't bear to think about the mess out there. 'Your present! It was in a bag.'

'Don't worry about it. I'll get it. Why didn't you just go to bed? You could have phoned me. We could have gone out another time.'

'But it's your birthday *today*. I just – I wasn't going to tell you.'

'Oh, Luke.' She takes my hands. 'I think I'd have noticed.' Her eyes aren't just sparkly, they've got make-up on, something silvery and glittery, and they're huge and beautiful.

I pull my hands away and rub them over my face. I turn on the taps, rinse out my mouth with cold water. I can't trust myself to speak without screaming or something.

'It doesn't matter. It's just one of those things. Come and rest in my bedroom. I'll get you some more painkillers. Do you want me to phone Sandra?'

'They're out.'

Let me stay with you. It's more a feeling than a thought. I move closer to her, push my head into her soft hair, breathe in her perfumey clean smell.

She rubs the back of my head. 'Come on.' She takes my hand and leads me back down the beige hall and opens a door. Her bedroom. I have an impression of white paint and fairy lights and books but the only thing I'm really focussing on is the bed. White cover, looks so soft, loads of cushions. I could bury my head in one of those cushions for ever.

'Get into bed properly,' she says, pulling back the duvet. 'You're freezing. I'll go and put the heating on. I won't be long.'

Lying down in Esther's bed feels wonderful. It smells clean and laundryish but there's a faint scent of Esther herself, the smell I remember from the first time, from her cardigan. Her duvet is warm and light round me. On a shelf beside the bed I see the card I made her. I wonder if she liked it. I wonder if she remembered the joke. I press my head into her pillow.

'Luke? Are you asleep?'

'Huh?' I drag myself back to consciousness and struggle to sit up. She stands above me, her dark hair falling round her shoulders. She hands me two tablets and a glass of water.

The room's warmer now, and my trousers are steaming on the radiator under the window.

'You look cosy.' She sits down beside me, and it's only a single bed so I scrudge up and we're really close, only she's outside the duvet and I'm inside. She puts her arm round me and I lean against her, and she presses her lips against my forehead, and I want to say that we'll go out tomorrow instead but I don't think I get the words out before I fall into sleep.

Esther

Happy birthday, Esther.

But the funny thing is I am weirdly happy. Going out for dinner would have been lovely. And I wish for Luke's sake it hadn't been spoilt, because I can see how angry and embarrassed he is. Or was; he's asleep now, his lips slightly parted, his eyelashes dark against his cheeks, his hair a blond tousle against my dress, one arm thrust out across me. I reach down and kiss his hair – so soft, tasting of shampoo – and he doesn't wake. I don't want him to wake. Being here, like this, with Luke's body a slightly uncomfortable but welcome weight against mine is more special than being in a restaurant with ordinary strangers and waiters and music and food. This is just me and Luke, closer than we've ever been.

If he wakes up the spell will be broken.

I've imagined Luke in my bed. Though not like this. The sound of his breathing shifts a little, and his weight against me increases, as the enchantment deepens. I catch sight of the carrier bag Luke had with him, which I brought in with the painkillers. I know my present is in there, and I won't open it until Luke's awake, though I can't help wondering what it is. I peek in the bag and see that my present isn't the thing that made it heavy. My present must be that neat book-shaped parcel. A book. Well, of course I'm the kind of girl you buy a book for. I feel slight panic. I can't help feeling that whatever he's chosen will be some big statement of how he really feels about me.

But I don't need a statement. He dragged himself here, clearly feeling terrible, just so he wouldn't let me down.

Anyway, whatever the book is, it's small and light: what made the bag heavy was the bottle of red wine.

I've never really drunk. There's never any alcohol in this house, and it's not like I get invited to parties. But the bottle has a dark, promising glow. And it's my seventeenth birthday and my boyfriend is out cold in my bed and the house is so quiet with only his breathing and, if I listen closely, mine. I pick up Luke's empty water glass, and turn to the wine. I move really cautiously so I don't disturb Luke but he's totally out of it. One of the kids at summer scheme used to sleep for hours after a seizure. Another one used to bounce back like nothing had happened.

Lucky it's a screw top. You wouldn't find a corkscrew in 45 Palgrave Crescent. It splashes into the glass, darker than I expect, not really red but purplish like Ribena. It doesn't taste like Ribena. The first mouthful is bitter and makes my teeth shiver, but it curls a warm passage down inside me and I like the thought of it, a secret red ribbon threading through me. I wish Jasmine could see me now: sitting on my bed, beside this beautiful sleeping boy with the glass of wine in my hand, about to pour myself another – after all it's my birthday.

I spill a little on the white duvet and it doesn't look like Ribena, so I drain the glass and set it carefully on the shelf beside the ice-skating pony. Luke doesn't stir at all. I try to match my breaths with his. I stroke his hand with one finger and, unexpectedly, wonderfully, his hand closes round mine.

I press my lips against the nape of his neck. I am so happy.

'Esther! Esther! What on earth? Pamela! Come here!'

The room explodes into shouting and confusion. Dad's face in the doorway, purple. Luke's weight against me, Luke's eyelids flickering.

I struggle to sit up and my head reels and my stomach sloshes. In a moment I remember – the wine. *Happy birthday, Esther.*

'Pamela! For goodness sake come and –' Dad looms closer.

'Dad – it's OK. It's not ...' But I can't find the words to explain and my tongue feels twice its normal size. My eyes flit round the room, lighting on the wine bottle, half empty, Luke's trousers on the radiator.

Luke shifts and murmurs beside me.

'You – get out of my daughter's bed.' Dad actually *shakes* him, and Luke wakes up faster than I knew anyone could, springs into instant alertness and swings back his arm in a punch –

I scream. 'Don't!' I grab his arm, yank it down, shocked at its rigid strength. 'For God's sake – *Dad*! It's *not ...* '

Mum appears in the doorway, her mouth an O of disbelief. 'Oh, Esther. We trusted you – you said you ...'

'It's not – it's honestly *not* what you think. Luke was just –'

'Don't bother.' Luke wrenches away from me, pushes past Dad, pulls his trousers off the radiator and yanks them on. He looks round for his shoes and pulls those on too, without a word. His face terrifies me. The post-seizure daze on his face has been replaced by an ugly mask of hatred.

Dad rants. *Trusted you – that kind of boy – drunkenness –*

I *try* to explain. I *try*. But when I try to get up he's right about one thing. If this swirling, room-spinning, dry-mouthed, heaving panic inside me is drunkenness then I am very drunk indeed –

– and Dad's shouting and shouting, 'Get out and don't ever come back to this house, and stay away from my daughter, do you hear, stay away –'

– and Luke's storming out –

– and now it's me who's suddenly puking, horribly red, all over my dress and the cream carpet.

Luke

At the top of Esther's street I look round, half-expecting to see her dad's sweating bulk coming after me. He's mad enough to.

I'm not really checking for Big Willy. I'm checking for Esther. But she's stayed with *them*.

Two kids are snogging in the bus shelter. He has his hands round her bum and keeps kneading it, dirty little bastard; he's only about thirteen.

And who are you to –

Not now.

She has hanks of his long shaggy hair wrapped round her fingers. They both give me death looks every time they come up for air, but it's raining and tonight's been shit enough without getting a soaking. My watch says it's nearly ten o'clock. We must have slept for ages. And that bit of it hadn't been shit. I remember the feel of Esther's arms holding me, her breath warm against my neck.

'Ouch,' says the boy. 'You pulled my hair, you stupid bitch.'

I decide I'd rather stand in the rain.

The bus, when it finally lumbers up, is pretty empty; it's the next one, the last one, that'll be full of drunks. When I reach into my pocket for the fare, I realise I don't have my phone. I can't remember if I had it earlier or not.

The headache, which had faded away in Esther's bed, has been conjured back by the rude awakening, the running, the rain and the bus, and by the time I'm walking down Sandra's street, dodging a heap of chip wrappers abandoned under a streetlight, I'm knackered. I'd like to creep up to bed without talking to anyone, but the Skoda outside and the light in the window tell me they're home.

I look at the slightly scraped blue paint of their door. It feels like days since I locked it behind me but it was only a few hours ago. I step into the hall and breathe out.

Sandra's voice drifts over the noise of Saturday night TV. 'You're back early.' I push open the living room door. They're side by side on the sofa. Sandra has her feet in Bill's lap and Bill's rubbing them. I've never seen them like this before. Jay looks up from the other armchair and yawns.

Sandra twists her head to smile at me. 'Had you a good time?'

'All right, son,' Bill says. 'There's tea not long made if you want a cup.'

'Thanks.'

'Well?' Her face is as eager as her voice.

'Och, Sandra, leave the lad alone. He doesn't want to tell us every detail.'

'It was …' I look down at the plate of KitKats on the coffee table. I'm starving. I reach out for one and unwrap it.

'You can't have had a great dinner when you're still looking for biscuits.'

'Och, Sandra, growing lads.' Bill winks at me.

They're so normal, so nice, so *themselves*, so not the kind of people who'd do what Big Willy's just done, that I end up telling them.

'We didn't go,' I say. 'I had a seizure. I'm fine!' I add when I see the concern in Sandra's eyes. 'I'm completely fine.'

Sandra and Bill look at each other. I look at the KitKat in my hand. I run my nail along the fold between the two fingers.

'Och, son,' Sandra says. 'Did you take your medication?'

I'm about to give my usual indignant reply to this, when I remember. I got up late and rushed around all day. I didn't even think about my pills. 'I forgot.'

Sandra raises her eyebrows. 'Well. What do you expect?'

'It's the first time.'

'Och, but there's other things, Luke, you know there are – not getting enough sleep.'

Check.

'Getting stressed out.'

Economics test. Yuck. Maths test. History essay. Check, I suppose. She's been reading her leaflets like a good foster carer. And watching me.

'You're right. It's my own fault.'

'That's not what I said. Why don't you take a few days off school, get yourself back to normal? Take your pills and catch up on your sleep?'

'I can't – I have a test –' The familiar panic surges in my chest.

'Either you take a few days off or we're going to the doctor.'

I could miss the test. And not have to see Wilson till he's cooled down.

But then I wouldn't see Esther.

Esther who *let* her dad throw me out of the house like a thief, who didn't even *try* to defend me?

Sandra's looking at me in that way which is bossy and kind at the same time, and for once it's a relief just to give in. So I drink the tea and take my meds, and then I go to bed and sleep for fourteen hours.

Esther

So this is a hangover. Yuck. I skulk in my room as long as I can, trying not to look at the stain on the carpet. The room smells of carpet cleaner. I swallow down a fresh wave of nausea as I catch its chemical whiff. Mum must have cleaned up.

Around eleven the need for water forces me out to the kitchen. Mum's peeling potatoes at the sink.

'Oh,' I say. 'Why are you not at church?'

She sniffs. 'After the last time we left you on your own? Your dad's gone.'

'Mum, you wouldn't let us *explain*.'

'You were drunk. You were in bed with a boy. Half dressed.'

'I wasn't! I was *on* the bed. Fully dressed.'

'We knew there was something going on before we even got into the house,' Mum goes on as if I hadn't spoken. She stabs the peeler into a potato and digs out an eye. 'There was – evidence – on the doorstep.' She shudders with disgust. 'So *he* must have been drunk before he even got here?'

For a moment I haven't a clue what she's on about. Then I remember.

'Mum! You've got it totally wrong. *Luke* wasn't drinking! He was sick because he'd had a seizure. You know he has epilepsy. He shouldn't have come out but he didn't want to let me down because it was my birthday. His trousers got a bit' – I'm not squeamish but I feel a bit too delicate for all the details – 'so I made him take them off while I sponged them. He went for a lie-down and he fell asleep. *We* fell asleep. And that's *it*, Mum.'

I can't tell her how lovely it was before they came along and spoilt it. What it felt like holding Luke, the relaxed oblivious weight of him against me. And I don't remember exactly how it ended; I just have a confused memory of shouting and screaming.

Mum runs clean water into the basin of peeled potatoes. My sand-dry mouth cries out at the lovely cold splash, but I don't dare to push past her for a glass.

'That's *not* it, Esther. You'd certainly been drinking, even if he hadn't.'

'It was my *birthday*. I didn't mean to have such a lot – it was meant to be for the restaurant and I just – I know it was stupid. But you can't blame Luke. He wasn't even *conscious*.'

Mum sighs. 'You're so *naïve*, Esther – maybe that's our fault. I know we've protected you. But there was never any restaurant booking, was there? That boy intended to get you drunk and take advantage of you – and clearly you allowed him to.'

'*Mum!*' It's so far-fetched it's nearly funny, but only nearly, because she believes it. And because it's so much the opposite of how things really are with me and Luke. 'That's rubbish! Dad just doesn't like Luke. But I thought you'd make up your own mind. If you have one.'

Mum's face stiffens into hurt. Then Dad walks in in his church suit, and my stomach lurches.

'I hope your mother's made our feelings about last night perfectly clear?' He looks challengingly at Mum.

The need for water is urgent. I take a glass from the cupboard and fill it at the cold tap. I could do with some painkillers too but I daren't look for them with Mum and Dad both here. I drain the glass and turn to Dad.

'I've explained to Mum,' I say. 'And it was *nothing* like you think.'

Mum looks unhappy.

'Pamela?'

'I don't know, Alec. We may have been a wee bit hasty –'

'Hasty?' Dad gives one of the snorts that people at school imitate. 'It was quite clear what had been going on. She was completely incapable – that boy could have done anything.'

'He never *touched* me – not the way you mean. He never has. I'm a virgin.' I raise my voice. 'OK? I'm. A. Virgin.'

'Esther!'

'But that's what this is about, isn't it? You think Luke's – violated my honour.' I've started sounding as ridiculous as them. Maybe I'm still a bit drunk. I take a deep breath. 'Look, I'm sorry for getting drunk – but that is the *only* thing I did wrong. That and being stupid enough to think you'd treat my boyfriend with any kind of respect.'

'*Respect*! Did you *see* our doorstep?'

I put my head in my hands. I can't go through this again.

'I'm going out,' I say.

Mum shoots Dad an uneasy look.

'You most certainly are not going out. You're grounded!' Dad snaps.

'That's ridiculous! I'm seventeen. You can't *ground* me.'

'Either you *promise* not to see that … that boy again – or you're grounded indefinitely.'

'Of course I won't promise!' I need to see Luke *now*; I can't wait until school tomorrow. 'Mum?' I turn to her. 'Will you please tell Dad I can't be grounded?'

Mum bites her lip and shakes her head. 'We can't trust you, Essie.'

'Obviously you'll go to school,' Dad says, 'and if you'd like to resume going to church activities – well, that would be fine. But that's all.'

'Ruth's house?' I could pretend to go to Ruth's, but really see Luke.

They exchange looks again. 'I could take her, Alec,' Mum says, 'and pick her up again.'

Dad hesitates.

'Don't bother.' I storm out and back to my room.

I lie on the bed and try to smell Luke's hair on the pillow. He hasn't texted or phoned. I want to speak to him so badly, but I'm kind of nervous too. In the end I just text.

World War 3 here.
Grounded for ever.
Haven't opened your
present yet, want to be
with you. Meet at WM,
before school?

There's no reply. I alternate between anger and worry. Maybe he didn't get home OK last night. After all, he was still in that woozy post-seizure state. I shouldn't have let Dad throw him out; I should have gone after him. I blush when I think of the state I was in which meant I couldn't. The wrapped-up book sits on the shelf beside the ice-skating pony.

I hear voices from the living room but not words.

My phone stays silent. My hangover abates enough for me to have an equally silent Sunday dinner with my parents. Mum's been crying. So have I.

I get to the war memorial as early as I can, but it's not that early because Dad made me get a lift with him. I wait in a chill drizzle until the first bell goes. OK. So he's really pissed off. But it isn't *fair*. I can't help having Victorian parents. By the time I've got to the door of tutor group, with my hair frizzing damply and my nose burning with cold, I'm ready to fight with Luke. How dare he punish me like this! I've given up thinking something has happened to him – surely I'd *know*.

'Hurry up, Esther,' Baxter says.

Luke's place is empty.

Jasmine leans over to me. Her silky hair brushes my arm; it makes me think of Luke on Saturday night. 'No Luke?'

I shake my head. I pretend to look at my homework diary, crossing off the homeworks I've done, smiling at my desk the whole time.

He's late on purpose. He's avoiding me.

He's dead. He had another seizure on the way home. He fell under a car. And his phone got crushed by the car, so Sandra couldn't get my number.

He's just trying to punish me.

What for?

At the end of tutor group I wait till everyone's gone and hover at Baxter's desk while he's shuffling his bits and pieces together.

'Yes?'

'Sir – you know how Luke's not in? I was just – I wondered if there was anything – if you knew why?'

He looks at me over his glasses. 'Good heavens, Esther, I have no idea. You sixth formers aren't renowned for your punctuality. No doubt he'll swan in when it suits him.'

He doesn't.

I text him – Are you OK? – and there's no answer.

After school, hating myself for doing it, I take the landline phone into my room so he won't recognise the number if he's screening his calls. It goes straight to voicemail.

I lie on my bed and tears run into my ears. Mum has changed the bed so the smell of Luke's hair has gone from the pillow. When Mum calls me for dinner I yell back that I'm not hungry. I hear Mum's voice, worried, and Dad's – 'Let her; it won't hurt her to lose a few pounds.'

Thanks, Dad.

It's only seven o'clock. How do people get through times like this? I turn on the radio but it's all love songs. I need distraction that isn't going to make me think about Luke. I need a book. I heave myself off the bed and stand sniffing in front of the bookcase. Nothing. The books I need are under the bed. I hunker down, avoiding the stain on the carpet – I know if I get close enough I'll still be able to smell it – and reach under. My hand closes on the box of children's books – just the feel of it, full of Jacqueline Wilson and *Anne of Green Gables*, is enough to make my heart just a fraction lighter – but it also hits against something else. Something small and hard. I pull it out.

Luke's iPhone.

It's died, and I can't put it on to charge because nobody in this house has an iPhone, but at least it means he hasn't been ignoring me.

The next day Luke's absent again. But now I have a plan. After tutor group, I go to assembly – because Dad might notice if I don't – but then, on the way to English, I turn back to the lockers, shove my bag in, and start walking purposefully towards the side door. I meet McCandless, who twitches her beard at me and asks me what I'm doing out of class and I say I'm going to the toilet, and she sniffs but she can't say anything and I don't have my bag so I don't look like I'm about to walk out. I dodge out the side door and meet no-one.

According to my phone, there's only one Lilac Walk, and it's the other side of town. The bus takes forever, and my stomach feels the way it did on the day of my hangover. I don't know what I should be prepared for. He must be sick, or he'd be at school. And why hasn't he been in touch some other way?

When I step off the bus at the entrance to a council estate I think, this can't be right. Nothing here – the painted kerbstones, the tattered flags hanging from streetlights, the concrete walkways between small houses – chimes with the Luke I know.

But I find Lilac Walk easily enough, and count off the houses – 3, 5, 7 – oh, gosh, please let it not be that one with the bins in the front garden – but no. Number 11 is spruce and painted, with shrubs in the small garden and a cheerful blue door.

Luke answers the door. Not under a car. Not sick. When he sees me his eyes widen.

We speak at the same time.

'What are you –?'

'Why aren't you at school? I was really worried.'

He shrugs. 'Sandra made me stay off. It just took a bit longer than usual to – you know – bounce back.'

I look at him closely. He's nearly as pale as he was on Saturday, and he has a rash of spots across one cheek, but compared to the under-a-bus scenario he's fine.

'Why aren't *you* in school?' he asks.

'I mitched,' I say airily. 'I'm tired of being good. After getting off my face on Saturday night, and being grounded for the next two years, I thought, what can I add to my new career of debauchery? *Plus* I hadn't heard from you and I was convinced something terrible had happened.' I'm working up a little indignation now that the relief of seeing him has worn off slightly.

'Look – come in properly. And I haven't a clue what you're on about.'

'Where's Sandra?'

'At the shops.'

I follow him into a cluttered living room. The walls are covered in photos – baby photos, school photos, wedding photos. I count at least six different kids. I wonder if there'll be a picture of Luke here some day, and I wonder where all those kids are now. A gas fire hums in the grate, and the cushions on the squashy, patterned sofa are scrumpled as if Luke has been sitting there. An economics book lies face down on the coffee table, and a small black cat blinks at us from an armchair, then settles back to sleep.

'I thought you hadn't been in touch because you were angry with me,' I said. 'About my dad being so ... I was texting you like mad. And then last night I found your phone under my bed. It must have fallen out of your pocket.' I thrust the phone at him.

He tries to turn it on and sets it down on the coffee table when it doesn't respond. 'I suppose I was a bit pissed off. I thought you'd at least come after me. I didn't think you'd just stay and let them –'

'How could I have come after you, the state I was in? I could hardly walk!' I burn with shame. 'I was puking my guts up.'

Luke shakes his head. 'What? It was me who –'

'I drank the wine. Well, most of it. You were asleep and it was there, and I just – I just did. And then I fell asleep too. And when everything kicked off I *tried* to stick up for you; I tried to explain, but I was – kind of *incapable*.' Dad's word – ridiculous and OTT but sadly accurate. 'But you *knew* all this.'

Luke shakes his head. 'All I knew was your dad went mental.'

'Well, you missed me making a complete fool of myself.'

I'm so relieved that Luke *hadn't* seen me with red puke all down my dress that I could sing. For the first time I *get* what it must be like for him, knowing people have witnessed him in similarly humiliating situations. All the epilepsy websites in the world couldn't tell me that.

'So – you're grounded?' he asks. 'For how long?'

I blow out through my fringe. 'At first it was indefinite and I was banned from seeing you. Now it's for two weeks and I'm – *encouraged* not to see you. I think Mum had a word with Dad. They know if they forbid me to see you it'll just make me more determined.'

I have a sudden fear that he'll think it's not worth it; that *I'm* not worth it. 'It's only two weeks,' I say, 'and I'm here *now*.'

I lean forward and kiss him, gently at first, then harder, and I push him backwards on the sofa. I straddle him as best I can in my school skirt, and kiss him and kiss him and kiss him, and it's lovely –

Until he groans and twists my hair in his fingers, and then he shakes his head and pushes me away.

I shiver with rejection, but then the front door slams – maybe it's not me; maybe he heard the door. When Sandra comes in, lugging Lidl bags, we're at opposite ends of the sofa though I know my face is burning. Sandra is a big woman, not as fat as Mum but sort of solid all over with thin frizzy grey hair and a strong-featured face that looks as if it smiles easily. She's smiling now.

'Och,' she says, 'you must be Esther.' Then her face changes. 'Should you not be at school?'

'I had a free period,' I lie. As if any free period could be long enough to get all the way out here and back.

'Well,' she says, 'it'll give Luke a wee lift to see you. He's been a bit down.'

'*Sandra.*' Luke shakes his head at me. 'I'm fine. I'm just going to walk Esther up to the bus stop, OK?'

I feel dismissed, but I know I should get back to school. I can spin Donovan some story, but it's French after break and Madame Sudret's not so gullible.

Luke takes my hand walking to the bus stop. He says he'll be back tomorrow. He asks me to ask Toby to text him what he's missed in economics. We get to the main road and, even though I want to be with him for longer, I'm so nervous about getting back to school that I'm half-relieved to see a bus coming down the hill.

'Oh,' Luke says, 'you haven't told me if you liked your present?'

'I haven't opened it.'

'Well, do!' He kisses me quickly. 'See you tomorrow.'

From the bus I watch him walking away down the hill, past the boarded-up community centre and the drooping flags. Even though he's wearing an old hoody and track bottoms he doesn't fit. He looks like an actor walking through a film set.

Luke

'Your dad won't actually *spy* on you, will he?' I glance behind me through the gap in the war memorial hedge. In the far distance a teacher patrols.

'Course not.' But she doesn't sound totally confident.

We sit on the bench, close but not touching – because you can't get away from the fact that this is *school*, however little it feels like it. Esther takes my hand and traces a pattern on it with her finger.

'I reckon Big Willy was just waiting for his chance. He was *delighted* to find me in your bed –'

Esther leans her head on my shoulder. Then she raises it and says, 'It's only two weeks. One and half now. It's not that long. Only I'm scared –'

'What?'

'You might get fed up with me.' Her voice is small. 'There's plenty of girls whose parents aren't on their case all the time.'

Plenty of boys who'd be a much better bet than you, Lukey.

'Shut up!'

'*What?*' Her eyes widen in shock.

I shake my head. 'I mean – don't be daft. They aren't you.'

Sandra knocks on my bedroom door. 'I've called you three times. Your tea's ready.'

'I'm not hungry.' I hardly look up from my sketchbook. The picture of Esther is coming on well, even though it's mostly copied from a photo on my phone. You can see the shine on her hair and the lovely roundness of her. But I can't get the eyes right – dark and serious but ready to sparkle with life. Maybe it's too much to expect pencil to do that.

Sandra gives me the look I'm getting used to, and folds her arms across her large chest. 'Sorry, son – not an option. You know the score.'

She's turned into the seizure-control police. She even bought me one of those pill boxes with a compartment for every day of the week, like I'm a senile old man, and she stood over me while I filled them all for the week ahead. But I suppose she's right: not eating, not sleeping, getting stressed – all major triggers. And I do feel better than I have for ages.

Yesterday the school nurse asked me to talk to a second-year girl who's just been diagnosed with epilepsy and keeps crying and refusing to come to school because she's so scared of having a seizure in public. I told her about my first day and how it was kind of mortifying but I got over it because you have to. I made her laugh. I suggested that Esther and I should talk to Lauren's friends about how to help if she has a seizure. 'That's a great idea,' the nurse said when Lauren had skipped back to class. She looked at me with the kind of approval I used to get all the time from the staff at Belvedere.

I go down, sit at the table and eat pasta, and listen to Bill talking about a man at work who keeps chickens in the back garden and does Sandra think it would be a good idea? Sandra thinks it would be a terrible idea and they argue about it cheerfully all through the meal.

'You seeing Esther, son?' Sandra asks when we're finished. I hesitate. 'You know she's welcome round here any time.'

Bill nods. They've obviously discussed this.

They don't know about Esther being grounded.

I shrug. 'She has something on. Some family thing.'

I go back upstairs. Jay is on my bed. He looks up and yawns when he sees me, then curls up again. I take out my sketchbook. I take a new page and start drawing Jay. It's a good way to pass time because I get so engrossed in trying to show the way his paws are tucked so neatly under, without it looking like he has no legs, that when my phone buzzes I actually jump and the pencil slides out of control.

It's an unknown number.

Just checking you're free
to come to my birthday
party next Saturday.
And Esther of course.
Jasmine x

I wonder where she got my number. I don't like the way she's put Esther's name as an afterthought. And I don't like the x after her own name, which doesn't look like an after-thought at all.

Esther

They aren't keeping me prisoner. In fact they drag me with them everywhere – Tesco; Gran's house; they even ask if I'd like to go to a special young people's praise service at church.

'I hate the phrase "young people",' I say. 'It sounds ridiculous.'

'Well, they're people and they're young,' Dad points out. 'Don't go if you don't want to.'

If I can't see Luke I don't want to see anyone.

But then Ruth texts.

Adam n I put loadsa work in2
it wd luv u to be there xxx

I think I might as well. Maybe it will sweeten Mum and Dad up. I even make gingerbread men. Mum smiles when she comes into the kitchen to find me putting trays into the oven.

'Essie, it's like old times, seeing you baking.'

As opposed to seeing me drunk in bed with my boyfriend? I don't say it out loud. I give all the gingerbread men identical bland smiley faces.

My stomach squeezes as I push open the church door. I know pretty much everyone, and they've known me all my life. Even though it's supposedly a Young People's event, our church – I mean, *their* church – is quite small, and everybody goes to everything. So when I walk in, clutching a pink biscuit tin, and looking desperately for Ruth, noticing that there are new blue curtains, but that the old poster with the

144

peeling edges that says CH_CH – WHAT'S MISSING? is still up above the door, lots of people troop up to me, all smiles, their words caressing me.

'Och, Esther, you're welcome back.'

'There's Esther!'

Mum and Dad aren't here – I think it's a test to see whether they can trust me. I can imagine them phoning Pastor Greg as soon as it's over to check I haven't sneaked out to meet Luke. I speak to everyone who speaks to me – which is everyone apart from a couple of new Lovely Young People. Then Ruth bounces up, her hair in curly bunches, pulling a stocky, jolly-jumpered guy by the hand, and squeaks, 'Essie! I'm so glad you came! This is Adam.'

Adam and I nod our hellos.

'I am *so* nervous,' Ruth says. 'I'm leading the worship.'

Adam gives her an affectionate squeeze. 'You'll be wonderful. Once you get them joining in all those new choruses, they'll be ready for anything.' He can't keep his hands off Ruth, while never actually deviating from what's acceptable for Lovely Young People in the church hall.

It's so long since I heard words like *worship* and *choruses*. I want to sit near the back but Ruth pushes me into a seat in the front row. 'I want to see you,' she says bossily. When the choruses start I can't stop myself joining in – I love singing and I've known these all my life.

We are one in the spirit; we are one in the Lord ... I felt one with Luke, when he lay in my bed ... *And they'll know we are Christians by our love, by our love* ...

Ruth, bent over a honey-coloured guitar, looks up and smiles straight at me. Light from the high stained glass window makes her ruddy hair into a halo. She looks happy and in the right place. A few people wave their hands in the air. I would make so many people happy if I came back here. It wouldn't be difficult. I *want* to believe it. I *liked* believing it. When I started not being sure it was horrible, like falling off something I'd thought was a wide path but turned out to be a narrow ledge. Maybe God will speak to me again; if I'm back in the church I can be listening better. And maybe he'll speak to Luke too, and we could come together – and Dad would approve of Luke and everything would be brilliant.

But I know I'm kidding myself. I still don't know what I believe, but I do know this isn't the place for me any more.

And if Luke were ever to find God, he'd find him somewhere austere and beautiful, not in a suburban evangelical church with lots of Lovely Young People waving their hands. Or maybe he'd like Quaker meetings. All that silence.

Ruth speaks at the front, very sincere, nervous at first but then stronger. She makes a joke I don't get, something about fish and Pastor Greg.

Then it's time for what Dad calls the bun fight. My appetite has diminished since all the trouble, but there's something about caramel squares and cupcakes that makes them very easy to eat. Ruth squeals when she sees my gingerbread men, and introduces me to a boy called Ben. He's shy, and a bit weedy, but he tells me how much he loves our church and what great work Adam does. He has green eyes, proper green eyes, large and strangely beautiful. If I had met him before Luke I can imagine liking him quite a bit.

Ruth brings me a glass of Schloer and I tell her she was brilliant. She giggles. 'I was *so* nervous.' She glances over her shoulder. 'So?' she says.

'So what?'

'*Ben.* Isn't he lovely? I knew you'd like him. I've told him all about you.'

'He seems nice.'

She waits. 'And?'

'*And* I have a boyfriend, in case you'd forgotten.'

Ruth plays with one of her red ringlets. 'I thought – I wondered if maybe you weren't still…'

I wonder what my parents have said to her parents.

'Well, we *are* still.'

Dad taking me to school is a nuisance. I only get in in time for tutor group, and Luke – and Jasmine – are always there before me. At least he's not talking to her today; he's at his desk, reading.

Jasmine smiles at me as I'm putting my bag down. 'Like the hair,' she says.

I don't know if she's being sarky or sincere, as all I've done is put it in a ponytail, so I just smile back at her.

'Test?' I ask, sliding into the place beside Luke.

He nods. 'Thought I'd get out of it, being off, but she gave it to me to do over the weekend. I'm just checking over it.'

I squint at the pages of Luke's neat writing. 'Looks boring.'

'It is.'

'So – is that what you were up to *all* weekend?' Apart from texting and Skyping me from a bedroom that looked so freakishly tidy I wondered if he'd cleaned it up for the occasion.

'Pretty much. I had two days of notes to copy up.'

'So you might as well have been grounded too?'

'Uh-huh.' He frowns at the notes, and then smiles. 'Missed you.'

147

'They let me go to this thing in the church last night. Brought me to the door, and Ruth's dad left me home.' With me and Ruth hardly talking the whole way.

'Sounds wild. You aren't going to go all holy on me, are you?'

Before I can say anything, Toby comes up and says, 'It was a nightmare; I reckon we've all failed,' and Luke says, 'I certainly have,' and then Baxter comes in and the school day takes over and whirls us away from each other.

'I can't believe *you're* invited to Jasmine's party.' Because it's Toby it doesn't sound mean.

It doesn't seem such a big deal to me now, except that it's on the first day of my release from being grounded, so it becomes the night that's going to make up for my disastrous birthday.

Everything has to be perfect. I have five days. I persuade Dad to drop me off at the chemist's on the main road on the way home from school – and even *he* knows I'm not going to be meeting Luke in a chemist's shop – and I stock up on face packs and lipstick and bendy things that are meant to make your hair curl.

The trouble is what to wear. My jade dress was the most beautiful, perfect dress there's ever been, and there won't be another, even if I had the money. I saw it on the washing line, so I know Mum must have washed it, but I couldn't bear to go and examine it closely, so it's languished in the ironing basket ever since. As soon as I get in from the chemist's – shouting a loud, 'I'm back!' so they both know they can *trust* me – I make myself go to the utility room and rummage in the ironing basket. I pull it out, the soft jade fabric all twisted and rumpled. It looks fine – but that's the back, with the label sticking out at the neck. I hardly dare to look at the front. Puke and red wine – even separately they're bound to stain horribly, but together – it must be lethal. There's no point …

The front of the dress is fine. Those horrible streaks have gone. I take it to the window, hold it up to the light, but the jade fabric just shines with a lovely dull unblemished sheen. *Thank you God*, I breathe – some habits are hard to break. I take out the ironing board and plug in the iron. And on a whim, because sucking up does seem to be working, after I've ironed the dress I tackle the rest of the stuff in the basket too – three of Dad's shirts; a couple of voluminous skirts of Mum's; my spare school cardigan. I quite like ironing: the clean steamy smell of it, the weight of the iron making everything smooth and perfect.

Mum comes in just as I'm finishing off a very large and ugly blouse.

'Goodness, what's got into you?'

'I ironed my dress for the party.'

I don't want to dwell on either of these things too much, but Mum looks closely at the dress, hanging on its hanger from the jamb of the back door.

'It's come up good as new, hasn't it?'

'Um, yes.' It suddenly strikes me that never mind thanking God, it was Mum who'd saved my dress. 'Mum – thanks for doing that. It can't have been – um – very pleasant.'

'Oh, well. When you have children …'

'It won't happen again.' I busy myself folding a tee-shirt to hide my embarrassment.

Mum reaches behind me and switches off the iron at the wall. 'Esther – we don't mean to be unreasonable about Luke.'

I chew my lip.

'We're just concerned because Luke's background is so – well, different from what you're used to. Growing up in care. It's not –'

'I didn't think *you'd* be so prejudiced.'

'I think ...' She takes Dad's shirts and lays them carefully over her arm. 'Luke deserves credit for doing so well. But... I didn't like the way he reacted when we came into your room that night. So – violently.'

'Mum,' I say, 'he didn't even know what was going on. Dad startled him. You *know* what people can be like after a seizure.' She's been bitten and punched enough times by some of the kids in her class. 'Luke's really caring. You should see him with Lauren – this wee girl with epilepsy that we're kind of buddying. He's so –'

'You didn't see his face like I did.' Mum isn't going to be distracted by my tales of Luke's good works. 'You were too ... anyway. He looked like he really wanted to *hurt* Dad. Totally out of control. I just want you to be careful.'

'I *am* careful.'

'I mean it, Esther. You've always been so sensible.' She starts towards the door and turns back just as she reaches it. 'Don't let yourself get carried away.'

Esther

I accept a glass of champagne from Jasmine's very solemn little sister Poppy and her giggling friend. They're being waitresses.

'For half an hour,' Jasmine says, 'and then they are going to bed and *not* showing their faces again.'

'Ruby's having a sleepover with me,' Poppy says, showing gappy teeth in a big smile. 'We're having pizza.'

'We're going to sit on the stairs and watch all the snogging.' Ruby covers her mouth with her small plump hands.

'You so aren't,' Jasmine says.

I wonder where their parents are. There are two BMWs in the driveway, but the house, a huge modern Grand Designs kind of thing perched on a hill overlooking Belfast Lough, is big enough to conceal any number of parents keeping a discreet eye on things.

Mortifyingly I was first to arrive; Dad insisted on giving me a lift, and Jasmine, coming out to hang balloons on the gate – 'They're *ironic* balloons, obviously' – saw me hanging nervously around the gate and made me come in.

Now we stand around the huge white-painted hall, being all nicey-nicey and checking each other out – Jasmine's wearing a tight midnight-blue shift dress with a deep V-neck. I sip my champagne out of sheer nervousness, and it's much nicer than red wine, which I will never drink again.

Then Cassie arrives, hugs Jasmine and whispers something in her ear, then stands close to her, as if to protect her from me. When Ruby thrusts a glass at her she shudders.

'Do you know how many *calories* are in that?' She grimaces at the bubbling pale liquid in my glass as if it's at least fifty per cent lard, and then at my stomach as if she can see me expanding as I drink.

But she can't; the jade dress is even more flattering than it was a fortnight ago. I catch sight of myself in the full-length mirror that takes up one whole wall. The bendy things worked, and my hair looks shorter than usual but fuller too in loose curls.

The twins come in, Zara in dark pink, Zoë in light, carrying a huge (pink) bouquet for Jasmine. Jasmine kisses their cheeks and exclaims at the flowers, calling for Poppy to come and put them somewhere safe.

'Jas gets hay fever, you know,' Cassie says to the twins, who turn to me and shrug, rolling their eyes.

And then lots of people pile in, glittery and loud. Some from school; some from God knows where. I try to speak to people; I want to look happy and integrated and relaxed when Luke arrives, even though I feel hollowed out with nerves. The rugby team arrive together. They seem to have won some match or other. Every so often one of them shouts out, 'Fifteen–three!' and they all high-five. One has a black eye he's clearly very proud of.

'Your dress is pretty,' says Poppy, who seems to have abandoned her waitressing duties.

'Thanks.'

I reach down and smile at its soft dull sheen. Luke must be on his way. Bill's giving him a lift. It was easier, logistically, to meet here. I hope he gets here soon. We've waited too long for this evening to miss a moment of it.

'Jasmine got a car for her birthday. *I* only got an iPad.' She gives her gappy grin again and I can see Jasmine at the same age, the ice-skating pony party days. 'Have you got a boyfriend?'

'Yes. He's coming soon.'

'Do you love him? Do you kiss him?' She giggles.

'Yes and yes.' I'm not sure, and not very often, actually.

Poppy nods. 'Ruby says when she gets a boyfriend he's not allowed to kiss her, just hold hands, only he has to use hand sanitiser first because Ruby has two brothers and she says you wouldn't *believe* where they put their hands.'

'Has Jasmine — has *she* got a boyfriend at the minute?'

Poppy looks wise. 'Well, she never *tells* me, but I think she's *working* on someone. She was going out with Simon – the one with the black eye? But she dumped him because – oh, well, I'm not meant to know why so probably I'd better not *actually* say – but that was yonks ago. Like *weeks*. So it's definitely time for a new one.'

'Poppy – you're not meant to still be here.' Jasmine swoops down and grabs Poppy's arm. 'Go on – Ana has your pizzas ready for you. *And* Coke. But you have to go upstairs now and not come back down.'

Poppy trudges upstairs, her plaits drooping.

'No Luke yet?' Jasmine says his name casually, but her eyes glitter harder than usual. She isn't drunk, but she seems jittery.

And then suddenly Luke's here. He puts his arms round me from behind and pulls me to him, and the unexpected contact, the clean smell of him, is so delicious that I swing round and hug him fiercely and find his mouth with mine. He tastes of chewing gum.

We break apart and I let my breath out in a slow hiss. 'I missed you.'

'I know. You look amazing.'

'Really?'

'Yes.'

'So do you.' He's wearing black jeans and a jacket I've never seen before. His hair looks blonder than usual in the light from the industrial-style chandelier.

The rugby players are playing a drinking game which involves a lot of chanting. Cassie and Jasmine are talking on the stairs to some boys I don't recognise. Jasmine gives one of them a play punch on the arm and he pretends to reel from it, but his grin splits his face. Through the open door of the living room – which is about the size of my entire house – I see people dancing, and the band. The music isn't overwhelming but it's good that there's about an acre of garden round the house.

'I wish all these people weren't here,' I whisper to Luke.

'You didn't expect it to be just you and me, did you?'

In a way I had. All I've thought about all week was being with Luke again. It's already after eight and I've promised Mum and Dad I'll get a taxi home before twelve. They wanted to pick me up but I persuaded them not to.

I nuzzle against Luke's chest. 'I just want to be with you.' I can feel his heart through his shirt. 'I thought we could – you know – find somewhere more private?'

'What do you mean?' He gives a tiny frown.

'Oh, Luke, what do you think I mean? Come on.' I take his arm and pull him after me. 'Let's at least get a drink, get into the party mood. There's champagne. I mean, actual champagne. It's like' – I have a sudden flash of brilliance – 'Gatsby's party!'

'Ess, have you been drinking?'

'*One* glass! It was lovely! Let's go and have some more.'

He pulls back. 'I don't drink.'

'Since when?' I ask. 'You were the one brought the wine for my birthday.'

'I know, but ...'

I look round at all the people, all the glass, and I know what he's scared of, but at the same time I want him to relax more, or maybe *I* want to relax more, and I don't want to drink on my own again.

'You won't have a seizure because you have *one* drink.' I'm pretty confident about this.

'I'm not risking it, Esther. Especially when it's been so good recently.' He smiles at me. 'Let's go into the garden. Did you see the fairy lights on the trees all up the drive?'

We get waylaid in the hall by Jasmine who gives Luke a kiss on the cheek. I stiffen in annoyance.

'Luke!' she says. 'You look gorgeous. So do you, Esther,' she says after a pause. 'That's a sweet dress. Isn't it the one you wore for the results party?'

'I'm surprised you remember what anyone wore that night, Jasmine.' Oh, thanks, Sassy Girl!

Her eyes glitter. I take Luke's hand and drag him away.

The front door is open – if you did that in Palgrave Crescent all the neighbours would know you were having a party and they wouldn't be long complaining, but all you can see here is the dark sweep of garden, the fairy lights and the lough below. I know the garden doesn't go down to the sea really – there's at least a mile of houses and motorway and normal stuff underneath it – but it feels like that. We stand on the driveway and look over Belfast Lough. There's a big ship in the harbour, all lit up against the black water. The Titanic building is a silver shark.

'Trust Jasmine to live somewhere fancy,' I say.

'I can't believe her parents let her have a party like this in their house.' Luke's standing slightly behind me; he rests his chin on my shoulder.

'I suppose they want to show it off. And she didn't put it on Facebook or anything. I don't think anyone would dare to do anything stupid. I think she'd make them pay for it. Though I suppose you might do something stupid without meaning to.'

'Says the girl who got blind drunk in her own bed.'

'Says the boy who didn't notice.'

He puts his arms round my waist and I clasp his hands. I could stand here for ever. Hardly anyone's outside. Music pulses out of the downstairs windows. I look up and see lights upstairs. Poppy looks out of a window and waves at me. She jumps up and down, her blond plaits flying round her. I wave back.

A boy and a girl I don't know run out of the front door, laughing, the boy holding a bottle, the girl with a pint glass. They glance behind them, then make for a dark clump of shrubbery, still giggling. I hear the chink of glass on glass then more giggles. Then silence.

'Luke.'

Desire shoots through me. I don't even have to summon up Sassy Girl. I turn round to face him, kiss him hard; tangle my fingers in his hair. He steps backwards, nearly losing his balance, and I fall against him and kiss him more and more and more, harder than I've ever kissed him before. I slip my tongue into his mouth, and my hands leave his hair and slide down his back and cup his bum and press him to me, tighter, harder. I don't want there to be any space between us at all, and –

'Whoa.' He takes my hands and puts me away from him. 'Steady on, Ess.'

The shock is like a slap.

'Don't.' He rubs a hand over his face.

I don't understand. Aren't boys meant to be pushing for it all the time? It's me; I'm not *arousing* enough, not desirable enough. But no – he said I looked amazing. Do I need to be more encouraging?

'Luke, I've missed you. Come on.' I take my hand from round his waist and place it on the crotch of his jeans. This is way out of my comfort zone.

Luke shudders. His face is crazy-patterned pink and green and blue under the fairy lights. He bites his lip and closes his eyes. Then he pulls away.

'No,' he murmurs thickly. 'No.'

'What do you mean *no*? I thought boys always wanted to –'

'Stop it!' He grabs my hands. His fingers burn into my wrists. 'Don't tell me what I want!'

I can't believe I've been so crass. I want to explain that I'm not some kind of nympho, I just need some reassurance that he actually fancies me.

But he so obviously doesn't.

Now it's me pulling away. The fear that's lurked for weeks surges up from deep inside. 'Why won't you admit you don't fancy me? You hardly ever *touch* me.'

'Don't say that.' He frowns, twisting his face as if it hurts. 'It's not *you*. I … really … like you, but –'

He leaves the 'but' hanging.

My chest swells with pain. I'm tumbling down the dark, scary hole where I've buried all the uncertainties about Luke and me, and I hadn't realised how deep it was until I started falling.

'But you don't fancy me? You only like me because you feel safe with me. Because I don't freak out about the epilepsy.' I'm sobbing now. That memory that I thought was so beautiful – Luke in my bed, feeling so close – he wasn't even conscious. He doesn't share that memory – it was just an illusion, it was just me making it beautiful and special when it was nothing of the sort.

'Esther! It is nothing to do with the bloody epilepsy. And I do fancy you.'

'Well, you've a funny way of showing it. And you know what – I'm tired of being your freaking comfort-blanket. Find another nursemaid.'

He opens his mouth and says one word: 'Bitch.' And walks away, leaving me standing under the fairy lights, tears streaming down my face.

Luke

I need to get out of here.

Drunken girls are splayed all over the drive – I have to step over them to get past and one of them goes, 'Ow, that was my boob. That was my actual boob!'

In the doorway, two girls are kissing, running their hands through each other's long shiny hair. They're drunk and pretty and their boyfriends are watching and laughing.

I've rammed down a shutter in my brain over everything Esther's just said, but bits of it creep out through the gap at the bottom.

You don't fancy me.

Find another nursemaid.

'Luke! What are you doing all on your own?' Cassie shimmies over to me. Her hair's piled messily on top of her head; you can see the dark roots. She holds out her hands to me. 'Dance?'

I shrug her off like a wasp. I'm leaving. But I left my jacket in there, in the cloakroom. It's my only decent jacket. I know I'll never get something that quality off Sandra and Bill – it'll be Primark all the way, not that I'd ever wear it – so, despite wanting to walk away from this carnival now, I have to fight my way back in for it.

The party isn't quite so civilised now. Two rugby players are arguing, loudly, on the doorstep – 'You frigging did – I frigging never – frigging did – frigging never.' One of them is the stubbly ape from the try-out I never had. I have to push past a girl crying in the hall. She has dark hair and a green dress and for a minute I think – but it's not.

The table in the hall is still covered in glasses, most of them empty. I've never tasted champagne. Isn't it meant to make you feel good? I stretch out my hand for one of the glasses and neck it back. The champagne is warmish, and flat after sitting out, but it tastes OK. Has absolutely no effect on me. I grab another couple of glasses for the road.

Halfway down the drive – the same girls are smoking, lying full-length on the grass now even though it's started to rain – someone grabs my arm. I swing round and the champagne fizzes over my hand before the bubbles die.

'Careless! That's £24.99 a bottle. Of course we only got the cheap stuff for my friends.'

Jasmine.

'You're not *leaving*? Where's Esther?'

I shrug. 'Somewhere. I don't know.'

The fairy lights make droplets of rain sparkle in her shining hair.

'You haven't fallen out, have you? How could anyone fall out with Esther? She's so *sweet*.' She widens her eyes. 'I hope you haven't hurt her feelings.'

Of course you've hurt her. You were always going to hurt her. Better this way. For her.

'Jasmine – it's kind of none of your business.'

She pouts. 'I'm sorry. It's just – you're my friends. Both of you. I don't want you falling out at my party. I want people to be happy.' She makes a balletic gesture with her arms and looks up at the sky. 'Happy!' she repeats. Her pupils are huge. She is either very drunk or stoned. 'Luke? Are you *un*happy?'

'I'm fine.'

'Cos you know you can talk to me.'

We seem to be walking down the drive together, threading through the trees. At least I'm moving in the right direction. And I don't want to leave too quickly in case I meet Esther at the bus stop. I take a sip of the champagne. This one tastes better – the bubbles fizz behind my nose and make me sneeze.

Jasmine laughs. 'One for a wish,' she says. She looks at me expectantly.

'What?'

'Two for a kiss?'

I haven't a notion what she's on about.

'*You* don't have to leave – even if you've fallen out with Esther –'

'I haven't.'

Bitch.

'– because you haven't fallen out with me, have you? And everybody's here. Next year, when there's a countdown of all the best parties in our leavers' yearbook, this will be number two. Number one will be my eighteenth,' she goes on, answering the question she clearly expected me to ask. 'Why don't you make friends with people? There's more to life than Esther Wilson.'

'I have friends. Toby.'

'Oh, *Toby.*' She leans in to me, overbalances a bit and giggles. She leans back against a huge tree. 'You know what everybody thinks about you and Esther?'

'I really couldn't care less.'

'Well – I'm not saying this to be mean – you know how she isn't exactly in your league?'

My second glass is empty now and if this girl doesn't shut up she could be getting it in her face. Black, sour anger surges through me.

'Jasmine, you won't get anywhere with me by insulting Esther.'

'And will I get anywhere with you any other way?' She puts her hand on my sleeve. My arm trembles. The glass trembles.

'Put that stupid glass down! The cleaner will find it in the morning.'

She takes it from me and throws it behind her. It lands with a smash on the drive. She's still caressing my arm with her other hand. I move back. She moves with me. The bark of the tree trunk is rough against my back even through my clothes.

'You haven't answered my question,' she says.

'Piss off.'

'Just a bit of fun? It's my party. It's my *birthday*. And you didn't bring me a birthday present, did you?' Her fingers stroke her neck. 'What about a birthday kiss, then?'

'No.'

'Oh, come on.'

She pins me against the tree with both arms. She's the same height as me; her lips are on a level with mine, her neck and cleavage are dappled with fairy lights.

I'm shaking.

My groin aches.

'Don't pretend,' she whispers. She moves one hand down my body, stroking me, over my crotch. '*See?* You do like me. You only think you don't.'

See? You do like it. Don't ever tell me you don't, you little pervert.

She leans in. Her hair tickles.

'Come on, Lukey,' she murmurs.

Come on, Lukey.

I grab her arms and fling her from me, so hard she slams against the tree. Her hands scrabble in the air and she clutches at the string of fairy lights. With a hiss the lights go out and the tree is plunged into dark.

Esther

I hate him.

I lie on my bed and the tears soak into my ears and I hate him and hate him and hate him. I listen to Taylor Swift and wonder how my life turned into one of her songs.

Mum hovers outside. I hear her heavy tread and feel her worry seep from behind the closed door.

When I arrived home at nine o'clock I told her I had a headache, thought my period was coming, and I'd just go straight to bed. I know she didn't believe me, but I was home before my curfew, sober and unmolested – practically untouched – so she couldn't do anything about it.

It's not you. Thanks for the clichés.

I pull the book down from the shelf. War poetry. Not love poetry. Well, of course not. And the card. Stupid ice-skating pony. *Bitch*. I plonk them both into the bin.

Luke

It doesn't make sense to feel this drunk. I had – I don't remember – but not that much champagne. But I feel like I did the few times at the start of this year when I was totally wasted. *Not* on champagne. I'm not falling-down drunk, but my steps weave a bit and I have to concentrate on keeping a straight line. I'm too wired to get the bus, so I walk. I don't know this part of town but some instinct takes me down into the city centre and eventually to the main road at the far end of Sandra's estate.

It's the rough end, where I never go if I can help it. Instead of terraced houses there's two grey high-rise towers, a short parade of mostly boarded-up shops, and a row of garages with graffitied doors.

I need to have my wits about me.

And I don't. My brain's skidding around like a pony on an ice rink, like I've just had a seizure but I know I haven't. When you have a seizure you fall, you land, and it's over. You feel like shit, and maybe you're bruised and you're probably mortified, but you get back up. You sleep it off. Now I feel like I'm still falling. And I don't know what I fell from, or where I'm going to land.

Three guys my age lean against a row of garage doors, smoking, and check me out. I breathe in the sweet smell of dope, and concentrate on not making eye contact. I wish I was wearing my usual jeans and hoody. I want to know the quickest way to Lilac Walk but no way am I asking these hoods. I miss my footing at the edge of the wet footpath and career into a streetlight, grabbing at a tattered remnant of Union Jack to keep my footing.

'Oy, mind our fleg,' calls one of the kids.

'We'll frigging do you if you touch that,' says his mate.

Something stupid in me nearly shouts abuse at them, because something stupid in me *wants* these lads to give me a kicking, to let the bruising and the walloping of my body to the ground blot out the memory of the party. But I'm not that pissed, and there's no guarantee that they'd stop at a kicking.

'All right,' I say, using the accent I used to turn on and off at the school gates at Belvedere for reasons of survival. I walk on, waiting for the jump behind me but it never comes.

This street is wider, and below me I can see the neon sign of the Spar, and I know my way from there.

Am I ever going to have a normal night out? I don't even know what went wrong tonight. Last time I could blame the epilepsy, but tonight – it was just Esther going all weird and then Jasmine – God, how did that all happen?

And what exactly *did* happen?

Come on, Lukey, she said.

My insides reel. I feel filthy, sick. I wish I could puke it all out, get rid of it, get rid of the whole horrible evening, let the rain swirl it all away.

Because you *are* sick.

But it started OK, Esther so gorgeous in her silky greenish dress, and so warm and happy to see me, and then so – what did she say – *Find yourself another nursemaid.*

Bitch.

And Jasmine –

No. Can't go there.

I want to go to bed and not talk to anybody but Sandra pulls open the living-room door just as I set foot on the first stair. Canned laughter booms from the TV.

'Good party?' Her voice is all hopeful and interested. 'D'you want a cup of tea?'

'No.'

'No, *thank you.*'

'I'm going to bed.'

'You're in a strange mood, son.'

'How would you know? You don't *know* me. And I'm not your fucking *son.*'

'Luke!' Bill zaps the remote at the TV and mutes it. 'Don't speak to your – to Sandra like that.' He sounds crosser than I've ever heard him. He looks at me closely. 'Are you on something, lad?'

You're right, Lukey. They don't know you. They wouldn't want to. But I do, don't I?

'No!' I slam out and upstairs and into my room. I don't turn the light on but as I lie on my bed I feel the walls and ceiling dip and swirl even though I can't see them. I don't know if I'm drunk or sober. I don't like the way I smell; I don't smell of myself or Esther, I smell of Jasmine's strong spicy perfume.

I wake up still on top of the bed, still in my clothes, and it's morning and I feel like shit. I stay in my room and try to read. I'm hung-over but I don't know if it's from drinking or something else. I'm desperate for air. I sit by the open window. I should go out for a run or a cycle or something, but the Sunday streets look like they're lying in wait for me.

I take out my sketchbook. It's getting pretty full now. I don't look at the pictures of Esther. I take out paints and try to paint without thinking too much, but all that comes out is a scribbled mess.

Sandra calls me down for lunch in the voice you don't argue with. I'm not hungry but I know there'll be a lecture if I don't eat so I choke down potatoes and roast beef. Bill talks about creosoting the back fence. I take my pills. I catch Bill's eye and he looks puzzled. I want to say sorry for being so grumpy last night but how can I? Better just act like it never happened.

Just act like it all never happened.

But it did happen, Lukey.

Like you always knew it would.

Esther

It's clear from the snatches of conversation behind me that the party got much wilder after I left. I write forward dates in my homework diary like it's the most important thing in the world to have all the subjects filled in until December.

'And I swear I am never drinking the blue ones again.'

'So I was just, like –'

'No way.'

'Did you see the pictures?'

This is a first for me. Actually having been – briefly – at the party all the gossip's about. For years this was my dream. Now it's a nightmare. At least I'm not important enough for anyone to be gossiping about *me*. I don't suppose Jasmine even noticed me leaving.

Luke comes in late. Baxter frowns. There's an empty seat beside Toby. Luke sits in it. He doesn't look at me, or anyone. He doesn't apologise to Baxter. The chat behind me dies away.

I hate him. I write it in my diary. Lightly, letting the pen just skate over the surface of the paper, then digging deeper. It stands out in blue.

I hate him. I outline it in red.

At the end of tutor group, Jasmine and Cassie flounce past Luke arm in arm, without a word, their hair swinging. Weird. Last week I'd have loved Jasmine to be ignoring Luke, but now – it's like there's something going on I don't get.

Luke and I arrive at the classroom door at the same time. How can you hate someone when the sight of their fingers on the door handle makes your stomach flip? When the familiar smell of their shampoo makes you forget to breathe?

If he apologises. If he says, *Meet me at the war memorial at break time*, I'll stop hating him.

'After you.' He waves me through like I'm an old lady in a bus queue.

I hate him.

Art and French are a relief. He's in economics, then maths.

At lunchtime I go to the sixth form centre. I sit in the coffee bar with a yogurt I don't want. I scrape the lid and concentrate on licking yogurt off my spoon. I play with my phone. There are no messages and it won't go online – the signal's always erratic in the coffee bar – but it's something to look at since I've forgotten to bring a book.

I become aware of someone sitting down opposite me. I look up. 'Cassie.' I haven't seen her without Jasmine for weeks. She's looking at me the way you'd look at someone whose entire family had just been gunned down by a maniac.

'Esther,' she says. Before I can stop her she places her icy white fingers on my arm. 'How are you – you know – bearing up?'

'To what?' A slurp of yogurt goes down the wrong way and I cough. Is this something to do with me and Luke falling out? Do people *know*? And what business is it of Cassie's?

'You shouldn't bottle it up,' Cassie goes on.

'Bottle *what* up?'

She plays with the end of her hair. 'I mean – Jas and I have been saying – God knows what *you've* been putting up with all this time. But there are people you can talk to.'

'Am I meant to know what you're on about?'

'Luke, of course. I mean – I saw the bruises. And she was crying – she was in a terrible state. Lucky *I* was there to look after her. It took me ages to calm her down. Poor Jas.' Her eyes gleam.

'*What* are you talking about?' The yogurt curdles inside me. Luke? Jasmine? Luke and Jasmine? But what does she mean *bruises*?

I know one thing. Whatever's going on, I don't want to hear one more syllable of it from Cassie Morris.

'Where's Jasmine?' I demand. Maybe I'll get some sense out of her.

'Don't you know?' Cassie bristles with importance. 'The nurse sent her home. She was in an awful state. I suppose – seeing him – it was just too much for her.'

I swallow down dread.

'Do *you* like it rough?' she goes on, as if she's asking me what flavour my yogurt is. 'I wouldn't have thought you were the kinky type.'

I find my voice. 'What exactly are you saying?'

Cassie steps back. Her panda eyes goggle. 'Luke. At the party. After you left. He *forced* himself on her. She only just got away.'

'That's – impossible.' I can hardly force the words out.

'I've seen the bruises.'

I stand up. The coffee bar spins and reels. Don't, I tell myself. Don't assume it's true. This is *Cassie*. Drama queen. Fantasist. Bitch.

I turn and walk away. I have to get out of the sixth-form centre before I cry or scream or throw up. I could do all three very easily.

The nightmare twists tighter.

He forced himself on her.

What does that even *mean*?

Words jab at my brain.

I've seen the bruises.

She was in a terrible state.

I blunder down the steps out of the sixth-form centre, thoughts racing round my head like frightened insects.

Luke wouldn't *do* that. If he was the *slightest* bit violent or – forceful – I would know.

What about that RE class? What about my birthday?

No. Those were completely different situations. And they were both directed at a man – at my dad – not at girls.

Be careful, Esther, Mum said.

The bell clangs right above me and makes me jump. It's history. With Luke. I can't sit in class and look at him. It was bad enough before; it would be impossible now.

My feet rush me out of the building, across the quad, down the drive. Just as I get within sight of the gate I see McCandless on guard, feet planted squarely, haranguing someone clutching a packet of chips. I wheel right and head for the war memorial. It's the only place I can get some peace, think what to do. And maybe sitting there, looking at the marble cross, reading the names of all the dead, might – I don't know – give me some sense of perspective.

Or maybe not. Because as soon as I reach the gap in the hedge I see him there, sitting on the bench, his back to me. He's drawing. Calmly sitting there *drawing*. My stomach clenches. He doesn't turn round.

'Aren't you meant to be at history?' My voice sounds clogged, as if I've forgotten how to use it.

'Aren't *you*?' He sets his pencil back in his pencil case, selects another one.

I breathe in deeply. 'Is it true?'

'Is what true?' He doesn't even look up.

'Did something happen with you – you and Jasmine?'

And now he looks up for the first time, his eyes guarded.

'Just tell me, Luke.' My breath shudders in my throat and I know Luke must hear it, but I force myself to speak. 'Cassie says you – you *forced* her. She says Jasmine was in a terrible state – and she's had to go home and – '

'*What?*'

I've never seen the colour drain out of someone's face before, but Luke's face bleaches whiter than the pages of the sketchbook he lets fall out of his fingers. Without thinking I bend down and pick it up, smoothing back the crumpled pages. A detached part of my brain registers that he's drawn the war memorial beautifully.

I hand him the book, and the fingers that reach out to take it are shaking. I look down at his hands – the long fingers, the squarish knuckles, the nails he says he's going to stop biting. I know these hands in a way I've never known anyone's. I've felt their gentleness, and their strength – and something about his hands tells me it's not true.

Of course it's not true.

It's weird and sick and twisted and I don't know why Cassie's saying it, but I *know* this boy – and he *wouldn't*.

'It's ridiculous,' I go on, with a sudden surge of confidence. 'They can't go round saying that about you.' For a moment I'm so indignant on his behalf that I've almost forgotten that I hate him. 'You *have* to go and sort it out.'

Luke's fingers close round the book. The knuckles are white.

He turns and walks away.

Luke

You have to go and sort it out.

I've walked out of school without really noticing, but if I go home at this time Sandra will fuss. So I walk. I walk into town and let the impersonal shop fronts distract me.

That night. I know now I was drunker than I realised. I read the small print on my drugs – *may increase the effects of alcohol.* But I wasn't *that* drunk.

A *Big Issue* seller thrusts her magazine at me outside Castle Court and I shrug her off.

It's ridiculous.

Esther's face. Hurt and angry, but loyal and trusting. She *knows* me.

She thinks.

I walk past the Central Library, cross the road and go up to the cathedral. I sit on the steps. The cold stone under my legs feels real.

An old lady comes out of the cathedral. She holds on to the rail for support as she struggles down the steps, tucking her walking stick under her arm. At the bottom she half turns and gives me a whiskery smile. 'Safely landed,' she says.

I hug my knees and rest my chin on them. My mind forces itself back. Trees. Fairy lights sparkling in the rain. Panic and – yes, desire. And violence. I remember that.

She says *you forced her.*

True colours, eh, Lukey boy?

You knew it was going to happen.

It was always going to happen.

I eat as much as I can of Sandra's dinner. I don't want her getting suspicious, but every mouthful is harder than the one before. The chips graze my throat and each pea is an indigestible bullet. My throat spasms and I have to put my knife and fork down.

'What's wrong with it?' she demands.

'Not hungry.'

She humphs. Relations have been strained since Saturday night. 'You know you need to make sure you eat properly.'

'I'm tired. I might go to bed.'

She looks at me suspiciously. 'It's only half six. Are you coming down with something?' Her voice softens. For a moment I'm tempted to say I feel sick – it wouldn't be a lie – and I could stay off school tomorrow, and not have to face Esther and, oh God, Jasmine.

'I'm fine. Just tired. I'll go on up.'

I get undressed and into bed. Every time I close my eyes I smell the resiny bark of the trees and Jasmine's perfume. And hear the voice. Louder in the dark.

There's a small tap on the door. 'Luke? Are you awake?'

I hold my breath. The door squeaks open a tiny bit and Sandra looks in. 'I've a wee cup of tea for you if you want it?'

'Thanks.'

I sit up.

She comes in and sits down on the chair and hands me the tea. 'Are you sure nothing's worrying you?'

I shake my head. Then nod. Not sure which is right. Sandra is soft and heavy and comforting and if there was something normal wrong I might tell her. But how can I say, *A girl is saying I attacked her and I can't deny it because it might be true?* Bet she hasn't got a leaflet for that.

'Where's Esther these days?'

I cup my hands round the mug. It's yellow with a smiley face on it. She always gives it to me. She calls it Luke's mug. I don't really like it; when I make the tea I always take the blue china one, but she never notices.

'We – sort of broke up.'

'Och, no.' She straightens the duvet cover a bit, then says, 'Yous'll maybe make friends again.'

I shrug. Some tea slops on the duvet cover.

'Well, you know where I am, son.'

I'm not your fucking son. I wish I hadn't said that. But it's true.

The tea makes me even wider awake. I lie and listen to Sandra and Bill come upstairs. Their bathroom noises. Someone shouts in the street.

The voice in my head gets louder. It hasn't let up much since Saturday night.

You're disgusting.

I try not to look at the green glow of the bedside clock. Try not to work out how much – how little – sleep I'd get if I fell asleep now, at 12.43; at 1.13; at 1.29.

At 2.08 I get up and sit by the window. Jay stands in the garden, looking up. He yowls up at me, and I pad downstairs to let him in, but when I open the door he's not there. I stand at the door for a bit, feeling the cold night air on my face. A siren blares from the main road. I wait until I'm shivering before I go back in.

Esther

Ruth hugs Mac and frowns over his furry face.

'He didn't *deny* it. That's the scary thing,' I say for about the tenth time.

'But Esther – you've been going out with him for weeks. Surely you'd have noticed if he'd been a bit – well, you know, rough or whatever.' She blushes, her cheeks clashing with her hair, and squeezes Mac harder.

I shake my head. 'No. Definitely not.' I think of the cool soft sketching of Luke's fingers on my face. But then those same fingers, contracting into a fist –

And how strong his arm had felt.

But that was different – Dad had startled him; he was half-asleep and it definitely wasn't *sexual*.

Totally out of control, Mum had said.

'Esther?' Ruth is looking at me in concern. She deserves more than this – I phoned her, blubbing so much she could hardly make me out, after Luke left me at the war memorial, and she'd said at once she'd come round straight after school. And she's been sitting on my bed for ages now, listening to my very confused and incoherent story, and only interrupting occasionally. The least I can do is be honest with her, no matter how embarrassing it might be.

So, with a kind of whooshing breath, I try to explain. 'He was always a bit – you know. Awkward. Backward.'

She looks at me, her eyebrows drawn together as if she hasn't a clue what I'm on about. 'You mean – physically?'

'We – we'd kiss – sometimes. But he never seemed to want to go any further.'

'How far did *you* want to go?'

I shrug. 'Just – you know. Normal.' Far enough to feel I turned him on.

Ruth plays with Mac's ears. 'What's normal? I've told you about me and Adam. We've decided we won't sleep together –'

'Yes, but –'

'Hold on. That's normal for *us*.' She frowns. 'I'm not saying it's *easy*. Did you even *talk* to Luke?'

I bite my lip. 'Not about that.' Not until it exploded into that terrible scene at the party.

'Esther!' She sets Mac on her knee and shakes her head at me. 'How could you *not* talk about it?' She makes it all sound so easy.

'Because I was frightened that he – that it was *me* ...'

She cocks her head on one side. 'I don't get you.'

'That he didn't fancy me,' I mutter.

'So why would he be *with* you?'

'Because he thought I was the best he could get? Because he wasn't confident enough to go after someone like – someone better?'

Ruth hurls Mac at me. 'Don't be daft! You're gorgeous. He was lucky to have you.'

'It isn't daft!' I dismiss the compliments. 'I thought at first – that he was just shy. But he can't have been so shy with Jasmine, can he?'

Ruth is silent for a long time. 'Esther – there's a bit of a jump between not being shy and actually *forcing* yourself on someone. And you don't really know much about him – I mean, his background –'

'Don't be so snobby!'

'I'm not. But kids aren't taken into care for no reason. Maybe there's violence in his background.'

I pick Mac up from the floor and smooth his fur. There's a bit on his cheek that I rubbed so much when I was young that it's worn away to a weave of threads.

My voice is very small and desperate. 'Cassie's not the most reliable. She'd do anything for drama.'

'And what about Jasmine?'

'I don't think she'd exactly *lie*,' I admit.

'Was she drunk?'

'I don't *know*. I wasn't *there*. But – she *does* drink a lot,' I tell Ruth. 'At the results night party she was a complete mess. Cassie was hopeless, so I kind of had to deal with Jasmine – hold her hair out of her puke, stay with her when she passed out.'

'Ew. I hope she was grateful.' Ruth speaks with the confidence of someone whose friends never need their hair held out of their puke.

'Jasmine doesn't do gratitude.' I try to think back to the party. Jasmine was drinking champagne – was she drunk? Not that I remember. But even if she was –

'Ruth? Are you saying if she was drunk she'd have *deserved* –'

'No! Of course not. That would be *worse*. If he took advantage of her. I just think you need a clearer picture of what happened.'

'How? Luke just walked away from me. I can't trust Cassie.'

'So ask Jasmine.'

'I can't.'

'You're scared of what she might tell you.' It's a statement, not a question.

And I know she's right.

Luke

I pause outside the English room with my hand on the doorknob, and breathe in. I don't exhale until I've given my late slip to Mr Donovan, and walked the long, long path to a seat at the back. I keep my eyes fixed on the Shakespeare poster on the noticeboard.

They're staring at you. They know what you are.

Esther doesn't look up from her copy of *Othello*.

Cassie rubs Jasmine's arm. I don't speak to anyone, except Toby when he turns round and tells me what page we're on. His face is pinker than usual.

I look down at *Othello*. The print blurs. Sweat breaks on my forehead. I don't know how I'm going to survive a double period, and then economics and then history, and then lunchtime, and then the afternoon, and every afternoon. For the first time ever, I wish I could have a seizure, just to escape from this. A bad one. I could hit my head and be unconscious for hours. Days.

As Donovan drones on about leitmotifs, I let my sweaty fingers bleed into the pages, and fantasise about it. It could happen. I haven't taken my meds since Sunday.

Esther won't look at me.

I can't look at me.

From my seat I can see the back of Jasmine's head. She leans over to whisper to Cassie and her hair parts on her neck. There's a vivid scarlet mark at the top of her nape. Like a thumb print. Like someone pressed really hard.

Horror surges through me like a wave of nausea. The air around me solidifies. My skin turns to ice.

I scramble out of the room. Don't know where I'm going, don't know where I *can* go. I'm falling, dying, can't breathe. My face burns; the skin's peeling off. I gasp for air but my throat's sealed. Panic slams me against the corridor wall; cold wall sliding down my back, head exploding, fighting to breathe, not a seizure, I'm dying, and maybe it's better –

Definitely better, Lukey.

'Luke? Luke! Are you all right?'

Someone stops. A man's voice tells me to breathe slowly. 'In and out, that's it. Slowly.'

My head subsides. Someone is breathing, harsh, ragged. It's me. I'm not dying at all.

The man beside me, telling me I've had a panic attack but that I'm fine now, looking at me with eyes that, magnified by their glasses, are brown and warm, like his daughter's, is Wilson.

We're both mortified. He asks me if I want to go and sit somewhere quiet for a bit. I say no, I'm fine to go back to class, and he nods and walks away. When he's turned the corner at the end of the corridor I just walk out of school and keep walking until it's time to go home.

———————

Someone's in the room. All this time I thought he was dead but I was wrong.

You thought you'd got away with it.

You thought you'd got away from me.

In my bed, twisting round my legs like a snake. I writhe and kick but it's not enough. The voice gets nearer; warm breath on my neck. The space round me gets smaller and smaller; walls that are soft to the touch but every time I push them away they billow back and smother me.

When it gets to my head I'll die.

You don't deserve to live.

I struggle, gasping, into consciousness, scrabbling at the monster pressing down on me, kicking at the snakes round my legs.

It's the duvet.

I'm in bed, awake, drenched in sweat, with the duvet tangled round me. My mouth is so dry I can't swallow. I grapple for the bedside lamp. My hand slips and falters on the tiny switch but at last I snap it and soft light turns the room back into my familiar bedroom. I check my phone. 3.24 a.m. I choke down some water from the glass beside my bed, and lie back down, heart pounding, breath shuddering through me. It's not real.

Except it is.

I can't go back to sleep and risk that again. I'll have to stay awake. I drag myself into a sitting position and look round for distraction. *Tender is the Night* is beside the lamp. When I first lived with Helena I used to get nightmares. 'Always keep a book by the bed,' she'd say, standing in my bedroom doorway. 'Nothing like it for taking your mind off things and getting you back to sleep.'

I was eleven, and it worked. It doesn't work now. The words dance around and tease me, and even when I force myself to concentrate on them, they only penetrate the very front of my brain. The rest of it lurches from the memory of the dream to the non-memory of the party.

You wouldn't do that.

Come on, Lukey; you know you want to.

You don't deserve to live.

A quieter voice tries to be heard. *You know where I am, son.* Sandra's next door. I could go and wake her.

But then what? What would I say?

181

What could she do?

What can anybody do?

Maybe I wouldn't feel so weird and panicky if I'd taken my meds. That's why I can't sleep, why I feel like I'm falling, why this nightmare is waiting to seize me every time I do manage to close my eyes.

I'm kidding myself. I know what the nightmare's about.

But I get up and open the drawer of the bedside table. There they are in the senile-old-man box Sandra got me, all counted out, two for each day. Sunday night, Monday and Tuesday are still in their compartments. It's Wednesday now. Or does it still count as Tuesday? I take Tuesday's, but then Monday's look wrong, forsaken, so I take them too. And Sunday night's. Maybe they'll knock me out until morning.

There isn't one moment when I decide to take them all.

Wednesday.

Thursday.

I walk to the window and lean my head against the cool glass. I don't know how long for. The street is quiet. When I close my eyes the street lights still wink in my head.

Street lights. Fairy lights.

Friday.

Throat itches.

Saturday makes me gag. Need more water. I stumble into the bathroom. A new red spotty towel hangs on the rail. Sandra brought it home today. It doesn't go with the green tiles but she said it was cheerful. The spots dance.

I bend over to fill my glass, and a rush of nausea hits me. It must be starting, this must be what it feels like. I breathe in as slowly as I can.

The water splashes in. The red spots dance, all different colours now.

My head's going to explode.

Need to get to my room. Lie down. Out on the landing a knife in my guts splits me in two. My hand squeezes the glass. The landing stretches for miles. I can't make it.

Pain bites harder, doubles me over –

Top of stairs –

Falling –

Grab for the handrail but hand jerks madly, a flopping fish, doesn't connect.

Still falling.

Head shatters –

glass

everything

shatters

Esther

I sit in French and try to concentrate on *L'Etranger*. Luke wasn't in tutor group and it was kind of a relief. But it's English next and I bet he's there. He probably arrived just in time for maths. I wish I didn't know his timetable by heart.

When will I stop being so *aware* of him?

There's a knock on the door and Madame Sudret frowns. 'I sincerely hope this is a matter of life or death,' she says, which is what she always says when someone dares to interrupt a lesson, and a few people titter obediently.

It's Dad. He says something in an undertone to Madame Sudret and goes back into the corridor. As always when I see him unexpectedly in school, I cringe and don't make eye contact. In the front row Cassie is already reaching for her bag, always ready to be the centre of any pastoral-care drama.

But it's me Madame Sudret calls out.

'Your father waits for you in the corridor,' she says quietly.

Why is Dad embarrassing me in school? I open the classroom door ready to be indignant.

And then I see his face.

Esther

The door of the side ward clicks open. I don't want to look round because I know if I take my eyes off Luke for even a second he will die. But part of me needs to turn away because looking at Luke's face the way it is now – bruised and swollen on one side, contrasting horribly with the greyish white of the other side, with a tube lying across it going up his nose – is so dreadful.

It's the curly-haired nurse, the one I like because she reminds me of Ruth. But I don't like her now because she frowns and says, 'Only two people at a time.'

I tighten my grip on Luke's hand. I can only hold his left hand because his right one is bandaged.

Bill and Sandra and Brendan, who is apparently Luke's social worker, all look at each other.

'Family only,' the nurse says.

'He hasn't got a family,' I say, and Sandra looks hurt.

'Probably best to keep it to adults,' the nurse says. She must think I'm about twelve.

'I'm staying,' I say and my voice comes out much stronger than I expected it to.

Bill and Brendan stand up. 'I should go anyway,' Brendan said. 'I've three meetings this afternoon.' He shakes his head. 'I don't know what can have gone so wrong. When I first took over his case, Luke was the one client I didn't worry about. He was fourteen – doing well at school, playing in the football team, fit, healthy, well-adjusted. One of our success stories. Ticked all the boxes.'

My teeth shiver with irritation. *Client. Case. Ticked the boxes.*

'I'll walk out to the door with you,' Bill says. He makes a smoking gesture and Sandra frowns.

'He's meant to be off them,' she says, as the door closes behind them.

The nurse bends over Luke, checks something on the monitor beside the bed and nods at us. 'That's better,' she says. 'Talk to him. Try to sound natural. Try not to let him pick up that you're worried.'

'Can he hear us?' Sandra asks.

The nurse shrugs. 'It's hard to know,' she says. 'But there's always the chance he knows you're here.'

Luke's face doesn't look like it knows we're here. Luke's body, mostly hidden by the white sheet, his chest exposed with things taped to it, doesn't look like it's ever going to move again. I haven't seen his bare chest before and I never thought I'd be seeing it like this. I want Sandra to go away, to leave me alone with him, but at the same time I'm grateful for her.

The nurse opens the door. 'I'll be back as soon as I have some results for you,' she says, and Sandra and I are left at opposite sides of the bed.

The results are to do with the scan Luke's just had. They know he hit his head when he fell down the stairs. They know he took an overdose of his medication, which – weirdly – caused a massive seizure. What they don't know is if he's going to make a full recovery. Or any kind of recovery at all.

Or why he took them.

'I thought yous two had fallen out,' Sandra says after a long silence.

I shake my head. 'It was complicated.'

'Complicated,' she repeats. She leans over the bed as if Luke is going to magically whisper some kind of answer to her and pushes a bit of hair out of his eyes. 'I wish he'd talked to me!' she bursts out. 'I knew he was in bad form, but I never thought … Finding him like that – all that blood and broken glass.' She shakes her head. 'I'm getting too old for this.' She breaks off, chewing her lip. Then sits back and squares her shoulders. 'Och, he was no trouble really. Until this.'

I stroke Luke's hand. The rhythmic gesture soothes me; I don't know if Luke can feel it. I don't want to talk because I'm scared I'm going to burst into ridiculous hateful sobs.

'Had you any idea?' Sandra asks.

I shake my head. 'We – sort of weren't speaking,' I admit. I can see her blaming me. I bite my lip. 'There was this party,' I go on. 'We fell out and I left, and then …' I look down at my school skirt through a blur of tears. She clearly hasn't a clue, and I can't say it.

Just then the door opens again. It's a doctor this time. He's not old but he looks grumpy and tired, as if he's had enough of teenagers hurting themselves.

'You're the mother?' he asks.

'Yes,' Sandra says firmly, 'I'm his foster mother.'

'Ah,' says the doctor in a kind of that-explains-it voice which makes me hate him. I try to focus on what he's saying, but it's technical. And terrifying. I thought pills just made you unconscious, but he's going on about brain damage and organ failure. Sandra frowns and nods. I tighten my grasp of Luke's hand, as if I can protect him from the terrible fates the doctor seems to be wishing on him.

'But that is worst-case scenario,' he says.

'And what's best-case scenario?' Sandra asks, catching my eye.

The doctor pinches the bridge of his nose. 'Many people make a full recovery. The pills weren't in his system very long.' My heart flips up. 'But there are the complicating factors of the brain injury and the epilepsy.' My heart flips down again. 'And of course, even if there is a full *physical* recovery …'

I don't let myself listen to the next bit. The bit about depression being common in young people with epilepsy. *No*, I want to say. *I don't think that was it.* Luke's seemed pretty cool with his epilepsy recently. That's not why –

But what would I know?

As soon as the doctor leaves, Sandra's face crumples. 'Our Joanne was against it from the start,' she says. 'She said at our age … But when Brendan told us he had this boy who needed somewhere in a hurry – och, sure how could I say no? He was seventeen; he'd be going off to university in a couple of years; and Brendan didn't think he'd be any bother.'

'So this was – after his mum died?'

'His mum had been dead a brave wee while. No, it was after Lady Muck decided she couldn't cope with his *special needs*.'

I don't want to admit that I've no idea who she's talking about. Except that it must be the *someone else* that Luke used to live with.

She gives a snort. 'If you ask me it was just an excuse. She couldn't wait to go and start her fancy new job in Dublin. Doctor bloody Scott.' Then her voice changes. 'Mind you, she probably knows him better than anyone. I wonder what she'd say if she saw him like this.'

I rub Luke's wrist. And think that even though I've felt closer to him than I ever have to anyone, there are ways in which I don't really know him at all.

'You made him happy,' Sandra says suddenly.

I bite my lip. 'Not enough.'

Sandra pulls at the thin gold chain round her plump neck. 'Oh God, I wish he'd just wake up.'

She doesn't say any more.

The room grows hot. I prickle inside my school shirt and my hand sweats around Luke's. I want to take it away and wipe it, but I can't bear to break the connection.

I love you, I say over and over in my head. And I think it's true, but yesterday I hated him. He walked into English and I wouldn't meet his eye, and he'd looked calm and sort of proud and distant. Until he smashed out of the room.

If I'd gone after him – and God knows it was hard not to; Toby had leaned forward and said, 'You should go,' and I'd shaken my head – would it have made any difference?

Would anything have made a difference?

Esther

'No.' Dad gathers up his car keys. 'You'll be better off at school.'

'I can't! Mum, tell him! How can I go to school when Luke…?'

They forced me home last night, and I've slept in fitful, nightmarish bursts. I dreamt that Luke died and then I dreamt that he was fine. I dreamt that I went into his room at the hospital and Jasmine was there, in the bed with him. When I woke up after that one, heart thudding, I switched on my laptop, which is going through a phase of behaving itself, and spent the rest of the night googling overdoses and brain injuries, and now my own brain's whirling with possibilities, all of them terrifying.

'Get your uniform on, Esther. I know we let you spend yesterday at the hospital, but this could go on for some time. You can't miss your education.'

'I phoned Sandra this morning,' Mum says quietly. 'She says no change. She's gone home for a rest.'

'So he's all on his own! You can't expect me to go and sit in school when Luke could be – could be *dying* –'

'You can go later,' Mum promises. 'I'll take you after work. Oh, no – I have a parents' meeting. I'll take you after tea.'

'No! That's too late.'

Dad loses whatever patience he had in the first place. 'Esther – get dressed; I've to do a special assembly and I can't be late.' He picks up a sheaf of papers from the table. 'Of course there's been gossip.' My ears prick at the word *gossip*. Just what does Dad know? 'The pupils have all got wind of it, goodness knows how. We're playing it down – focussing on the fact that he had a seizure and a fall – which of course is true. But –'

'You go on, Alec,' Mum says. 'I'll deal with Esther.'

'I don't need to be *dealt* with!'

'The water's hot,' Mum says. 'Go and have a shower. I'll make you some breakfast. And Alec – go.'

We both obey her.

The shower makes me feel better. Back in my bedroom I look at my uniform thrown over the chair. I get as far as picking up my skirt, and then I pull my favourite jeans out of my bottom drawer. And Wilfred Owen, rescued from the bin. Maybe it will sort of bring Luke luck.

In the kitchen Mum looks at me. 'Alright,' she says. 'I know you won't do any good in school. But I don't like you hanging round the hospital all day either.'

'He hasn't got anybody else.'

'He's got Sandra and Bill.'

I take a deep breath. 'Mum,' I say. 'I don't want to go against you and Dad, but I *will* go and sit with Luke. I have to. I can't just walk away from him.'

She sniffs and pours me out a cup of tea. I pour in the milk and wrap my fingers round the mug.

'I thought you'd fallen out?'

'I never said that!'

'Esther. I'm your mother. I saw the state you came home from that party in. *And* how upset you've been all week – long before this. And now suddenly you're at his bedside. It doesn't make sense.'

'I know.' I try to swallow some cornflakes. 'But I have to, Mum. It's just – right.'

Mum sighs. 'It's too hard on you. You're only a child.' Then she looks at me and sighs. 'No, you're not, are you?' She sounds sad.

I wish I was.

At first it looks like nothing has changed. Luke lies in exactly the same position, with the same tube going up his nose and the same things plastered to his chest. The same monitor shows the same lines and bleeps, and his breathing is the same regular, slightly rasping sound. The bruises on his face, which were red yesterday, are purplish. His hair is darkened with sweat, and when I bend over him he smells funny – not dirty, just kind of – sick. But when I pull the chair over beside the bed and sit down and take his hand, it feels warmer than it did yesterday. I don't know if that's good or bad. I give it a little squeeze. I'm so scared of hurting him.

There's a get-well card on the bedside cabinet that wasn't there yesterday. I lean over and pick it up. It's from Brendan – *Whatever's gone wrong, Luke, you know there are people to help you. Hang in there* – and a phone number.

Sandra isn't here. In a way it's scarier, being alone with this silent, unconscious Luke. I stroke my fingers up his arm.

'I'm sorry I couldn't stay with you all night,' I say. At first my voice sounds loud and strange but soon I get used to it, and it feels more natural to be talking, even if he can't hear. 'Mum and Dad made me come home. They tried to make me go to school today but of course I didn't.' I rub the little veiny bit on the inside of his wrist. 'Please wake up, Luke. Just wake up and be OK.'

My voice skids to a halt. It won't be as simple as that, will it? How does a person feel after taking an overdose? Will he be relieved to be alive, or angry? What does it mean to be suicidal? He can't have taken those pills by accident. I mean, I've felt sad before. Left out and hopeless and just plain *wrong*. Especially when I left the church. And after the party. But not like this.

Sudden anger at Luke crashes through me, making me gasp. How *dare* he put us through this! I think of the horror I felt yesterday when Dad told me it wasn't just another seizure – but that he'd poisoned this strong, beautiful body with drugs. On purpose.

I learnt in history that suicide used to be a crime. Like an actual crime you could go to prison for – if you weren't dead.

But Luke's a real person, and this hand I'm holding, with its bitten nails and the little patch of rough skin he always gets on the side of his thumb, is real, and this body that he did his best to destroy is real. Words like sin and crime are just too – abstract.

He must have felt so alone.

'Luke. Please wake up. We'll sort it out. I'll help you.' If you're still speaking to me. 'And Luke' – I squeeze his hand – 'I don't know what happened with you and Jasmine, but we'll – we'll get past it.'

How?

Am I just a fool sitting here holding the hand of someone who doesn't deserve it? Is part of me – a silly romantic part – in love with the drama of the situation? I imagine it as a headline in one of those trashy magazines Mum pretends not to read. *I stood by my rapist boyfriend!*

I pull my hand away and wipe it on my jeans. There is no reaction from Luke. His hand lies on the sheet like a dead animal. I wriggle my shoulders to try to shrug off the tension in my arms.

No. Everything in me tells me it isn't true.

Because you don't want *it to be.*

Why would he have done this if he wasn't guilty?

He didn't deny it.

Why don't you go and speak to Jasmine?

I stand up and press my hands into the small of my back. I go to the window and pull back the blind a little. Outside there's a wall. A carpark. Other bits of hospital. Everything is grey. The window doesn't open and suddenly I need air. I turn round to the figure on the bed. His hand has slipped a bit on the sheet. It's open and empty. I should go back and sit down, take his hand, take up my vigil again, show him I believe in him.

But I don't know if I do.

Instead I take Brendan's card, slip it into my bag and whisper, 'I'm just going to get some air, Luke. I'll be back really soon, I promise.'

The curly-haired nurse is wheeling a trolley full of drugs down the corridor outside. She looks at me quizzically. 'Had enough?'

'Just going to the loo – maybe get some air.'

'That's right. We'll be bringing a cup of tea round soon. You can have one.'

'Thanks. How long until he – wakes up?'

She frowns. 'I can't really –'

'Please. You must see people like this all the time.' How depressing that must be.

She considers. 'It's not so much the drugs now. They're pretty well out of his system.'

'So why is he still unconscious?'

'We-ell. He's still concussed. There may or may not be brain damage. We've done a scan and it looks fairly good – but you can't always tell until the patient wakes up.'

'So he could wake up and be – not OK?'

She looks uncomfortable. 'Honestly, I can't really say. I'm sure Dr Meyers will talk to his mum later.'

I can't be bothered to correct her. I take the lift down to the ground floor and even though the big windows show that it's raining outside I rush to the front door. I'm desperate to breathe fresh wet air but first I have to push past little groups of patients smoking. One of them's hooked up to a mobile drip.

Well away from the main building I sink down on a bench and take out Brendan's card. *Hang in there.* Unfortunate wording for someone who's just attempted suicide. I take out my phone and punch in the number.

After four rings it goes to voicemail. *This is Brendan Maguire. I'm at a conference for the next three days. If you need to speak to –*

I listen to all the options. None of them is, *If you're confused about someone in care and want to talk to someone who's known them since they were fourteen just in case they can shed any light on whether said someone could possibly have done something terrible …*

I don't leave a message.

I trudge back up to Luke's ward, suddenly scared that by leaving him I've made something bad happen, but everything is the same. I set the card back on the bedside cabinet. The nurse brings me a cup of tea. It's lukewarm and greyish but I drink it. I sneak a look at my phone and there's a text from Toby saying nice supportive things that make me cry. I'm about to check what people are saying on Facebook but it's kind of a relief when the nurse, coming in to do something with the drip, frowns at me and says I need to turn my phone off.

The day drags on. I'm half-asleep, still holding Luke's hand. I jerk awake when the door opens.

'No change then?' It's Bill. He's puffing as if he's walked up all seven flights of stairs to this ward.

I shake my head. I can't trust my voice.

'I'm just calling in on my way to my work. Sandra'll be up soon. She was here all hours last night.' He looks down at Luke and tuts, not crossly, just sort of hopelessly. 'Why could he not talk to us?'

'I don't know.'

Bill crosses to the bedside cabinet and picks up Brendan's card. He nods as he puts it back, and then sits down at the opposite side of the bed to me. He pulls at the knees of his trousers as he sits, the way my dad does. He pats Luke's arm in an embarrassed sort of way, then turns to me and lowers his voice. 'Don't you be blaming yourself, love. I know yous've fell out, but you're here now. That's the main thing.'

Luke has said almost nothing about Bill, except that Sandra's the boss. I know he's a school caretaker who likes a fry up and his garden.

'I should have spent more time with him,' he says. 'I tried to – tried to get him interested in the garden and – och, but sure yous have your own interests.' He scratches the side of his face. 'I was looking forward to having a boy again,' he goes on. 'I thought maybe he'd be into football or – och, well, maybe if he'd been a bit younger. But he always kept me at arm's length.'

You and me both.

'Now, he did help out the odd time in the garden, fair play to him. We'd a tree fell and he helped me chop it up to take to the dump.' He lapses into silence.

I wonder what it's like, taking on a succession of foster kids. Taking on all their problems.

The bruises on Luke's cheek are darker purple now. Weird that your skin still does all that – goes through whatever process it is that makes bruises change colour – while you're unconscious.

I wonder what colour Jasmine's bruises are today.

I raise my hand and very lightly touch the unmarked side of his face. His skin feels clammy. His eyelashes are dark against his cheeks, and his chin is roughened by stubble. That seems weird too – bruises change colour, hair keeps growing. The stubble makes him look older.

'You're a good girl,' Bill says suddenly. 'Whatever yous fell out about – I'm sure yous can sort it out. He was dying about you.'

Another unfortunate word choice. Even though the room is hot I shiver.

Nurses bustle in and out. I go to the vending machines for a Coke. The sky outside the window darkens. My eyelids flutter, if something so heavy can flutter. I lean closer to Luke's face. With the hand that's not holding his I push the darkening hair back from his forehead, as gently as I can. I don't know where his head injury is. There aren't any marks on the outside. His hair is damp with grease. He would hate to think that he's lying here unshaven, with unwashed hair.

'Bill was here,' I say. I lay my head down on the bed cover for a second. I need Luke to wake up. I imagine feeling his hands in my hair, cradling my head, soothing me, telling me everything's going to be OK.

But it's up to me to do that. 'I know we fell out,' I whisper. 'And if you just want to be friends that's OK. Just wake up.'

A hand touches my hair and I start. But Luke hasn't stirred. I turn round.

'Sandra.'

'I didn't want to wake you, love,' she says. 'You look shattered.'

'I wasn't –'

She gives a soft laugh. 'I've been here over an hour. You never stirred.'

I rub my hands over my hot face. My head's throbbing. I've slobbered on the bed cover.

'Let me give you a lift home, Esther. You look like you've had enough.'

'I can't.'

'Bill's heading back – come on and I'll give you a lift home.'

I feel guilty but I do want to get out of this airless room.

'My mum's coming for me later. She has to work late.'

'You can get your mum to pick you up at our house. Come on, love. You need to mind yourself.' Her combination of kindness and bossiness is irresistible. I wonder if she was like that with Luke. I find myself letting her take control, and even though I hate leaving Luke behind, it's magic to get out into the damp grey dusk.

Luke

Try to surface but everything's so heavy. Limbs pull me back. Eyelids leaden. Somewhere voices hum and die.

Esther

It's no good. The temptation is too great. I hesitate on the tiny landing, outside what I've worked out must be Luke's bedroom door, but only for a second, and then I'm in. I close the door behind me and lean against it briefly. It's a small, tidy space, with pale walls and white furniture. The blue-covered duvet is pulled up neatly, the desk clear. It's even more freakishly neat than when I saw it on Skype, because I couldn't tell then that all the books were in alphabetical order.

I pretended I needed to go to the loo but Sandra's not daft. I haven't much time.

I cast my eye along the bookcase, all the spines in line. One of the books is a notebook. Feeling terrible I slide it out. It's an academic diary. Empty. I replace it with a feeling of disappointed relief.

Would you read his diary, if he has one?

No.

Maybe.

But there isn't a diary. There are school books, his beloved MacBook Air, with a thin film of dust, his iPod and phone sitting neatly on the bedside table. I switch the phone on, and it buzzes into life but it's password-protected and I won't waste precious time trying to guess the code. I open the wardrobe and I breathe in the smell of his clothes – washing powder, mint and just *Luke*. His school blazer and trousers hang neatly on hangers beside the jacket he wore to the party.

There is nothing in here to help me. It might as well be a hotel room. There are no pictures on the walls, no clutter.

There is one card on the windowsill. I pick it up. It's from Lauren's parents.

Thanks so much for everything you've done for Lauren. We're so grateful that she can have a positive role model like you to show her that living with epilepsy doesn't have to spoil her life.

I open the top drawer and find neatly-ranged grey and black underpants that make me feel uncomfortable. Like some kind of pervert.

I go to close the drawer but it sticks. I reach my hand in and it closes on something that definitely isn't underwear. Something cool and hard. I pull out a sketchbook, A3, ring-bound, the same as my AS one. The sketchbook that made me so angry when I confronted Luke at the war memorial. I sit on the bed and open it.

The first few pages are pen and ink sketches similar in style to my birthday card. But there aren't any ice-skating ponies. There are sketches of this room, and the street outside, and lots of the big old houses near the park, very accurate and accomplished; not very revealing.

I turn over. Pencil sketches of Jay, the cat, in a variety of poses, some very detailed, some a mere dash and scribble. One of the war memorial, with tiny scratches for the names, so precise that I have to squint to make sure they aren't actual words. That's what he was doing on Monday – was it only a few days ago?

There's one of Dad! I can't quite believe it, but it's Dad alright, sitting at a teacher's desk marking. It's not a caricature or anything – it's lifelike and accurate. Dad looking tired at the end of the day – the slump of his shoulders, the hugeness of the pile of books to be marked, the little frown on his forehead.

The next page – my heart skips. It's a pencil sketch again, very delicate and soft. It's me. Only not me. I look – I swallow because I can't believe it – I look beautiful. Like me only seen by someone who really fancies me. Clothes are just suggested; you can see my shape. I don't look fat; I look voluptuous. I stroke my hand over my face as Luke has drawn it. My lips are full, my top teeth resting on my bottom lip in the way I've always been self-conscious about. The hands that drew this are the hands that have held back from touching me, the hands that made me think he didn't fancy me. But this picture says something different.

If this is how he saw me, why could he never show me?

There is only one more page filled in, and when I first see it I almost jump at the contrast. The whole page is covered in swirls of psychedelic colour – mad and angry, with harsh black lines bruising the page. The paint has smudged and messed up the opposite page as well. Just looking at it makes me feel dizzy. I run my hands over the page and feel the texture. The paint is thick and rough in places and in others he has scored so heavily with the black pen that the page is nearly in holes.

If the picture of me is about love, is this hate? Or violence? It doesn't look like it's been done by the same careful skilled hand that drew everything else.

Is this the same violence that made him attack Jasmine?

'Esther! Tea's ready!'

I shiver, close the sketch book and put it carefully back under the pants. A postcard falls out from between the pages. It's of a college building, old and pretty. Dublin City College is printed across the bottom. I turn it over. It's addressed to Luke Bressan, at this address. The handwriting is precise – rather like Luke's own – and the message is very short:

I thought you might like to see where I work. All going well here. Good luck with the new school and remember to aim for the top.
Helena

All going well here. Lucky Helena. Whoever she is.
Lady Muck. Fancy new job in Dublin. I know exactly who she is.

Luke

Words whisper from different places.
  Come on, Luke.
  Come back.
  You know you want to.
  You'll like it.
  See?
  You little pervert.
  Come on. Wake up.

Esther

The doctor looks at the chart at the bottom of the bed. He nods at me, frowns, and goes out.

My arm aches with holding Luke's hand. I alternate hands but all that happens is they both start to ache. I say the same things I said yesterday. Stupid things. The clock on the wall says it's eleven o'clock but it feels later. When the door opens and Sandra comes in, relief floods me.

'I'll sit with him for a while,' she says. 'Go on, love. Away and get some fresh air.'

There's a park just over the road. Even though it's cool and drizzly I find a bench and sit there. I lean back and feel the soft damp air on my face. After the hospital smell it feels like heaven. Quarter past eleven. Break time at school. Are people gossiping? What has Jasmine said? People will believe her. They don't know Luke.

Do I?

I suppose she knows him better than anyone.

I take out my phone. Helena's college is easy to find. I go through the list of staff and find a Dr Helena Scott. I click on her photo to enlarge it. She has a perfect chestnut bob and small dark eyes and good cheekbones. There are email addresses for all the staff. I tap out a message:

Hello Dr Scott.
I know you used to be Luke Bressan's foster carer until recently.
  Luke is very ill in hospital. I'm his – I hesitate – friend, and I would really appreciate it if you could contact me urgently.

I think it would help Luke if I could talk to someone who knows him as well as you must. Esther Wilson

It doesn't say enough, but when – if – she phones the words will come then. I add my phone number. My finger shivers over the SEND icon and then touches.

———————

A gentle knock at the door of Luke's room, but nobody comes in. I stand up stiffly and open the door.

'Ruth!'

'*They* won't let me in,' she whispers. She flips her head in the direction of the nurses' station. 'But I thought you might need someone.'

'I didn't expect to see you. I wasn't very nice to you on Monday.'

'Don't be daft. I don't walk away from my friends.'

'Me neither. That's why …'

We both look at the bed.

'I have to say,' Ruth whispers. 'I wouldn't have recognised him from the photo you showed me.'

I have nothing to say to this.

'Come for a coffee?' she suggests.

'I don't like leaving –'

'Just down to the canteen. You need a break.'

I turn back to Luke. No change. No life.

'Fifteen minutes.'

The hospital canteen is big and noisy. Ruth makes me take chocolate and a slice of cake as well as coffee. I slide my phone out of my pocket and chance turning it on. There's a new email.

Dear Esther, I am very sorry that Luke is ill but I do not see what help I can be. Luke has made it very clear that he wishes to have no contact with me. I do, of course, wish him a speedy recovery. Regards, Helena Scott

I pass the phone to Ruth because I know it can't *actually* say that. I'm just too tired to make sense of anything. She lifts her eyes to me in disbelief. 'That's *horrible*. Well, *she'll* be no use.'

'But he lived with her for years. She must *know* him. She must know *something*.'

Ruth spoons sugar into the grey-looking hospital coffee. 'What *exactly* are you trying to find out?'

I take a deep breath. 'OK. You know I don't believe Luke attacked Jasmine.'

'Esther. The evidence isn't looking great. Surely the fact that he –'

'I *know* how it *looks*. But – I … I feel as if there is something I should know, something I can find out that will prove he didn't do it, and …'

Ruth looks unconvinced. 'And you think this Helena will know what it is? If there is anything?'

'I don't know. But there is literally nobody else, and I can't just do nothing.'

'You should talk to Jasmine again. If Jasmine knows what's happened –'

'She must do. You know what school gossip's like.'

'Well – if she was – exaggerating or something, surely she'd have *said*? Knowing how serious it was?'

'Ruthie. I *can't*.' Panic wells up. 'It would just be a waste of time.'

'OK.' Ruth stands up and brushes the crumbs off her school skirt. 'So let's go.'

'Back to Luke?'

She shakes her head. 'Dublin.'

My cake sticks in my throat. 'We can't!'

She jingles car keys. 'I've got Mum's car outside. If you want to, I'll take you.'

'I – yes.'

At the door of Luke's room I hold my breath as always in case there has been some change in the twenty minutes I have been away. The bruises are purplish-blue today, his lips pale and flaky, his jaw slack and unshaven. He is a million miles away from the beautiful boy I sat beside on the first of September.

'I wouldn't have recognised him,' Ruth had said.

I take out my phone and take a photo. The click makes me feel really guilty, like I'm stealing something. I bend over and kiss his forehead, my lips recoiling slightly from the hot dry skin, the stale breath. Then I turn and walk away as quickly as I can.

Luke

Something flutters at my skin. Soft. Not to be trusted. I want to open my eyes and tell it to go away but my eyelids are too heavy.

If you stay still it doesn't last too long.

Somewhere, not exactly here but very near, is pain.

Better not to move.

Esther

I frown at my phone.

'Not happy?' Ruth asks. She peers through the streaming windscreen at the oncoming traffic. 'I'm never going to get turned here.' She chews her lip, looking suddenly young and scared.

'She thinks I should come home. And *rest*. But I'll rest when it's all' – I stop myself from saying *over* – 'sorted.'

'You lied to her.'

'I didn't *exactly* lie. I said I was with you. I just didn't mention Dublin.' I slip the phone into my bag and sit back.

Ruth gives me a quick sideways glance before returning to her fretful assessment of the traffic. Obeying the sat nav's directions onto the motorway out of Belfast is so fraught that I keep being scared she'll say it's a mad idea and we have to turn back. But at last we're speeding down the M1.

'I haven't driven on the motorway before,' Ruth says, after a huge articulated lorry cuts in in front of us and makes us both flinch and the little red Polo vibrate.

'Now you tell me.'

She relaxes against the seat and flexes her shoulders. 'God will look after us.'

I'm silent.

'Have you been praying for Luke?' she asks.

'Kind of.'

We try to spot the exact point where we cross the border, where the speed signs change from miles to kilometres, and the names in Irish as well as English. I don't know how to pronounce them but I love how they look: I let them roll over me. Dún Dealgan. Baile an Ghearlánaigh. Droichead Átha.

Ruth tries to distract me with chat. Lots of *Do you remember?*

Toll – 12km shouts a sign. I look at Ruth in horror. 'What does that mean?'

'Looks like you have to put money in. Euros.'

'I don't have ... I never ...'

I imagine us being turned away at the toll; having to drive all the way back to Belfast without even seeing Helena.

'There *might* be some euros in the glove compartment.' Ruth indicates to overtake a creeping silver car. 'From when Mum and Dad went to Donegal.'

My fingers scrabble in the glove compartment. Another sign for the toll whizzes past. My fingers close on cold metal, and my heart leaps but it's a pound coin and then, thank God, a two-Euro piece.

'Is this enough?'

'Hope so. Relax, Esther – you're making me nervous.'

We get through the toll. We pass the airport. The road starts to clog up with cars and lorries on both sides of us. Ruth's hands tighten on the steering wheel and she goes quiet. My insides fizz with fear at the thought of actually meeting Helena – I want to be there, talking to her, but another part of me wants the journey to last for ever.

Cars hurtle round us; the open road becomes a suburban street, with beautiful tall old houses and different street signs from home. Now we're driving down a long tree-lined road. It's a bit like the roads round school, but the buildings are on a different scale – gracious Georgian terraces with steps up to painted front doors, street names from history books – I know if I were here for a different reason I could love this city. Luke would too. I remember all the pictures of old houses in his sketchbook. I wonder if he'll ever see these streets. Or any streets again.

'You have reached your destination,' intones the sat nav. We turn into what looks at first like a big park and then a school, a mishmash of old and new, brick and stone and glass. Then in front of us looms the building from the postcard. Ruth pulls into a parking space, turns to me and breathes out through her fringe.

'We're here,' she says and grins. She high fives me. 'I can't believe I just did that.'

'You're brilliant.'

She waves this away. 'Come on. There's the reception. Just pray they let us in.'

There's a buzzer to the right of the glass doors, and they slide open when I press it.

'Now where?' I look round the wood-panelled hall. There's an office with a frosted glass door but nobody comes out and I'm scared to knock in case someone sends us away. Not that I would go, when we've come this far, but –

'There,' Ruth says, pointing. There's a board with a list of names, and two from the bottom is DR HELENA SCOTT ROOM 119.

'How will we find it?'

'We'll look.'

We go down endless identical corridors that look a bit like the nicer parts of school, and count off the numbers on the office doors, until finally we're standing outside 119.

I look at Ruth in sudden panic. 'What if she isn't here? She's probably in a lecture or – or a meeting or something.'

'Someone's here.' She presses her ear to the door. 'I can hear computer keys tapping.' She lifts her hand and knocks firmly.

My first thought, when Dr Helena Scott calls *Come in*, and I follow Ruth into the book-lined, tidy office is, you can't imagine her as any kind of mother or carer. She's tall and thin with a perfect sharp bob and an unwrinkled linen suit. She turns round from her computer and asks, 'Are you Sarah? About the essay extension?'

'I'm Esther Wilson.'

Her high-cheekboned face reddens. The air in the office crackles with unease. I try to look confident.

'All right,' Helena says at last. 'I suppose you should sit down.' She gestures at two plastic chairs, saves her document and then turns to us. She glances at the watch on her thin wrist. 'I have to see a student in a few minutes,' she says. 'I'm sorry, I shouldn't have been so – my email – it was just – thinking about Luke again after all this time. You gave me a bit of a shock. I can't believe you just came and found me.' I can't work out if she's annoyed or impressed. 'I don't know how you think I can help,' she says. 'Luke made it clear – well, keeping in touch wasn't an option.'

She looks defeated and much older than when we first walked in. Like Dad at the end of a bad week at school.

'What has he said about me that makes you think …?'

I don't answer for a moment. I wonder if what I'm going to say will hurt her as much as it should.

'He's actually never mentioned you. But I know he lived with you for years. Sandra's known him for a few weeks. Brendan's gone to a conference and there's nobody else. Believe me, I wouldn't have left Luke and come all the way down here if I'd had any choice.' I thrust my phone at Helena. 'Look,' I say. 'I don't know what Luke looked like the last time you saw him, but that's him today. That's what he looks like after trying to *kill* himself. And *that's* why I'm here.'

She winces. She looks at the phone for a long time. A little vein pulses in her cheek. She hands me back the phone.

'What did he do?'

'He took an overdose of his epilepsy medication.'

Beside me, Ruth is very quiet but I can feel her attention focused one hundred per cent.

Helena shakes her head. 'That doesn't sound like …'

My heart skips.

Then she sighs. 'But honestly. How would I know? He changed so much when his mother died. It was like – having a stranger in the house. He was always so … self-controlled. And then – he wasn't.' She rubs her hand over her face. 'Oh God,' she says. 'It's my fault. Why should he have been any different? I expected too much.'

'Can you tell us what you mean?' Ruth asks gently.

Helena sighs. 'I didn't set out to be a foster carer,' she says. 'I always expected I'd have my own kids and then – well, it doesn't matter, but it didn't happen. I decided to try fostering. I knew I could offer a lot to a child. A good home, opportunities, books – I was doing my PhD, working from home. There was a lot in the media about children in care being left behind by the system, falling through the cracks, not achieving at school – I thought, *I* could give a child more than that. So I did all the courses and everything and they gave me a little girl. Shelby.' The way she says the name shows exactly what she thinks of it. 'She was hard work. Very needy. Always wanting to cling round me, climb on my knee –'

'Look, I'm not interested in *Shelby*. I need to know about Luke.'

'It's relevant, though. Things didn't work out with Shelby – I wasn't the right kind of person. And when she left I thought I wouldn't try again. But I didn't like feeling I'd *failed*. Anyway, they told me they had a boy who was – I can still remember the words they used – *bright and self-contained* – the opposite of Shelby. He was so easy. Worked hard at school, loved books, loved sport – wanted to do well. I was ambitious for him. I kept reminding him he could be anything, do anything; being in care wasn't going to hold him back. We were – a good team. But ...' She frowns and I can't look at Ruth because I'm sure my face must be giving away my excitement that she's on the brink of telling me something helpful at last.

'But ...' I prompt her.

'There was always trouble when he had contact time with his mother – it was always sulk sulk sulk the whole way there. I think he blamed her for a lot. She'd *asked* for him to be taken into care because she couldn't cope with his behaviour – which I never really understood. He was as good as gold for me. I don't know why Social Services insisted on the contact. It obviously wasn't a positive experience for either of them. And then when she was killed ...' She shakes her head. 'It was terrible. The husband was killed outright but she wasn't – she was on a life support machine but it was hopeless. Brendan thought I should take him to the hospital, say goodbye before they turned the machine off. I mean – she was gone already, really, but – you know' – she makes air-quotes – 'closure. He wouldn't go. He said he had nothing to say to her, and what was the point when she was unconscious anyway.'

I shiver at this, at the memory of the unconscious boy I have been trying to talk to for the last three days, and Ruth leans over and squeezes my hand.

'He was very cold about it. He just went to his room and read. It was New Year's Day. But I *did* insist on him going to the funeral.'

She picks up a paper clip from her desk and starts unbending it. 'I told him this was his last chance to say goodbye and that he might regret it if he didn't take it. We got as far as the car park and it was packed. I hadn't expected a big funeral. His mum didn't have much in the way of family, but of course it was a joint one, with the husband. Anyway, suddenly Luke just lost it. He said he wasn't going in. I put my hand on his arm to try to calm him down, and he lashed out at me. Screaming, shouting, cursing – I'd *never* seen him like that the whole time he'd been with me.' She sets the unbent paper clip back on the desk. 'He hit me. I don't know if he knew he was doing it but …'

I shudder inside.

'He jumped out of the car – made a run for it. Didn't come home until the early hours. Very much the worse for wear. It was the first time there'd been anything like that.'

'Anything like what?' Ruth asks.

I'm carefully not meeting her eye at Helena's mention of Luke hitting her.

Helena runs a hand through her shining hair. 'Luke was always quiet, didn't mix much with the boys at his school – of course it wasn't the school *I'd* have chosen – but suddenly he was going out a lot, drinking heavily, and then once he was brought home by the police, given a caution – and it wasn't just drink that time. It was some kind of pills. He seemed to change personality overnight. He wasn't the boy I'd brought up.'

'His mum had just died,' I say.

'Of *course* I took that into account.' She sweeps her hands up the side of her face as if to hold it together. 'But – well, the epilepsy started the day after the police brought him home stoned.'

'You think there was some connection?'

Helena shrugs. 'Nobody knows. Epilepsy can start for all sorts of –'

'*And* for no reason at all.' *I* don't need a lecture on epilepsy. I've read every website going.

Her tone becomes harder. 'Look, it was a *nightmare*. Trying to get him stabilised. Trying all the different drugs. The mood swings … and the seizures. It scared me.' She sounds ashamed. 'There came a point where relations had just broken down too badly. He needed something – someone – not me any more. I'd been offered this job. I thought – a new start –'

'That's not very loyal,' Ruth says, and I squeeze her hand because I wanted to say that but if I open my mouth right now I'll scream.

Helena nods. 'Don't think I didn't feel bad about it. But if it's *loyalty* you're talking about – he wasn't above taking money from my purse to go out and buy drink and drugs. I don't think Luke has any loyalty except to himself. Children in care can be very selfish. It's a survival instinct, I suppose.'

'Well, Luke's survival instinct has clearly let him down,' I say.

'Yes.' She shakes her head. 'I'm sorry. I really thought he'd be much better off with Sandra and Bill. They seemed very caring.'

'They are.'

'I wanted to stay in touch. See how he was getting on. I was so *proud* of him – despite everything, he did so well in his exams, and getting into Mansfield – it was what we'd always dreamed of for him. But he's never once been in touch. I tried but he – he just cut himself off.'

Yes, I think. *He's good at that.*

There's a knock at the door and Helena doesn't even try to hide her relief. 'My student.' She stands up.

Ruth and I stand too, since there's no help for it.

'Ah – Sarah. Come in.' She manages to usher the nervous-looking girl inside and hustle us out at the same time.

'I hope he's OK,' Helena says. 'I'm sorry I couldn't help you much. Anyway. Better ...' She nods at us and goes back into her nice safe office.

Ruth leans against the corridor wall and lets out a long breath. 'Why didn't you tell her about *Jasmine*? I thought that was the whole point – to find out if she thought he was – well, if he could be violent.' Then she answers her own question. 'But you didn't need to ask, did you?'

'She didn't say *violent*.'

'Esther. He hit her.'

'It was a funeral.'

I take a last look at the very solid door of Helena's office and notice her full title. *Dr Helena Scott. Economics.*

I feel suddenly exhausted. 'Come on, Ruthie.' I slip my hand through her arm. 'Let's go home.'

Luke

Eyelids aren't as heavy now. If I really made the effort I could push off whatever is weighing them down.

I force myself as hard as I can but someone has glued them shut, or maybe stitched them. If I force it too much I'll only break the stitches.

Why'd you want to go back there anyway? You don't think it's going to be any different, do you?

Unless you're brave enough to wake up and take your punishment.

Esther

I can hardly make out what Sandra is saying – *He's awake.*
As far as they can tell there's no permanent damage.

I throw the phone on my bed, pull on any old clothes,
and only Mum's nagging forces me to stop long enough to
choke down a piece of toast which then sits uneasily somewhere in my oesophagus as if it knows there is no room for
it in the huge bubble of happiness inside me.

So it's an anticlimax to find Luke lying just as I left him
yesterday before the trip to Dublin, the bruises yellowing
now, his eyes shut. I stand inside the door, tears fighting
up my throat.

The skinny nurse appears. 'Ah, you just missed him. He
was awake for about half an hour.'

'I thought –'

'He's been out for the count for three days. You didn't
expect him to be dancing round the ward, did you?'

I thought he'd be looking forward to seeing me. I thought
he'd make sure he stayed awake until I arrived. I can't say
any of this without sounding like a child. It feels wrong
now, to pull up the chair and sit beside him, even though
I've done it for days. Then I realise that his breathing is
totally different from the way it's been – slow and steady,
like normal sleep, and I remember, not the last three days,
but the time in my bedroom when we fell asleep together,
and I feel ashamed and go over to him and take his hand.

'Hey, Luke.' My voice is a bit teary, and I cough to clear it.
I can't think of anything to say now that he is quite likely
actually to wake up and hear it, so I just squeeze his hand.

It feels warmer than before and it squeezes mine back, very briefly.

His eyelids flicker. My breath catches.

'Luke,' I whisper. 'Wake up.' I stroke his stubbled cheek with my free hand, as if I can stroke open his eyes, but they open themselves. He runs his tongue over his cracked, pale lips. His voice is rusty.

'Esther.' That's all he says and his eyelids flicker again, then he seems to make a huge effort to open them, and fixes his eyes on me. I stroke the greasy hair back from his forehead. His eyes look darker than usual.

'What day is it?' he asks. He looks round the room, moving his head gingerly and focusing through narrowed eyes.

'Saturday. You've been unconscious for three days. Um … how do you feel?'

He swallows. 'Like – a bad hangover.'

'Yuck.'

He closes his eyes. 'Yeah.'

'Just rest,' I say. I try not to let the disappointment creep into my voice – I mean, what did I expect? He took enough pills to kill him. And everything hasn't been magically fixed.

I can't believe how you guys never talk about anything.

'Luke? Do you remember what happened – *why* you're in here?'

He opens his eyes wide and stares at me. 'Oh, yes,' he says, and turns his head away. When his voice comes again it's much stronger, though he won't look at me. 'I don't know what you're doing here, but would you mind going away? I don't want to see you again.'

Luke

They ask me questions to find out if I'm mental now. Apparently not.

'Some degree of memory loss is normal after a head injury,' says the doctor, and Sandra and Bill hang on his every word because they're the kind of people to be impressed by doctors. Helena always demanded a second opinion. He goes on about having to change my medication and how I can expect headaches and tiredness for a while.

They talk about me as if I'm subnormal. Sandra keeps trying to take my hand.

The doctor wiggles his hands in the pocket of his jacket. 'So. Physically you are ready to go home; you probably just feel like you're sleeping off a heavy night?' He gives me a laddish grin that I don't return. 'But mentally –'

'I thought you just found out I *wasn't* mental? I thought that was what all those questions were for?'

And *home*? Who'd blame Sandra and Bill if they said, *Sorry, this isn't what we signed up for*? I don't make eye contact with anyone. If they've changed their minds they won't tell me directly. It'll come through Brendan. I know how the system works.

'Look, Luke.' The doctor grimaces, maybe because that sounds weird. 'The reason you are in here is that you took a huge overdose. Which caused a massive seizure. You're lucky you're still with us. We need to deal with what made you feel like that.'

'Hmm,' I say, since I'm obviously expected to say something.

'Well – what will happen is you'll be assessed by a psychiatrist and they'll recommend what happens now.' He sounds businesslike, saying *psychiatrist* as naturally as you'd say *dentist*. 'For now, just try to – well, rest.' The laddish grin is gone.

Rest. As if you can do that when every time you close your eyes you get the same litany. All this time I've been out of it, he's been gathering strength.

Didn't even manage to do away with yourself properly, Lukey boy.

No, and I haven't managed to do away with him either.

You don't deserve to live.

I know.

Esther

Dad finds me crying on a bench outside the hospital.

'Oh, love.' He wraps me up in a hug. I can't remember the last time Dad hugged me or called me *love*.

I hang on to him and sob and sob. He feels so different from Mum. Solid and male. That makes me cry harder. I snivel and wail. 'He doesn't want me. He told me to go away.'

'Esther.' His voice is firm and he holds me away from him and gives my shoulders a shake. 'Look at me. You didn't honestly think that everything would be fine now?'

I look down at the blistered paint of the bench, notice how my hands are clasping it tight, notice that my fingernails are as bitten and raw as Luke's. 'N-no,' I whisper, but it's a lie. Once I'd heard he was awake everything else disappeared. In a film, his waking up would be the ending. We'd kiss – maybe there'd be tears, but romantic attractive ones, not snot and gulps like the way I'm crying now, and Luke would say what a terrible mistake he had made and how my love had shown him that life was worth living. And Jasmine would come in and say it had all been a mistake.

Luckily I'm not so far gone as to say all that to Dad.

'Esther, Luke tried to take his own life,' Dad says. 'He's going to need help to get back on track.'

'*I* would help him!' It's not like I hadn't taken on board how serious it was. I just didn't think he'd wake up and still be falling.

'Professional help.' His voice is very calm and non-judgemental and for the first time I see why they made him head of pastoral care.

He takes off his glasses and presses the bridge of his nose. He looks tired – he looks like Luke's picture of him.

'Esther – I feel bad about what happened too,' he says. 'Luke was clearly in a bad way about something and –'

'You don't even like him,' I remind him.

'He was partly in my care. I – maybe I could have read the signals a bit better.' He looks at me as if he's making up his mind to tell me something, but he doesn't say any more.

'Well.' I sit up straight and force my shoulders back. 'He doesn't want to see me, so I – there's nothing more I can do.'

'No,' Dad agrees, 'but he won't keep on feeling like this. Give him time.'

I give a huge sniff. 'I thought you'd be glad he didn't want to see me.'

'Part of me is,' he admits. 'You're my only child.' He strokes my hair off my forehead. 'And yes, I wish I could wrap you in a blanket and keep you home and not let anybody ever hurt you. Because that's how you feel about your child. But you're growing up so fast and –'

'I don't think anyone's ever felt like that about Luke,' I whisper. 'His mum gave him up to social services, and that Helena – I think she tried but she wasn't very – well, *caring*.'

'And you are. Maybe too caring.'

'Not anymore.' Exhaustion swamps me. I can't do this any more. And he doesn't even *want* me.

We stand up and walk away from the hospital for the last time.

Esther

I walk into tutor group with my head high. If anyone looks closely they'll see I'm wearing makeup to cover my sleepless face, and that my eyes are red. But the good thing about being me is that nobody ever does look closely. Nobody ever did. Until –

Stop it.

'Esther!' Toby makes room for me to sit beside him. 'Is – is everything OK now?'

'Kind of.' I start asking about homeworks and notes – anything to keep him talking about safe things.

Cassie whispers to Jasmine but I tune them out. Just like I don't let my eyes see that Jasmine's wrist, when she reaches across my desk to hand a magazine to Zara across the aisle, is sporting a bracelet of fading yellow bruises. Baxter looks embarrassed to see me – kind of, *Oh no, now I'm going to have to deal with this; why couldn't she just have stayed off* – but he dutifully keeps me back – even though we'd both much rather he didn't – and asks how Luke is.

'He'll be OK,' I say. This is the answer I have decided on.

'And you? Are you – um – OK?'

'Yes,' I say firmly, 'thank you.'

Toby has waited for me outside. I've never been so grateful for him, and I chatter inanely about anything to keep him off the subject of Luke. Despite my tuning-out efforts, I pick up before breaktime that people *aren't* gossiping about Luke – it's probably so much less exciting now he's not going to die. There's a party at the rugby club at Halloween and that's what people are obsessing about.

All the same, I do catch a few interested glances, and when I walk into art the twins stop talking suddenly and become very intent on their easels. Mihai, who normally just does his own thing, nods at me in a kind way.

'Good to see you back, Esther,' says Beauman. 'We're doing portraits this week.' She explains the logistics of who is drawing whom, and all the time all I can think of is Luke's picture of me.

No. I *have* to stop thinking about him. He's not thinking about me. He made it clear he doesn't want me.

Luke made it clear – keeping in touch wasn't an option.

Maybe you're too caring.

Never again.

I'm drawing Zoë and she's drawing Zara and Zara is drawing me. They witter about how funny it will be if my picture of Zoë looks the same as Zoë's picture of Zara. I'm tempted to say that since I can draw and Zoë is only really happy with sequins and crayons, I very much hope it won't, but I can't be bothered. At least having something to focus on closely helps, though all the time part of my mind is checking perspective and shading, and getting the right shine on Zoë's gold earrings, another part is betraying me by wondering *when* Luke did that picture of me, and if he ever planned to show me. And how he felt about me when he painted it, and how that had all gone wrong.

I can't bear to go to the sixth-form centre at lunchtime, and Toby always goes to chess club on Mondays so I can't rely on him for refuge. I'd like to escape from school and hide out in Jus, but I walked out of the house without my purse, so I head for the library. I've missed three days of school and I can spend lunchtime catching up a bit. At least there's only this week to get through before half term.

I don't let my mind formulate the thought that sooner or later Luke's going to be back at school, and I have to be weaned off him by then.

Somehow.

I push open the door of the library and am met with the noisy fug of excited juniors. Wee Lauren, surrounded by her friends, waves out at me, all smiles. I back out, cursing. Monday's junior book club, once the highlight of my week. How could I have forgotten?

I hesitate at the door of Dad's office. I've never hidden out there in school – I've gone out of my way to avoid him – but I'm *nearly* desperate enough to knock. But just as I raise my hand I catch voices from behind the door. He's either in a meeting or pastorally caring for someone. I let my hand fall.

Not the war memorial – but then I square my shoulders. It was *my* place for years before it was *our* place. Maybe going there, reclaiming it, will help.

I trudge through the grounds. Junior boys kick a tennis ball in a game of about thirty-a-side. Girls swing their legs on walls and clutch each other.

The war memorial is the same as ever. It's stood for nearly a hundred years and it doesn't care about me and Luke. It doesn't even care about the eighty-three names engraved on it. For the first time in ages I read down the names, trying to imagine what the boys were like. Old-fashioned names – Piers, Frank, Cyril. No Luke. Stop it! Alec. Same as Dad.

'Esther? *There* you are.'

I look up. Toby. 'Why aren't you at chess club?'

'Doesn't matter.' He looks round. 'Haven't been here for years.' He sits down beside me. He's so soft and pink and safe compared to Luke, and for a moment I lay my head on his shoulder.

'Esther,' he says, 'why won't you talk about Luke?'

'What's the point?'

He opens his eyes wide. 'The *point* is there's something weird going on.'

'Yeah, I kind of got that.'

'No. Listen. What really happened?'

I sigh. But it's Toby – he's my friend; he's looking at me in concern, just like Ruth, except unlike Ruth he knows Luke too. 'OK. I don't know if this is common knowledge, but it wasn't just a seizure.' I lower my voice even though there's nobody around. 'He took an overdose.' I know Toby won't gossip.

Toby sucks in a breath. 'Ouch. Some people *were* saying that. But then Cassie was bleating to anyone who'd listen that it was definitely not true. And I wasn't sure because – you know – *Cassie.*'

'That's weird.' I frown. 'Not like her *not* to want the most dramatic story possible.'

'Maybe she only likes the drama to be about her.' Toby looks thoughtful. 'But *Luke…*? I mean – he has *everything* going for him.' He blushes and looks down at his hands.

Oh Tobes, I think. Not you too. 'I don't *know*. We broke up.' Which is far too simple to describe what actually happened. 'But I suppose it must be something to do with what happened with Jasmine.'

'What?' He looks totally bemused.

I stare at him in disbelief. 'Toby – even *you* must have picked up on what people were obsessing about at the start of last week. Jasmine's birthday party?'

He looks blank. 'I know it was quite decadent,' he says wistfully. 'And Strong Drink Taken, and some say Illegal Substances. And two of the first fifteen had a fight over that girl – the one with the eyebrows.' He shudders. 'But I didn't hear anything about Luke.'

'Well' – might as well say it – 'Luke and I fell out and I left and after I'd gone he and Jasmine …' The words stick in my throat. 'Only *she* says – well, actually Cassie says, I haven't spoken to Jasmine – that he – well, forced himself on her. And he's not denying it.'

The words spew out now – everything that's happened since the party – and it's horrible, but a relief too. Mum and Dad have been surprisingly amazing, but I can't tell them *this*; and Ruth has been fabulous, but there's nothing more she can do.

'And you think it's true? That he actually – *attacked* her?' Toby's eyes are round with disbelief.

For a long time I don't respond. Then I give a slow nod and feel the tears gather at the back of my eyes. 'I didn't want to believe it. But I've seen the bruises.'

'You *have* to talk to Jasmine.' Toby sounds surer of himself than I've ever heard him.

'What's the point?'

'Uh – the *truth*? Because I don't believe it.'

I give a hard little laugh that scratches my throat. 'You mean you don't *want* to. I *know*. I've spent days refusing to believe it – trying to prove that Luke wouldn't be violent. But that's *not* what I've found out. I told you what Helena said.'

'That was *totally* different.'

He sounds so fierce. I don't know if it's friendship for me or a crush on Luke – and how could I not have noticed that? Have I really been so blind to everything but my own feelings? – but he's saying the things I said to Ruth days ago. Before I gave up.

'Look,' I say, 'he didn't deny it. And I can't talk to him because he basically told me to walk away and leave him alone. And I – I do have *some* pride.' I scrub at my eyes with a disintegrating tissue I've unearthed from my blazer pocket.

'So you're too scared to talk to Jasmine? You'd rather take Cassie Morris's word? Cassie who hates you?'

'She doesn't *hate* me. Maybe she's a bit –'

'Oh, come on. She's never forgiven you for telling on her when she bullied you. And she's jealous of anyone Jasmine even speaks to. Look at how mean she is to the twins.'

'Well, I suppose –'

'Shut up.'

'Toby!'

'Sorry.' He pats my knee absentmindedly. 'I mean – I'm thinking. *Jasmine* never actually said it?'

'I saw her *bruises*.'

'And people *haven't* been talking about it.' He sounds thoughtful. 'Even I wouldn't miss *that* kind of talk.'

'Maybe Jasmine's embarrassed.'

'Why? *If* she was just an innocent victim?'

'Toby – I know what you're trying to do, and it's really sweet of you, but I've been through all this with Ruth. Jasmine was probably off her head – but *that* doesn't excuse –'

'But it might explain *her* taking Cassie's word just a *bit* too seriously.'

I try to think back to that horrible conversation with Cassie. I go over it with Toby even though I hate remembering it. *He forced himself on her. She was in a terrible state. Lucky I was there to look after her.*

'Well, *I've* seen Jasmine in a terrible state,' I say. 'And she was lucky that time that *I* was there. Cassie was useless. But even if she was drunk it wouldn't explain the bruises and it *certainly* wouldn't excuse anyone taking advantage of her.'

'You *have* to talk to her.' I've never heard Toby sound so sure of anything. 'You go all the way to Dublin to talk to some scary-sounding stranger, and you won't talk to the one person who might actually be able to help.'

'But –'

'Look at the facts: Jasmine has *not* been gossiping. In fact now I come to think of it she's been pretty subdued this last week –'

'Maybe because it's not very nice to be attacked!'

'And *Cassie* – Drama Queen herself – has been going round insisting that *no way* did Luke try to kill himself. Which doesn't add up unless –'

'Unless she couldn't bear the guilt if it were true?'

A tiny flare of hope flickers in my heart. And is immediately doused. Because the bottom line is – if that's why Luke did it, then *he* thinks it's true. And surely he'd know?

I blurt this out to Toby.

'OK,' he admits. 'That's an added complication. But we *must* tackle Jasmine. What could be worse than what you're thinking now?'

She's easy to find – she's in the squashy sofas at the back of the coffee bar where only the cool people sit. One of the twins is painting silver stars on the other's nails. Jasmine and Cassie are blowing on their own starry nails to dry them. All four look up when they see us.

'Do you want silver stars?' Zoë-or-Zara asks. 'Or I can do hearts.'

'No, thanks.'

'Toby?' She raises her eyebrows suggestively and Cassie sniggers.

'I'm gay,' he says clearly. 'I'm not a *girl*.'

Eight perfectly made-up eyes widen in amazement, and there's one of those moments when the whole room seems to go silent and listen. I try not to gasp, but I find Toby's hand and squeeze it. As far as I know this is the first time he has ever said the word *gay* out loud in public. When he squeezes my hand back I know why he did it – because if he can be brave, then I have to be too. And I don't care that Sassy Girl hasn't been near me for ages – because I've grown out of her now. I can do this on my own.

'Jasmine,' I say. 'I have to talk to you. About your party.'

She looks wary. Cassie puts a hand on her arm. 'Jas. You don't have to –'

'In private,' I say.

The twins look at each other. 'Come on, Zo. We can finish this in the loos.' They gather up their stuff and go. Cassie digs her skinny bum deeper into the sofa and looks at me challengingly. Toby gives my hand a last squeeze, then backs off, fiddling with his phone to show – or pretend – he isn't earwigging.

'Is Luke going to be OK?' Jasmine asks unexpectedly. Her face, now I'm looking at it closely, is pasty, her eyes baggy behind the mascara.

'Yes. I think he's getting home today.'

'Good.'

Cassie is watching both of us carefully. 'I told you he'd be fine, Jas,' she says brightly. 'I mean – it *was* only his epilepsy, wasn't it?' Her voice rises to a little squeak.

'Not exactly.'

'Your dad said he had a seizure and a fall.'

'*After* taking an overdose,' I say.

Jasmine's hand flies to her mouth and for a moment I think she's going to be sick. 'But not – on purpose?' she chokes out.

'Oh, yes.'

'*Why?*' she whispers.

Cassie darts little glances at me and then at Jasmine. She rubs her tongue over her lips and pulls at Jasmine's arm. 'Come on Jas. This has nothing to do with you.'

'Is that true, Jasmine?' I ask. 'Or has it something to do with your party? With *you and him* at your party?'

Jasmine twists a long strand of blond hair round her thumb. 'I haven't – I haven't said anything about him at my party.'

'Cassie has. She accused him of something.'

'I did not!'

'You did to *me*,' I remind her. 'You *said* Luke forced himself onto Jasmine. You *said* she only just got away.'

'Well, that's true! I was there. I had to pick up the pieces.' She thrusts a protective arm round Jasmine.

'Jasmine was there too,' I say. 'But maybe *she* doesn't remember very well? Because she was a bit – drunk? Like on results night, maybe?' My heart is banging but my voice is very cool.

Jasmine looks away. She doesn't say anything for ages but her throat moves as if she's trying to find words. Or maybe she's going to cry. She doesn't cry. She heaves a long in-breath and says, 'I have *bruises*, Esther. Do you want to see?' She holds out the undersides of her arms which have bracelets of fading yellow. 'I mean, that's *proof*, isn't it?' she asks.

'Proof of what? That he tried to rape you?' The word stabs the air and Jasmine winces.

'I *never* said … Jasmine rubs her arms. 'Look, Esther – I was drunk. He was drunk. Things got a bit – out of hand.'

'What kind of *things?*'

The bell rings but we all ignore it.

She opens her mouth and words tumble out, all mixed in with sobs. 'I ... I'm sorry! I never thought ...' She hugs herself, and fights for control. 'OK,' she says after some pretty disgusting sniffing. 'I was pretty out of it. I took some pills. I don't usually – but it was my birthday and I wanted it to be amazing.' She looks up, her eyes starry and smudged with tears. 'I wanted Luke. I admit that. I'd fancied him for ages.' She looks me up and down. 'And, no offence, Esther, but I never thought *you* were a keeper.'

'Thanks.'

'When you stormed off – oh, I saw you go   I thought it was my chance. *He* was drunk too.' She sounds suddenly haughty.

'So what? You got off with him? You had sex with him? *What?*'

'I ...' She looks at Cassie, her mouth trembling.

'Don't ask *her!*' I shout. 'And don't say you can't remember because it sounds to me like you remember pretty well.'

For a long time she doesn't speak, but her mouth works as if it's trying to decide what to say. 'No,' she says finally. 'I – I – he wouldn't play.'

'Wouldn't *play?*'

She sounds sulky now. 'I tried it on. OK? It was my birthday and – well, I'm not used to people saying no. I thought – we could hook up. Nothing serious – but he – he just pushed me away. Like – *hard*. That's how I got the bruises. *And* I whacked my head off a tree. Lucky for him I wasn't knocked out. All I did was try to kiss him.'

She caresses the bruises on her wrists. The scene she has just described is ugly and sordid and – yes, violent – but it's a million times better than the scene that's been haunting me for a week.

'And lucky for *you* he didn't – oh, it doesn't matter.' All of a sudden I'm sick of her, and her creepy friend. 'Just – tell me straight – did Luke try to make you do anything you didn't want?'

She sighs. 'No.'

'Right.'

I turn round. Toby is still standing behind us – I'd forgotten about him. 'Come on, Tobes,' I say. Now that I've done my brave bit, my voice is thick and I know I'm about to burst into tears. 'We're late for class.'

'Never mind class.' He half-runs to catch up with me, grabbing my arm. 'You were brilliant. *And* you got the truth. I knew he wouldn't –'

'I know.' I don't think the relief has hit me yet. 'But Toby – it doesn't change what Luke did. What he *thinks* happened. I don't think I can get Jasmine to confess that all again in front of him. Even if he was speaking to me, which he isn't.'

'No need,' Toby says.

'What do you mean?'

He waves his phone at me. 'What did you think I was doing? Updating my Facebook status? Texting my mum?'

'I don't –'

'I've got it all,' he says. 'On video. If you want proof for Luke, you've got it.'

Luke

'If you could make a *bit* of an effort, Luke?' I've pushed Brendan through his entire repertoire of tones of voice, and now I've finally driven him to pissed-off.

I sigh. 'I told you, I don't know. It's not – *one thing*.'

Yes, it is one thing, Lukey – it's you.

'Maybe have a go at telling me some of the things?'

'Brendan – you're not my *counsellor*.'

Though someone else is going to be. Twice a week. One of the conditions of getting out of here today. Christ knows what we'll talk about.

'No,' he agrees. 'But harsh as this might sound I *am* the only person in your life right now who has known you for more than two months. And it's my job to care about you.'

'Your *job*.'

'That came out wrong – I mean, I care about you. For God's sake, Luke – why do you think I'm here?'

'You probably have to fill in an incident form.'

I look up at the ceiling. There's a tiny grey stain that I think is getting bigger. I've been keeping tabs on it. It's the shape of a dick.

Pervert.

Brendan gets up to leave. 'Luke – I'll see you in a day or so. You'll be home this afternoon anyway.'

'Home?' I try to keep the anxiety out of my voice. I haven't asked.

'Sandra and Bill's.' He sounds surprised. 'You didn't think – oh Luke! They've coped with this kind of thing before.'

This kind of thing. Sorry to be such a standard-issue-foster kid. See, Helena? You were wrong. Always telling me I wasn't like other kids in care. I was special. I was better. I was going to be a success. What would you think if you could see me now?

'So they aren't chucking me out?' To my annoyance my voice falters slightly.

Brendan sits down again. He tries to put his hand on my arm but I flinch away. He sighs. 'Of course not. That's the last thing they'd do. Luke – you've had far too much to deal with in the last year. Your mum. Your epilepsy. Leaving Helena. But none of it was your fault. You need to let people help you. You need to let people *in*.'

I don't reply.

'Look – I'll call in and see you in a day or so.'

'Can't wait.'

He leaves.

I study the ceiling.

Esther

Sandra answers the door. She looks older and greyer. And not that surprised to see me, which presumably means she isn't up to speed with the whole Luke-wanting-me-to-stay-away situation.

'He's not very sociable,' she warns me.

'I've got something that might cheer him up.'

She smiles sadly. 'A miracle? Go on up. I'll put the kettle on.'

I wonder if I'll get to stay long enough for that.

I knock on the bedroom door, remembering the spying I did last week.

'Luke?'

There's silence from behind the door. I call again, louder. If he's asleep I don't want to wake him, but on the other hand – what I'm holding in my hand is going to make all the difference to him.

'Luke? I've got something for you.' I can hear Sandra bustling round the kitchen, so presumably she can hear me too, which stops me saying exactly what I've got, because I don't know how much Sandra knows.

Silence. I stare at the USB in my hand. Transferring Toby's video only took a few minutes. It looks so tiny. I can't risk leaving it on the floor outside the door.

'OK,' I say, just in case he isn't asleep but just ignoring me. 'I'm going to leave it with Sandra. It's something you'll want to see. Honestly.' I feel really stupid standing here talking to a closed door. At least when I talked to him in the hospital we were in the same room, even if he was unconscious. 'OK, I'm going now. I hope – I hope you're OK. And please – watch the video, Luke.'

My voice cracks a bit on his name and I rush back down the stairs, noticing for the first time how steep they are, and that there are dark stains on the carpet and wallpaper. You can tell that someone's tried to clean them, but it's obvious what they are. The stairs end in a tiny hall. No wonder he hit his head. Probably on the front door.

I find Sandra in the kitchen. She turns round in surprise. 'That didn't take long.'

'There's no answer.'

'I don't think he's asleep. He was down having his tea twenty minutes ago. Not that he's eating much.' She shakes her head. 'Will I go up and give him a shout? Did he know it was you?'

I put my hand on her arm.

'Look,' I say, 'I don't think he wants to see me. I mean – ever.' I frown to stop my stupid voice shaking again. 'But will you give him this?' I hand out the USB. She takes it, her eyes quizzical.

I take a deep breath. 'I don't know for sure,' I say, 'but I *think* – Luke might have been so upset because of some-thing he – thought – he was being accused of. But there's evidence on this that he *didn't* do it. Please – will you just give it to him? As soon as you can?'

'Of course I will. God, anything's worth trying. But you'll stay and get a wee cup of tea?'

I shake my head. 'Thanks. But no. I just want him to see the video.'

She sees me out, holding the USB carefully in her hand. Walking down the street to the bus stop I don't let myself turn back to look up at his bedroom window.

Luke

It's only a few minutes before the door knocks again. Jay, who's taken up residence on my bed, looks up and meows. I bite my lip. I can't stand this. Why won't Esther take the hint? She's better off without me anyway. She doesn't know how much better.

But the temptation to open the door –

Yes, Lukey. Let her in and then she can be your next victim.

I roll over and hide my head in my pillow, as if that was ever enough to block him out.

'Luke?' It's Sandra, not Esther. Relief and disappointment slug it out in my mind. Her voice is followed by her head round the door, even though I didn't say come in. I suppose I've forfeited the right to any privacy.

'Esther left you this.' She hands out a tiny yellow USB. 'She says it's a video and you'll want to see it. She says it'll make you feel better.'

'I don't want it.' It's probably Esther talking to me, asking me to let us start again, reminding me how good it was –

And oh God, it *was* good.

Too good for you, Lukey.

I shake my head. 'I don't want it.'

'I don't know what's going on with you *or* with that wee girl. But you either take this and watch it *now* or I'm going to put it on and watch it myself. It's up to you.'

'You can't do that. That's a breach of –'

'Well, get down off your bloody high horse and watch it yourself then.'

I don't say anything. But I hold my hand out for the USB.

I don't get it. I watch it a second time, a third.

Esther like an avenging angel – strong and beautiful and fiercer than I ever thought she could be. And Jasmine.

So he didn't force himself on you?

No.

No.

It's in the sixth-form centre coffee bar. Who took it? Could it be a hoax? No – of course not. It's Esther. Esther in the video and Esther who wanted to make sure I had it.

I didn't do it.

It doesn't matter that I don't remember properly. I still didn't do it.

You didn't do it *this* time, Lukey. Doesn't mean you're off the hook. Doesn't mean you deserve to live.

Shut up. Go away. I didn't do it.

I DIDN'T DO IT.

I haven't realised I've said this out loud.

I haven't realised I must have shouted it. Jay jumps off the bed with a yowl.

'Luke?'

It's the first time Sandra hasn't knocked. She stands in the doorway, her hands full of cutlery and drying cloth. 'What's going on?'

'I didn't do it,' I whisper.

I realise that she hasn't a clue what I'm talking about. I also realise there are tears on my face.

She sets the cutlery, wrapped in the cloth, down on the desk beside the laptop. She sits down on the bed beside me and it creaks under her weight. I know she wants to hug me, but I can't let that happen. I might never stop. I blink the tears out of my eyes.

'I'm fine,' I say.

'It was meant to cheer you up.'

'It did. It's just – complicated.'

'Can you *try* and explain?'

I look down at my hands. The right one is still bandaged. Apparently I was holding a glass when I fell. I know Sandra deserves something, but I don't know where to start. I shake my head.

'Luke, you can't keep on like this. Are you going to talk to your counsellor?'

I shrug.

'What about Esther?'

I shrug again.

'Luke – you do know that wee girl hardly left your side, don't you? I know yous were fell out – no, I don't know why, and I don't care – but she was up at that hospital night, noon and morning.'

I shiver. 'I didn't know.' Esther's face when I told her to go away.

'If you won't talk to me, will you at least go and talk to her? For *her* sake. It's not all about you, you know. At the very least you can thank her for being there for you. If you want to go now, I'll take you. Before *Coronation Street*, if you don't mind.'

She gives me a bit of a pat on the shoulder, picks up the bundle of cutlery, and leaves.

I can't help shivering as Sandra turns into Esther's street. Not sure if it's bad memories, nerves, or just that I've been cold ever since leaving the overheated hermetic world of the hospital this afternoon.

'It's just at the bottom of the hill, on the right,' I tell Sandra.

An ambulance is parked at the corner house, across from Esther's. I see Sandra look at it and for the first time I think about what this has all been like for her. Finding me. Waiting for the ambulance. Sticking with me now.

She brings the car to a quiet stop at the end of the Wilsons' driveway. 'OK? Just call me when you want picked up.'

I nod. 'Sandra –'

'What, love?'

'Thanks. For – you know. Everything. I'm glad – I like living with you. And I'm sorry …'

'Och, son.' She pats my hand and I make myself not snatch it away. 'I know what you mean. Now, get on and see that wee girl before I miss the start of *Corrie*.'

I note with relief that Big Willy's car isn't in the drive. Maybe they're all out. But lights shine from behind the living-room curtains and as I reach the front door I hear the theme from *The One Show*.

Esther answers the door. She's in her school uniform and furry slippers and her eyes are smudgy and tired.

'Oh,' she says, 'I thought you didn't want –'

'I came to say – I don't know. Thanks. For the video and – being with me at the hospital and – everything.'

'OK.' She nods. 'You're welcome.'

'And – sorry?' I suggest. 'I mean – *I'm* sorry.'

She pulls the door aside. 'Come in.'

The warmth of the house reaches out to me. A candle burns on the telephone table. It smells like Christmas.

'Come into the living room,' Esther says. 'Mum's out with Ruth's mum, and Dad's at one of his church meetings.'

Their living room is tidy and warm with books in two bookcases on either side of the gas fire. There are family photos on the wall. Big Willy on his graduation day with hair – dark, shiny hair like Esther's. A gap-toothed Esther beams over the handlebars of a pink bike. The real Esther sits on an armchair and picks up a cushion to hug.

I sit on the sofa opposite her.

'Um. So how are –'

'Who made the vid–'

Esther gives a tiny awkward laugh. 'Toby. I didn't know he was even doing it. I just wanted Jasmine to tell the truth. He was the one thought of getting proper evidence.'

'So you and Toby – were you – like – *talking* about me?'

She flips up her chin. 'What do you *think*, Luke? You do something – *dramatic* like that, you can *expect* people to talk.' Her voice softens. 'But – no. People aren't gossiping about you. Not in a bad way. And they were *never* talking about the party. At least not about you and Jasmine. Which is what made me and Toby kind of suspicious.'

'I wasn't trying to be – *dramatic*. It wasn't like that.'

She looks down at the cushion she's hugging. Then looks up. Her face is screwed up with intensity. 'So what *was* it like? Did you actually want to *die*?'

Not even for Esther do I want to remember this. But I know I have to try. 'Nothing was any good. *I* wasn't any good. I felt like – I was falling. And I didn't know how to land. And then – I don't know. I just let go.'

'Because of what happened at the party?'

I nod, willing the pressure at the back of my eyes to go away.

'But you heard what Jasmine said: *she* was the one who came on to you.'

'I still hurt her, though. She had bruises.'

'I know. You pushed her away. But what did you – what did you *think* had happened?'

'What – what you said. What Cassie said.' I can only whisper.

'That you'd tried to *rape* her?'

Nausea twists in me. Not even *he* has said that word.

'I … I couldn't remember. I was drunk, and –'

Her voice seems to come from far away. '*I* was drunk on my birthday. I don't remember everything that happened when – well, when Mum and Dad came home.' She shudders. 'But if someone told me I'd – I dunno – snogged a rabbit or something, I wouldn't believe them because deep down I would know I couldn't *do* that.'

'Because you're *normal*!' The words fly out before I've even thought them. Maybe it wasn't even me. Maybe it was *his* voice.

'*What?*'

I shake my head. 'I don't know. I can't – don't ask me.' Panic, fear, and the sudden desire just to *tell* her fight with the cold horror inside me.

'Luke. You're shaking.' She sets down her cushion, gets up and sits beside me on the sofa. She takes both my hands. Hers are warm. She smells the same as she's always done.

I trust her so much.

I trust you, Lukey. You won't give away our secret, will you?

'What do you mean?' Esther whispers. 'Why would you even think you *could* hurt someone like that?'

I shake my head harder and harder until something in my neck cracks. 'Don't. You don't *want* to know.'

She rubs her hands up my arms, makes me look into her steady warm brown eyes. 'Did something happen – I don't mean Jasmine – I mean – some other girl? That made you think maybe –'

'No! I've *never* hurt anyone like that. I promise I haven't. You're the only girl I've ever ...' My voice comes out high and childish.

Esther's eyes widen. 'Did someone' – she hesitates – 'hurt *you?*'

I look down at my knees. There's a loose thread on the seam of the left leg of my jeans. I feel my breath shallow and quick in my throat.

It won't be the first time I've told. But the other time –

She didn't believe you because it was your own fault. *You* made it happen. You *liked* it.

Esther's hands cup my elbows. It's like she's holding me together. All I have to do is open my mouth and say the words.

But if I do, everything will fall apart.

Don't you dare!

Shut up. You're dead.

You need to let people in.

I can't fall apart.

A clock on the wall strikes eight. When I finally say something it's so quiet and scrambled that Esther looks at me quizzically.

'Luke?'

I try again. 'I'd sort of – not forgotten – not really but – you know ...'

She nods. 'Take your time,' she says.

She sounds older. Calm. The way she was on the first day of term.

'My mum's boyfriend. Stephen ...' My voice chokes to a standstill on the name.

If she's shocked she doesn't show it.

'He wasn't like some gross pervert. Like Jimmy Savile or someone. I mean he was just normal. Nice even. When we went to Tesco he used to make Mum get me the mini-boxes of cereal – you know the selections? She'd never get them because she said they were a waste of money, there was always one I wouldn't eat, and he said whatever one I didn't like he would eat. God, it sounds so stupid.'

I pull at the loose thread in my jeans, wind it tight around my middle left finger until the top of my finger starts to throb.

'What age were you?'

'Ten. He moved in. I was glad – he made Mum happy; she was crap on her own. She kept saying how lucky we were. He took me to football, bought me stuff – it was like having a dad. I'd never – she'd had other blokes but they never really bothered with me.'

'You trusted him?'

'I suppose. And then – he started coming into my room. He used to run Mum a bath – and she'd go in and close the door, and she'd have the radio on – and he'd come in.'

I didn't know I remembered all those details, but just saying it out loud – orange bubble bath smell stings my nostrils, sickens my stomach. I swallow. 'At first he just talked to me and I – liked it. The attention. But then he asked me to – well, touch him. You know.'

'Yes.'

'I didn't like it but I – I didn't *hate* it. I sort of blanked it out. He gave me stuff. Trainers. Money. A *phone*. I know I shouldn't have taken them.'

'You were a *child*.'

You let it happen. You asked for it.

But the more I speak out loud, the weaker Stephen's voice in my head gets.

'But then it got – more.'

'What kind of more?'

I look down at her hands on my arms. The first time I was ever aware of Esther her hand was on my arm. 'At first he was only getting me to feel him up – wank him.' I squeeze my eyes shut so I don't have to look at her. 'But then ...'

'Did he start to touch *you*?'

'He said I would like it, he said I wasn't a kid any more and I might as well learn what it was all about.'

'You *were* a kid.' Her voice, which has been so calm and reassuring, is suddenly fierce.

'I was old enough to – you know – respond. I mean – physically.' I swallow down a sudden hot sickness in the back of my throat.

Yes, you were, you dirty little boy. The voice strengthens again.

Esther makes a little movement. I wait for her to flinch away. **Because you're disgusting.**

But she lifts her hands and her fingertips blot the tears I hadn't realised were on my face. 'It wasn't your fault,' she says. 'It doesn't matter how your body responded. That's just – mechanical. Or something. You were a *child* and he was an *adult* and if I had him here I would – I would ...' Her dark eyes flash with indignation. 'I'd kill him.'

'You can't; he's already dead.' I start to laugh, but it's the kind of laugh that explodes into hacking sobs. I fall against Esther. I shatter into pieces, and every piece is jagged and every piece hurts. 'I'm sorry,' I splutter into her chest.

And Esther just holds all the pieces together. She whispers into my hair that it's going to be OK. She hugs me so hard it nearly hurts but it's the kind of hurting that feels really good.

We sit like this for a long time.

Distantly I hear the clock strike again. Quarter past. I pull away, sit up and try to rub my face with my sleeve. I'm hot and sticky and my head's pounding. I can't remember the last time I cried. Or talked that much. Certainly not about –

Stephen. I make myself think his name.

I told her. She believed me. She's still here.

I fell apart but I'm OK.

'I think we need a drink,' Esther says shakily. 'This house is an alcohol-free zone. Maybe just as well. Coke OK?'

I nod and go into the bathroom to wash my face. A red-faced boy, shocked, battered, but whole, stares back from the mirror.

In the living room, we sit side by side, drinking Coke.

'Luke – have you never told anybody before?' Esther asks, setting her half-empty glass on the coffee table, and threading her fingers through mine.

'I told my mum. After the – what I just told you about.'

'And?' she prompts.

I give a dry laugh that hurts my raw throat. I take another sip of Coke. 'She didn't believe me.'

I close my eyes. I see me, just about eleven, and Mum, her long blond hair, her purple skirt, her big eyes pleading with me to stop talking, stop spoiling everything.

'She said, *Don't be disgusting. Stephen's been so good to you – to both of us. He treats me like a princess.*'

Esther shudders. 'What about how he was treating *you*?'

'She said I was a dirty little boy, making things up.'

'Your *mum* said that?'

I shrug. 'She said I watched too much TV. She said I was just jealous. Because she was pregnant. They were getting married.'

The diamond flashes in the corner of my right eye. I blink.

'So what did you do?' she asks.

I grimace. Mum not believing me was far worse than anything Stephen did. 'Acted up. Running away, getting into fights at school and with her – we had this big row one time and I – I well, I kicked her – and after that she told Social Services she couldn't cope.'

'And what about the baby?'

'She lost it. She kept having miscarriages – it was a bit ironic. She had me when she was sixteen, after some random shag – and then when she met the love of her life she couldn't give him a baby.'

'And what about Helena? Did she never know?'

I shake my head. I didn't think I'd ever mentioned Helena to her, but my brain's all over the place at the minute.

'It's not like I've gone round thinking about this every day of the last six years, you know. Sometimes I'd forget all about it for months – years, even. Living with Helena – it was good, really. When she realised I was quite bright she kept me at it, working hard, helping me with my homework. I didn't have time to think about anything else. And best of all she wasn't – well, I knew she wasn't going to come snuggling into my bedroom any time. I knew where I was with her. Until …' I trail off.

Esther's round cheeks suddenly blaze red. 'Luke,' she says, 'I don't know how you'll react to this.' She chews her lip. 'I've met her.'

'You *what?*'

'You were unconscious. I felt – I needed *someone* to help me understand why you could have hurt yourself so badly. Brendan was away at some conference and then – I thought of Helena. I knew you'd lived with her for ages so I thought, well, whatever she's like she must at least *know* you. So I – er – tracked her down and went to see her.'

'You went all the way to *Dublin*?'

Esther nods. 'Do you mind? I didn't tell her about Jasmine or anything. Just about the overdose. She – I think she felt bad about – how things had ended up.'

'Yeah.' Thinking about that time is nearly as bad as remembering Stephen. 'Helena was OK,' I say, trying to be fair. 'If it hadn't been for her I'd never have got into Mansfield. She was always telling me the statistics about kids in care, dropping out of education, and she made me feel I could do anything, *be* anything – but then … it all changed. Mum died –'

'And Stephen? Helena said it was your mum and her husband.'

'Yeah. I was so *angry* with them for dying. It was like he'd got away with it. I went *crazy*. Did some stupid stuff. Helena just freaked. She only knew me as this good, quiet boy who just wanted to do his homework and read and play a bit of football and suddenly she had to deal with this – I don't know –'

'Normal person?' Esther suggests drily.

'The epilepsy was the final straw. It was hard not to see it as some kind of – judgement.'

'Luke, you *know* that's daft. It's a physical thing. It's just electricity in your brain.'

'Yeah.'

This is what all the leaflets and doctors say. It's what I've told Lauren, whose epilepsy is far worse than mine. But it's different when Esther says it. And now – after everything that's happened – the epilepsy doesn't seem that big a deal.

Esther squeezes my hand. 'Luke – can I ask you something?' Without waiting for an answer she says, jaggedly, as if the words hurt, 'I totally get how you might have believed you could have hurt Jasmine. Because of that bastard making you think …' She looks down at our twined fingers. 'But when you were – when *we* were – together – you always seemed to be – well, pushing me away…' She looks up at me, frowning. 'Was that also because …?'

For ages I don't know how to answer. 'I'd never been with anyone before. I kept hearing Stephen's voice: *You liked that, didn't you? Don't pretend you didn't like that.* I hadn't thought about him for – years. Being with you – it's the best thing that's ever happened to me, but it brought it all back too.' I shudder. 'Christ, Esther, I was so scared. Of hurting you. Of being – *like that.*'

'You thought you'd *hurt* me?'

'I suppose – I associated anything sexual with …' I swallow. 'I thought I wasn't normal.'

'*I* thought you didn't fancy me,' Esther whispers. 'I thought you liked me and were – you know – *comfortable* with me, but that that was all.'

I look down at our clasped hands and wonder how two people can love each other and still get things so wrong. And I realise I've never thought the word *love* before, but I know it's right.

'You're beautiful. I did fancy you,' I whisper. 'I mean, I … I *do.*' I cup the back of her neck with my free hand and pull her head towards me, very slowly.

It's a brief kiss, a nervous kiss, but for the first time it isn't interrupted by Stephen's voice.

I wait. Nothing. Just Esther's breath, and the thump of my own heart. So I kiss her again.

Esther

Luke and I walk into tutor group together. It's his first day back. He was meant to wait until after half term, but Dad suggested coming in for one day, just to break the ice, sort out his new timetable now that he's switched from economics to art, and let people get used to seeing him round. I know he's nervous because he's told me – we've done more talking in the last week than we have since we met – though he looks detached and calm. But when I find his hand and give it a quick squeeze his fingers close on mine tightly.

Jasmine and Cassie perch on their desks in poses designed to show off their legs. They look up when we walk in, and Jasmine blushes so hard you can see it beneath her makeup. Cassie keeps on talking. The twins give identical small smiles and one of them says, 'Hi.' Nobody else bothers much. There's a holiday buzz already.

Toby makes space for us. He grins at Luke. 'You're *so* lucky you're dropping economics,' he says. 'You should *see* what she expects us to learn over half term.'

'Yeah, colouring-in's going to be far better,' Luke says. 'Tell me what we did in maths.' He gets out his homework diary and for a moment, as Toby starts talking incomprehensibly about maths, panic flits across his face.

'Hey,' I say softly, 'you don't have to catch up all at once.'

'Are you going to the Halloween party tomorrow?' Toby asks, tactfully abandoning maths.

Luke and I exchange glances.

'Hadn't really thought about it,' I say.

'I'm going,' Toby says, 'with' – his cheeks flame – 'Mihai.'

'*Mihai?*'

'I know him from chess club. He – um – asked me last week. Says he *thought* I was gay but didn't like to make a move because he wasn't sure, and … anyway. You can come with us if you like.'

'Yeah,' Luke says. 'Esther?'

'OK.' Fourth time lucky for the jade dress.

Baxter comes in, sees Luke, accepts his absence note without any fuss – clearly the teachers have been briefed about how to treat him, probably by Dad – and packs us all off with stern warnings about being careful with fireworks. Like we're *seven*.

I have French; Luke has maths. We pause at the classroom door, and he rubs my arm, which I know means, *Public displays of affection in school are tacky, but if we weren't in school I'd kiss you.*

And in a few hours' time we'll be free of school for a whole week. Luke has counselling twice a week, and he says it's like pulling scabs off a sore, but he supposes in the end it'll make the sore heal better – but we've loads of plans for the other days: going to Dublin for a day on the train, meeting up with Ruth and Adam, going sketching along the tow path if the weather's good enough. And I'll do some girl stuff with Ruth too. She wants me to help her plan her eighteenth.

Luke heads out with Toby. Mihai's waiting outside, and I see Toby introduce him to Luke. I hear a quick burst of laughter, then the three boys walk away together.

Luke turns just before they go through the double doors at the end of the corridor. 'See you in art,' he says, and he smiles.

THE END